The
Curse

Marian Nichols

Copyright © 2008 by Marian Nichols.

Library of Congress Control Number: 2007910261
ISBN: Hardcover 978-1-4363-1312-4
Softcover 978-1-4363-1311-7

All rights reserved. No part of this book may be reproduced or transmitted in any form or by any means, electronic or mechanical, including photocopying, recording, or by any information storage and retrieval system, without permission in writing from the copyright owner.

This is a work of fiction. Names, characters, places and incidents either are the product of the author's imagination or are used fictitiously, and any resemblance to any actual persons, living or dead, events, or locales is entirely coincidental.

This book was printed in the United States of America.

To order additional copies of this book, contact:
Xlibris Corporation
1-888-795-4274
www.Xlibris.com
Orders@Xlibris.com
43199

CONTENTS

Chapter One:	The First Encounter	9
Chapter Two:	The Psychic	19
Chapter Three:	Possession and Astral Flight	31
Chapter Four:	Visions Of The Past	41
Chapter Five:	Return To The Manor	49
Chapter Six:	Battle Preparations	60
Chapter Seven:	Underworld	67
Chapter Eight:	Return To The Surface	88
Chapter Nine:	Gaurdian Discloseur	100
Chapter Ten:	The Wedding	105
Chapter Eleven:	Eydasi's Return	118
Chapter Twelve:	The Conception	128
Chapter Thirteen:	The First Challenge	136
Chapter Fourteen:	The First Attack	145
Chapter Fifteen:	The Dragon And The Birth	156
Chapter Sixteen:	The Other Birth	165
Chapter Seventeen:	The Garden Party	176
Chapter Eighteen:	Training For Knighthood	189
Chapter Nineteen:	Sir Seth	202
Chapter Twenty:	Arthur Battles Mordred	212

Epilogue 225

I am dedicating 'the curse!' to the members of a site I have been a member of for about five years. This forum's members are like family to each other. It is the support forum for the Serene Screen Marine Aquarium, which is created by Jim Sachs.

I wish to express my gratitude to each and every one for their friendship, support and advice on any number of subjects that may arise in everyday life. They do not hesitate to give freely without expecting anything in return, except your friendship!

First to Morgan, who started the support forum.

Then to Michael. who helps administrate the forum.

Jim Sachs, for his creation and personal association with all members.

Then in no particular order, I wish to say;

Thank you!

Frank, Steve, SuferMinn, Sandy, Tiny-Turtle, Marshmarigold, Doc, Ed, Cliff, Celine, Pat, James, Nancy, Ralph, Loud516

CHAPTER ONE

THE FIRST ENCOUNTER

As thunder rumbles with each flash of lightning, the lone figure hovering in the far recesses of the manor is momentarily illuminated. Although no one living inhabits these premises, this unfortunate apparition makes for itself a home here. Far from the world of the living, nevertheless it can enjoy the material luxuries that this mansion once offered. Having found no joy or peace when it walked the land as a mortal, it now reflects on the reasons why it cannot enter the other plane of existence. These issues must be resolved before passing on to the next level; but having no idea how this will come about, it ponders its resources. It seems as if it has existed here for an eternity; that time has no value, and does not move forward into the next day. It is forever darkness, with little chance of the tiniest bit of brightness breaking the gloom.

Unexpectedly, there is a knocking on the large oak double door at the front of this residence, a sound that startles even this recluse from humanity. Thinking to itself that some lost traveler has found their way to this abandoned and isolated area, it hopes that they will soon tire of their long wait for an answer to their request for entrance, and seek shelter elsewhere. However, it is not to be, for with persistent shoving at the rusting latches, the door protests with a groan, then swings open, allowing the cutting bites of rain to infiltrate the reception hall.

There stands an ambiguous form, small, and clutching her arms tightly across her breast, as if she can stay the chills from penetrating deep into her bones. The entity studies this wisp of a girl, for she is young and obviously cold and scared. It wonders how such a waif finds herself stranded in the middle of nowhere. A flash of lightning abruptly lights the hall as bright as day, while the roar of thunder shakes the very foundation of this extremely old estate. At that moment, the girl is bathed in a distinct radiance that defines her small figure, and gives a feeling of awe to her being. She has hair the color of spider's silk; long to her waist, very straight, not a hint of curl, but it is wet and hanging in long blades down her back. She is quite pretty, so exquisite is she that she appears to be a portrait instead of a living person. She is dressed in a light blue sundress, for this is the season of summer, mid-July.

She hesitates for a brief moment, and then deciding that inside is much better than outside . . . she quickly enters, not bothering to close the door behind her. So here she stands, wondering as to how she will ride out the storm and if she will be able to locate help in this god-forsaken place. The hall is pitch black and only with the lightning's strikes is she able to make out a little of her surroundings. It is quite apparent that the house has been unoccupied for an incredibly long time, for all is desolate, with cobwebs spread from ceiling to floor. There is no color left to the walls, which are now muted shades of gray. High to the ceiling, the windows are dark and broken, allowing only bits of light from the storm to flash eerily about the room. What once were drapes now hang in tattered strips down each of the tall panes. There are a few pieces of furnishings scattered about, odd pieces that are broken and very dusty. There, in a far corner, she notices a divan, with a section lying broken on the bare floor and one end raised up at an angle.

Using the light from the storm, she cautiously eases her way across the shattered room, leaving small footprints in the dust as she goes. Having brushed dust and cobwebs from the settee, she eases her small form into a comfortable position. The settee sinks from her weight, but it feels so good to get off her feet for a brief time. Clenching her hands tightly together, she contemplates her difficult situation.

All the while, the phantom is studying her every move and marvels at her nerve to enter herein. This at least breaks up the monotony of its day-to-day existence. Where has she wandered from, for this estate is many miles from any settlement, not receiving visitors for more than a century? This is the phantom's place of damnation, doomed to wander these halls until someone would come to break the spell cast over it a hundred and fifty years before. It has long ago relinquished the hope of ever being released from this living death.

Wet as well as cold, the young visitor removes her sandals and pulls her legs up close to her body, wrapping her arms about her knees in an effort to retain her body heat as she sits there shivering. Being ever so weary, she drops her head down on top of her knees; with the sound of the rain pelting the mansion, she is soon lulled into a light sleep.

Noiselessly the entity drifts over to where she is slumbering; it knows that she will not detect it, so it takes its time examining her. There is not anything too unusual about her, per se, only that she awakes a longing in the spirit that it has thought long dead, a longing for more life. A feeling of great protectiveness comes over it, and it is unable to fathom why. It has had no concerns for mortals since its demise some hundred and fifty odd years ago.

So, through the long night it stands watch over the slumbering girl, at some point she slopes over to one side and rests her head on the arm of the sofa. The storm continues unabated until the wee hours of the morning, when it promptly ceases as quickly as it had begun.

She stirs. The entity, in silence, retreats to a far corner of the hall, where it can still watch her in seclusion.

Myra opens her eyes slowly. For a moment, she does not recognize her surroundings, but then her memory returns of the previous evening. However, it is morning, how could she have slept so soundly all through the night? The storm is gone and her clothing has dried. She feels somewhat better, but famished, having not eaten since the day before at noon, "I am sure there is nothing in this old place to eat." She speaks aloud and it is strange to hear her own voice echo throughout the room.

It is also disturbing to her unseen host, for it has not heard a mortal speak for as long as it has been here. Old memories return to haunt it.

Myra rises and stretches, then slides her feet back into her sandals and smoothes the wrinkles from her dress. "I must be a fright," she speaks audibly again, "but I just must explore this old house, there ought to be some old antiques or relics up these stairs. I could find something really unique." So with that she ventures off in the direction of the stairs. Not a spiral staircase but still it turns back on itself, leading up to the second floor.

"I wonder if these steps are sturdy enough to hold me," Myra asks herself. "Well there is only one way to find out, that's to give it a try." She reaches out her hand and places it on the banister, and with a determined gait, she proceeds up.

The entity did not foresee *this*, thinking that surely, this young girl would have left at dawn, but no, instead, she seems inclined to stay and explore the manor. It decides to follow her around to learn what she might uncover, and so it stays a slight distance behind her while floating above, so not to give her a sign of its presence.

Myra quickly advances up the stairs. On reaching the landing, she halts briefly to survey this part of the mansion. As with the downstairs, everything is covered with cobwebs and dust; where did it all come from, there must be centuries of it? Myra shudders abruptly; an odd chill is here. "Old place is drafty." She turns around, halfway expecting someone to be behind her, but of course, not a living soul is there. "I'm getting paranoid," she speaks softly to herself, just in case.

Myra has detected its presence, the specter realizes. It had strayed much too close, so to give her more space, it backs off and continues to shadow her.

Myra studies her surroundings intensely, and assured of being alone, she makes her way to the first door. The entity is immensely amused as it follows her. Since her intentions are unknown to the specter, it feels that it must accompany her on this excursion. The landing is ten feet wide and runs the length of the house, with a balustrade along the perimeter. There is an alarming drop of about twenty feet to the floor below. Here are six doors, some open, others shut. Myra pauses at the first one; it is partially open, so she leans against it and it creaks open, but only far enough to allow her to pass through. There is not much to see here, for it is empty, the walls have peeling plaster, revealing the wooden slates underneath. The next room appears to be a nursery, with an old style cradle, and an ancient rocking chair that is slightly moving, as if just vacated. Adjoining the nursery to the left is a smaller room, with the door taken off the hinges and propped against the wall. Here is a small bureau with a porcelain pitcher and washbowl sitting atop, and a cot with a feather mattress and nothing more. "This must be the nanny's room," she remarks and in here as well, are more cobwebs and dust. A large window is directly across from her having no drapery, but darkened panes. Further along the hall is the third door, which is shut and locked. It cannot be opened, and it is as if a supernatural power is holding it fast. "I'll try it later," she mumbles.

She has more luck with the fourth door. It is slightly open and she enters easily. Here is a four-poster bed with a canopy, bedclothes on the bed looking like a just made bed, even though it is covered with dust, while cobwebs hang from the canopy railing. In here also is an old-time sideboard, a freestanding garment closet, and a small chair at a dressing table; all are as dusty as the rest, with even more cobwebs. She tiptoes further inside with her invisible host close behind, "This must have been a beautiful room at one time," she imagines. On the outside wall is a stone fireplace with a wide mantle over it; on each side of the fireplace are two tall windows with heavy dusty drapes completely covering them, not allowing any light to pass through. Above the mantel hangs a life size painting of a young woman. She is stunning, with pale straight hair, which has the luster of mother-of-pearl, and flowing loosely to well past her shoulders. Alabaster skin, large violet eyes with dark arched brows, a finely trimmed perky nose and soft full pink lips with a hint of a mischievous smile. These features are all set in a small oval-shaped face. She is magnificently dressed in a purple evening frock reminiscent of the Victorian era.

While concentrating on this portrait, Myra realizes she is looking at an identical rendition of herself, but how could that be! This discovery is extremely disconcerting.

This is not lost on the phantom, now it understands why it feels such a compassion for this uninvited visitor!

Myra exits this bedroom, with a feeling of déjà vu. The whole mansion has a musty and rancid smell, "A good airing would certainly improve things," she declares. Myra is able to enter the fifth room but it has little to offer, other than an aged spinning wheel with a stool standing beside it, looking as if it is waiting for its mistress to return and finish the spool. "How odd," she remarks as she walks around this piece of history. "Spinning wheels aren't that easy to find. I've got to have it, I'll come back later for it," Myra speaks to herself again.

There is one more room, the sixth, with a closed door, but with a little effort, it swings open. WHOOSH! Something rushes out with a great swish, a flurry of wings, all flapping, trying to escape. Bats! As they swirl over Myra's head, she waves her arms frantically, trying to ward off the intruders. Swooping down to the reception hall and out the opened doors, the bats make a hasty retreat. Myra leans against the wall with her right hand above her heart, allowing herself to recover from this shock, "I think I have had enough for today," she says breathlessly.

Things have changed causing the entity to be apprehensive; for well over a century and a half, no one has found their way to this isolated manor, but a young girl on this ferocious night has done so unaided. What force has guided her here? There is only one explanation; she is for certain a descendant of the Worthington Family!

Myra retraces her steps back along the landing while deep in thought about how uncanny it is that this house seems somehow tied in with her life. At the third door she halts, "I'll try it just once more."

Again, she leans against the door with her full weight, but still it will not open! "Enough is enough, I got to get out of here and find help so I can go home!" she cries softly. Absentmindedly she descends the stairs to the reception hall below and takes a final look around the downstairs area. In a way, she hates to leave, but she must and she heads for the door. As she approaches, it suddenly slams shut with a BANG!

"*The wind?*" she wonders. Taking hold of the handle, she shoves and tugs, but something is blocking the door. This was easier last night.

"There's got to be another way out." She runs her hand through her hair; it needs combing, she needs a bath, it is getting hot and she is still starving!

She turns back to the interior of the room and is horrified; she puts her hand over her mouth and lets out a low gasp! There is a bluish mist surrounding what appears to be the resemblance of a woman. She is a striking figure with long flowing colorless hair; she is semi-nude, lucent, and floating three feet off the floor!

This being the first time Myra has ever seen a ghost, she tries that much harder to get the door open, but to no avail. Tears are welling up, and running down her cheeks. On this level, there is another exit; she heads for it but the spirit obstructs her. She races for the front; again, the spirit blocks the way. Tired of running, Myra stops, looks at the spirit and wails, "What do you want from me?" At that, the apparition points a slender finger out and up. "Must I go back up the stairs?" she cries.

Silently Myra follows the spirit, feeling she has little choice. At the third door, it pauses, and then vanishes.

After materializing, the spirit feels drained, having never used this ability before, but feels it is essential to keep the girl from leaving the manor. There are certain things, which need revealing to this girl before she leaves here. The spirit is convinced that she is the one who will liberate it, releasing the spirit from the haunting of Worthington Manor.

"I can't open this door!" Myra declares, "I've already tried."

While speaking a flash catches her eye. "A key?" she asks. It is jutting from the lock and with trembling hands, Myra turns it cautiously, remembering what had happened with the last door.

A rush of stale, stagnant air greets her; a sickening taste rises in Myra's throat causing her to gag. She feels she is suffocating, and she runs from the room to get fresh air into her lungs. She takes great gulps of air, coughing and choking, seeking relief from the burning in her mouth and throat. Several minutes pass before she is able to take an easy breath.

"I don't think I can go back in there," she speaks directly to the ghost, although it is not visible. With that, the specter reappears and directs Myra's attention to the partially open door, encouraging her to enter, then again, it vanishes.

THE CURSE

Myra faces the open door and with an enormous effort enters. Her eyes slowly adjust to the darkness; against the wall to her right sits a massive writing desk with a roll down front and five drawers, two on the left and three on the right. A huge French window directly facing Myra has shredded curtains and dark, cracked panes. A dusty French sofa with a low table in front stands to her left, but what is lying on it sends chills up her spine. There lies the corpse of a woman; Myra wills herself to look more closely, and, as she draws nearer she can tell that the body is mummified. It is wearing a dark red dress made of velvet and old lace. She effortlessly identifies the corpse as that of the lady in the portrait and protruding from her chest is a knife!

MURDERED! Myra is suddenly struck with pain as she grabs her chest with both hands and with a cry, she faints and collapses to the floor.

The specter also feels this agony and remembers its own death! It scrutinizes Myra lying in a heap on the floor; it draws nearer to the girl and tenderly attempts to touch her brow. Myra opens her eyes to find she is gazing into the face of her captor; it is wearing a look of concern that turns into a smile of relief. Myra now knows that the spirit means her no harm. She struggles to her feet feeling very weak and wobbly. She concludes that this spirit, the portrait Lady and the murdered woman are the same individual.

This is an earthbound spirit and a horrible tragedy has befallen it, and this magnificent house. Myra now understands the need for something to be done to release the specter from this earthly plane and allow it to proceed on to the next realm.

With the entity gently urging her, Myra crosses the room to the desk, brushing away dust and webs with a silk scarf found on the floor. The top of the desk squeaks, as she rolls it back. Here are the usual things, mostly in an advanced state of decay, nothing helpful here. She checks each drawer; in the left top are papers that disintegrate at her touch into dust. The drawer below has a pair of ladies gloves and earmuffs. The top right drawer has a tarnished silver letter opener, a quill or two, and a bottle of dried up black ink. The middle drawer contains more decaying papers; in the bottom drawer is the family Bible. She picks it up and blows the dust from it.

She leaves this third room and heads back down the staircase where the light is better for reading. Here she opens the Bible to the first few pages, where they commonly keep records. There are listed marriages, births and deaths of all family members and the family name is *Worthington*. In the center sections of all the listings, in faded handwriting are these names—Abigail Mason married to Don Worthington, June 17, 1840. Three children are listed, all boys, Theodor, Philips, and Lawrence, their birth dates, marriages and offspring. The oldest son, Theodor had married a Mariah Long in 1868 and a son had been born to them, Richard Worthington, on February 29, 1868. This is all of the handwritten record. What had happened to the others? No one had notified the authorities, but why? Somehow, this tragedy had gone unreported all these years. The manor house gives the appearance of having been wrecked, as if someone had gone on a rampage and destroyed as much as possible, leaving no clue to the perpetrator's identity.

Mariah, the spirit, knows what the Bible reveals and that Myra now has the essential information she will need to help solve this mystery. Although the murderer is long dead, before Mariah will be able to rest, he must be identified and she must discover the fate of her infant son.

"Mariah? Is that your name?" Myra speaks to the seemingly vacant room. "I can only tell you I will do what I can to right this dreadful wrong done to our family, because I feel we are related somehow." Myra pauses, waiting to see if there would be a response but there isn't. "My name is Myra, and I am desperately in need of help, my car is wrecked and I am miles from anywhere. Will you let me go if I promise I'll return?" The double door now opens with no assistance and Myra knows she can leave. "I'll take this with me," she indicates the Bible.

Although completely understanding what Myra is saying, Mariah's energy is depleted and she is unable to respond just now. She feels a strange sensation in the depths of her soul, that very soon she will have the answers she seeks.

Myra slips through the partially opened doors onto the fair sized veranda, with four towering columns supporting the roof, to the nine steps that lead down to the vast courtyard. She spins around to review this aged manor house. There are more than two stories, at least three, with very tall and steep roofs and several dormers, located on both the north and south sides. They have miniature rectangular windows, which are dark even in daylight. Tall stately pines are scattered about the back, while oaks grow along what used to be an access road. Trailing vines cover much of the house and thick shrubbery clusters around the front steps. Marble appears to be the building material and Myra guesses its age at around two hundred years, dating back to just after the Revolutionary War.

Myra heads down the winding road until she reaches the thick forest. She looks behind her but can no longer see the mansion for a grey mist has risen, hiding the manor and now she can barely make out the path. She does not remember all of this underbrush being here; maybe this is not the way she came. She is amazed that she was able to find the old mansion in the first place, in the middle of a tall pine forest like this. As she emerges from the thicket where she had abandoned her car last night, there is a State Trooper examining it.

"Good morning, sir," she addresses him.

"Good morning ma'am, by chance is this your vehicle?" he asks.

"Yes sir, it is. As you can see, I ran off the road last night during the storm and had to take shelter in the old Worthington mansion until the storm let up. My cell phone wouldn't work so I spent the night there," explains Myra.

"Did you say an old house is back in those woods?" he replies looking strangely at her.

"Yes, Worthington Manor, back up that road there, I stayed there last night."

"Road? I see no road, are you certain?"

"Yes sir, there," Myra points towards the path but, to her shock, it has vanished.

"That's odd," says the trooper, "I don't recall any manor or house being in this area, and I am from around here. Are you sure it was back in those woods and not further down this road. As you can see there is nothing along this stretch of road for miles."

"Yes sir, I am definitely sure about this."

"Well we will check this out later, right now we need to get you home. I've phoned your parents and told them that I had found your abandoned vehicle and your father is on his way right now."

"There's one other thing," Myra speaks haltingly. "There is a corpse of a murdered woman on the second floor."

The Trooper looks sharply at her, "What do you mean?"

"It has been there for a number of years, you can see that."

"I will call the Nash County Sheriff and report this. They will have some questions for you, so expect a visit from them." All this time he is taking notes on a pad.

Not too long after Myra's arrival back at her car, she sees her father's car coming down the road. She rushes into his outspread arms and despite herself, she begins to cry. He comforts her and they get in the car and head for home.

• • •

Mariah watches from a second story window as Myra makes her way across the courtyard, giving Mariah a feeling of dread. A black mist hovers over Myra's head that only Mariah can see. It trails Myra until Mariah loses sight of her, with Myra totally unaware of this nomad. This is the Dark Spirit that at times occupies the third floor. It is capable of leaving the mansion but Mariah is not. Mariah is not certain of who or what this wraith is, but she does recognize it as malevolent, and now it has followed Myra!

CHAPTER TWO

THE PSYCHIC

Weeks have passed since the occurrences at the deserted mansion; it is now the second week of August. The local sheriff questioned Myra extensively about the corpse discovered there; she passes on everything she knows *except* the *knowledge* of Mariah. Reluctantly she gives them the Bible and they promise to return it to her. Myra's safe return relieves her parents but they think it is unwise for her to travel alone again.

Although Myra is thankful to be home, she is at odds with herself; tense nerves, sleeping restlessly with horrific nightmares, little or no appetite and hallucinations! She is seeing fleeting, bizarre shadows in her peripheral vision, and transient, blurred faces in mirrors. She readily lays this on her paranormal experience with Mariah, and the stormy night spent in Worthington Manor. The county had provided a funeral for Mariah at the cemetery in Pine Grove and she visits the grave almost daily in anticipation of contact with the spirit.

Since then, Myra has been uneasy whenever alone. At times, when in her bedroom with Bandit, a blue-eyed Siamese, the cat reacts to an imperceptible foe, with hunched back, bushed tail, bared claws, hissing, and then taking refuge under the bed or a chair. She feels continuously under surveillance, and feels she is losing touch with reality for there seems to be no reason for her apprehension. She conceals this terror from her parents; she feels she cannot confide in them just now, for definitely they will bring in a psychiatrist. She has no resources to aid her in solving this mystical dilemma; she needs an expert, she needs a *psychic*.

• • •

Meanwhile, Mariah's existence has settled back into the same monotonous routine. The authorities investigate the interior and exterior of Worthington Manor using strange yellow tape to block off portions of the house. The most traumatic episode is when men in white coats come to remove her body, but now at least she will have a Christian burial and a final resting-place. Oddly, Mariah is able to attend her own funeral by forces yet unknown. Since then she has met Myra at the gravesite consistently, although she has not materialized.

With summer vacation nearing an end, Myra is very aware that time is fast running out for her to bring this crisis to a resolution, for she returns to college in the fall. She tackles the Internet and performs detailed searches until she identifies and locates the one person who could possibly assist.

Dr. Adrian Grey is a well-known intuitive; Myra sends multiple e-mails yet he does not reply. She finally confides completely to him before he responds:

"Hello Myra,

I am intrigued by your problem and will be in your area this weekend. Send me your phone number and I will call you when I arrive.

Dr. Adrian Grey."

• • •

His call comes through at two thirty Friday afternoon and they agree to meet that evening at five, on the front steps of the public library. Myra drives alone to meet Dr. Grey.

After arriving at his motel, Dr. Grey contemplates the vague information that this young woman has given him. Anything concerning the paranormal is magnetism to his *psyche* and he cannot ignore it, especially an actual sighting of a "spirit," much less a verbal encounter with one. He must prove to himself that this encounter is not a hoax and there is only one way to do that; he should investigate it for himself.

He calls Myra later that afternoon, arranging to meet her that evening at the public library on Falls Road.

Adrian stands a little over six feet tall with a lean muscular frame and distinguishing good looks. After a mid-day meal at the motel's restaurant, he calls a cab and leaves for his appointment with Myra.

• • •

While stopped at a traffic signal, Myra checks the rear view mirror but instead of the expected traffic, she sees a horrific creature taking up most of the rear seat. It is a hideous, malformed ghoul with enormous, blazing, red eyes; a large, a fire breathing snout; drool drips from its mouth; it has yellow, jagged teeth with two elongated fangs, which are twisting over the enlarged bottom lip. The skin of this demon is rubbery gray and scaly like a snake.

Myra quickly turns away, hoping this is just another hallucination. Gathering her nerve, she looks again but the creature remains. The ghoul suddenly grabs her with grotesque claws, and the vile odor of its searing breath nauseates her. Myra attempts to scream, but it clasp her by the throat, depriving her of air. She endures the heat of its flesh as it burns her skin and she feels herself slipping into unconsciousness, then it vanishes!

Thankfully, the signal light is still red, the other commuters have not noticed anything out of the ordinary, and all seems normal, even to her.

This attack happened at the intersection near the library and quickly she pulls her car into the parking lot and hits the brakes hard causing the tires to squeal. Hastily she climbs out of her car and, trembling uncontrollably, calls for help. Seeing her distress, a stranger, of about thirty, comes to her aid. He can tell she is in shock, so he gently guides her by the arm to a bench in the library parking lot.

"Are you all right, Miss. What happened? Are you injured?" he asks with great concern. Myra gazes vaguely into his face; he has serene, bluish gray eyes, a slight Roman nose, a deep tan and a kind smile. His muscular arms are still supporting her and before she can answer, he speaks again, "How did you get these burns?"

This stranger looks trustworthy enough, "I am so sorry but I glanced in my rear view mirror and there was this . . . thing . . . sitting in my back seat. I guess I over-reacted, but it looked so real, and it grabbed my throat, trying to strangle me. I know there was something there, why else would I have these marks on my neck," Myra touches the burns and they are painful.

Taking her by the upper arms, this stranger assists her in standing, then stares directly into her tearful eyes and says, "I bet you're Myra." She nods her head; "I am Dr. Adrian Grey" he pauses, "I know we had an appointment for this afternoon, just didn't think it would be this dramatic," he chuckles. Lifting up her hair, he inspects the burn marks, "These seem to be superficial, no scarring I think, but you should be seen by your doctor. Would you like me to call someone for you?"

"No, my parents have gone out, and I don't want to ruin their evening, I'll be fine," Myra's voice quivers. "I'll go home and put on an ointment . . . but my car." Her voice trails to a whisper.

The doctor interrupts her, "Not to worry. I would find it a privilege to drive you, only I came here by cab. We'll need to take your car. Think you can make it?" he asks with concern.

"I'm not too sure, it might happen again!" she is genuinely frightened.

"Wouldn't dare with me at the wheel!" he proclaims with a confident smile, meant to calm her fears. Again, she nods and allows him to guide her to the passenger side of her car. After fastening her seat belt he remarks, "Ordinarily I would not advise a young lady to go with a stranger, so to make you feel at ease with me, here are my credentials." He pulls out his wallet and shows her his driver's license, and a business card, stating he is a medical doctor with John Hopkins Hospital in Maryland.

"I am a medical doctor but paranormal activities are sort of a sideline with me, but I do have a PHD in parapsychology."

"Dr. Grey," she pauses," your reputation precedes you and I feel quite safe, thank you."

"Please, I'm Adrian to my friends, Dr. Grey was my father," he gives her a modest smile and a perceptive wink, and then climbs into the driver's seat. They talk seriously about Mariah and the demon that attacked her, while she gives directions to her home.

"This case, I sense, involves a spirit that's trapped on the Earthly plane, also known as the Quantum plane, due to a disaster beyond its control. *And until it is rectified the spirit will linger here until The Judgment*," Dr. Grey glances at Myra briefly to see her reaction.

"It has been, what, well over century now and the one who killed her has long ago died without his crime discovered or punished. So that spirit, too, is trapped in the Quantum plane the same as Mariah. Neither of them can move on until *he* is confronted with his crime. When this occurs, Mariah will be free to go to a higher plane. I think *what* attacked you is probably a demon; spirits do not have the ability to touch mortals. Somehow, these two entities are working together, a demon and a spirit. I have heard of this before. It is rare, but in some way, each will profit from keeping this spirit earthbound. What that is I can't say just now." The doctor pauses and takes a deep breath then glances at Myra for a response.

She also takes a long breath and replies, "So what this *creature* wants, is to prevent us from exposing it?" Myra looks to the doctor and he nods deliberately.

"I see!" She finishes.

"To *it*, eternity, free here on Earth, is better than the alternative which is Perdition." This time Myra nods her head.

"We're here, this path goes up to the house," Myra indicates a long drive that leads to her home. The one level, modern, brick residence is set fifty feet or so back off the main drive, so the doctor turns the vehicle onto this path and steers it down the unpaved gravel entrance. Approaching the house, a well-kept lawn can be seen, with low shrubs growing close to the front and sides. A magnolia tree is on the west corner of the lot and a very old, gnarled oak that is older than the house, grows on the east lawn. Behind the house in the very back, grow five or six tall, thin pines, standing at attention, slightly swaying in the warm summer breeze. Magnificent roses are growing in the side garden, with day lilies and tall sunflowers placed at the back. Situated near its center is a goldfish pond with a fountain spurting an umbrella spray. Around it are arranged smooth stones with cattails and water lilies floating on the glassy surface. Adrian maneuvers the car with ease and stops it at the front steps of her home; he leaps out, swings around to her side and assists her from the car.

"Well this is it" she sighs. "I see Mom and Dad aren't home yet." She looks about then asks, "Care to come in?"

"Tell you what, I will, but just long enough to call a cab," he replies.

"I am so sorry for this, having to bring me home and then call a cab to go back to your motel," she apologizes earnestly. With that, she leads him to her front door, he unlocks it for her with her set of keys then hands them to her.

"If you would, call a cab for me and I'll wait out here."

Myra starts to argue, but he stops her with, "No argument now, your folks aren't home so this is best for now." She goes and does as she is bid, returning a few moments later.

"The cab is on the way. Let's sit in the garden while we wait," she suggests. There are concrete benches scattered about, and they choose one close to the goldfish pond. The water is clear with sparkling bits of white light dancing across its surface. Waves are slightly lapping at the sides of the pool, and you can easily see the little orange fishes lazily swimming. The butterflies, bees and an occasional dragonfly, darting here and there, give this warm summer evening a feeling of tranquility. The gurgling song of the fountain, the chirping of birds, croaking of frogs and the clicking of unseen crickets, together create one of nature's melodies.

"You know you really should have those burns tended to," he takes a closer look at them.

"I did, I smeared a bit of ointment on, whilst inside. Really I am feeling much better," she assures him.

"Well, that's good, so what do you do with your time, Myra?" he asks.

Myra enlightens him about her future plans. She goes to the University of North Carolina, and starts her third year this fall, although she is only eighteen. She explains how she graduated from high school two years early for she is an advanced student with an IQ of 145. However, her parents objected to her placement too far ahead, feeling she would be deprived of her childhood. She is an English Major working on a bachelor degree, while also studying economics. She is also taking courses in business management and accounting, wanting a well-rounded education.

"You really have a lot on your plate. Ever feel overwhelmed?" he inquires.

"No, not really, though I don't get to do everything I would like. I don't seem to have the same interests as the other girls. They are more concerned with partying and boys than with getting an education and the *boys* are so juvenile," here she wrinkles up her nose, "I don't have a lot in common with most of them, so I pretty much keep to myself."

Adrian throws back his head in a hearty laugh. "Well, I must say, you do speak your mind. But tell me, your hair," he touches it lightly, "Is this natural?"

Smiling passively, Myra glances his way and heaves a sigh; she is asked this question numerous times. She explains that a gene in her mother's family line causes a few of the females to have hair without the necessary pigments. The hair is not white; it just lacks color. This gene is also associated with the higher IQ and the violet eyes. It skips every other generation; both male and female carry the gene but only the females have the trait. A woman with the gene and the trait will pass it on to both son and daughter though neither will show the trait. They in turn will also pass it to son and daughter, but the daughter will most likely, but not always, actually show the trait. Myra is the first one in two generations to have the hair color, eye color and high IQ!

"We have been told that it is a form of albinism, although instead of pale blue eyes, I have purple or violet colored eyes." Myra pauses for a moment waiting for a response. When none is forthcoming she continues, "You know, A—Adrian," she stumbles over his given name, "I'm sorry, Adrian, I haven't told you this yet but the ghost Mariah, and I looked a great deal alike, we could be identical twins."

"You need to fill me in with the particulars," his instinct tells him there is a great deal more than currently has been told, so Myra relates the missing bits.

"I know we must be related somehow, this form of albinism is too rare for us two not to be relatives," Myra concludes.

"I think you are probably correct which, in all probability, explains why you were on that stretch of road that night," he examines her face. "I don't believe it was just by coincidence, an infinite force guided you there. Myra, because you do look precisely like Mariah, this has me believing that you will play a large part in saving her," he states this emphatically. "You contend that the heavy rains caused your car to hydroplane and swerve, then hit the ditch, which I'm sure is the case, but the rest was out of your control. You were uninjured also, am I accurate so far?" Myra nods in the affirmative. "This confirms more than we first suspected." Adrian pauses for a brief breath then presses on. "This manor house is set back off the main road, it is impossible to be seen by anyone on a clear day, much less during a thunder storm," again, he studies her.

"But I did see it quite clearly, and it was only a few feet from the road on that particular night," she insists. "It took me just minutes to reach it, and strangely enough after entering the old house I felt quite safe, protected even. I fell asleep and slept the whole night even though the storm was furious. I had no worries or concerns the next morning when I went exploring, I felt like a child playing hide-and-seek, a game," this said in wonderment.

"In the bedroom where Mariah's portrait hangs, it felt so familiar, you know that feeling of *déjà vu*," she emphasizes. "But when I did leave, it took nearly an hour to make it back to my car," she pauses briefly, digesting this revelation. "Mariah *is* my ancestor, I don't know how, but I am sure of it. I am committed to proving it too, with some major research," she states frankly, "but haven't had the opportunity as yet."

"But *we* will!" replies Adrian with emphasis on "we." Suddenly, Adrian stands, seizes Myra by her upper left arm, pulls her to her feet and drags her unceremoniously in the direction of the house. In astonishment, she starts struggling, thinking him mad. "Run Myra! Your life depends on it," hearing this, and the obvious warning in his voice, she starts running!

Unseen and unfelt to Myra, Adrian senses the Darkness, a pulsating blackish gray mist giving off electrical sparks and hissing as a snake, advancing on them, but Adrian with his inner sense is forewarned! Together they rush into the open front door, where Adrian quickly shuts it, breathing fast he looks at Myra; "I can't leave you here alone."

"What was *it*?" she asks with fear plainly revealed.

"I'm not positive, but most likely it's the beast that attacked you while you were driving," he explains. "It is determined to get you, and it will unless you are protected. *And* it looks like I'm the one chosen for the job. You are not aware of it when it is invisible, only when it materializes do you know it is nearby and by then it could be too late. I sense that it is getting stronger with each attempt that it makes, but now I am also one of its targets." Adrian speaks rapidly as though this information needs revealing quickly or it might be too late.

"What can we do?" asks Myra.

"We need to talk with a minister or a priest and have your home blessed, so you will have a place of safety, where you cannot be molested." He looks around the room.

They are standing in the foyer, to the left is the living room and to the right is a long hall. The first door, along the hall, leads to a small study. He chooses the living room, and leads her in that direction.

Myra sits down on the edge of the sofa and clenches her hands so tightly together that the knuckles turn white; she turns a questioning face up to Adrian who is standing a little above her, silently asking him what to do. As if reading her mind, he smiles and sits beside her, and, taking her hands in his, he speaks in soft tones, "Things are going to be just fine. I'm asking a nice lady I know to come in and be your companion until this is over. She also has psychic powers; she's my mother. She's in upper New York State; I might be able to get her here by Sunday. Is that okay with you?"

Again, Myra nods with a blank stare. He cups his hand under her chin and lifts up her face, she raises downcast eyes up to meet his, "Myra, are you all right?" Again, she nods, "I think you need a drink." He heads for the liquor cabinet and locates a bottle of brandy. Pouring her a small glass, he carries it back to her. "Drink this slowly," he places it in her hand and guides it to her mouth. She sips it; looks at him and a faint smile forms on her lips. "There now, that's better." Looking at his watch, he sees it is nearly nine, and the sun is almost set beyond the horizon, "Your folks will be home soon and my cab has come and gone, so we'll just wait for them."

Thirty minutes later Myra's parents arrive home and, in a few minutes, enter the house. On reaching the living room, their daughter and a stranger greet them. Myra's father, Jonathan O'Keefe, a man of forty-nine with graying temples, is a lawyer. Her mother, Frances, forty-four, a petite auburn-haired beauty, is a high school history teacher.

Myra makes the introductions and the explanations begin. Myra is grateful for Adrian's presence, for without his calm demeanor and intelligent input in this unearthly subject, her parents, practical and steadfast people, would never have believed the story. When all explanations are completed, her folks look at each other in bewilderment. What to say, what can they say; this is too preposterous for words. They embrace their daughter tenderly, demanding to know why she has not come to them before now.

Adrian continues with the outline of what plans they have hastily drawn up:

First:	They will not leave Myra alone.
Second:	He will fly in his mother to act as Myra's companion.
Third:	Arrangements will be made for the minister to bless the house.
Fourth:	Adrian will move into the guestroom.
Fifth:	Serious research will begin, to learn Myra's family history.
Six:	Back to Worthington Manor.
Seventh:	Will take care of itself.

• • •

Mariah is concerned for Myra's well being, for she knows that Myra is in immense danger from the Dark Spirit, who had pursued her from Worthington Manor. This incubus will do its utmost to stop the mission now begun. An ally has rallied to assist in this venture for Mariah's liberation, a psychic with immense powers even he does not know he possesses. He recruits his mother to be Myra's companion, for she is most vulnerable to attacks when left alone. A blessing on Myra as well as her home will give a measure of protection against this incubus. Mariah seeks to give aid and bolster Myra's spirit, for bleakness has taken over her personality; she carries a heavy burden in her heart, the same one Mariah carries. Mariah visits Myra in her dreams and the two have developed a closeness shared only by mothers and daughters. Mariah helps her increase her strength so she can endure the unendurable, for the worst is yet to come.

A stage is being set at Worthington Manor; Mariah knows that Myra and Adrian must make a return visit to the manor. The wraith has taken up residence once more on the third floor, reserving its energy and growing stronger to do battle with this atypical army. Having lost one skirmish of this war, the Dark Spirit is biding its time until the battle returns to Worthington Manor.

• • •

Mr. O'Keefe invites Cyrus McGregor, the family minister from the Sunset Baptist Church across town to Monday night dinner, which he graciously accepts. Reverend McGregor is in his early seventies, a gray haired, portly gentleman, whom most people love right from the start. He has an infectious smile and a benevolent way of speaking that makes you yearn to hear him.

Dr. Grey's mother, Dorothy, by now has flown down from upper New York and has settled in with Myra, and both share the queen size bed. She is in her early fifties with dark hair peppered with white, worn mid-length and parted on one side. She is rather tall for a woman; about five foot ten, with wire-framed glasses, a slender build and is stern faced, with a no-nonsense attitude.

A little before seven on Monday evening, Reverend McGregor arrives for this dinner invitation. The entire family greets him warmly, but with the perception of wisdom, he quickly sees the uneasiness of the whole household.

Family and company make their way to the dining area at the back of the house. This is a long narrow room running the length of the house with the exterior wall constructed mainly of several large one paned windows, which allows for viewing the beautiful garden. They are seated, and Adrian and Myra sit next to each other.

The family cook serves a real southern meal with the traditional favorites, for which she receives high praise Gerti has been with the O'Keefe family since before the birth of Myra.

"Aha, y'all ain't taste nothin' yit, wait 'till yous gits a load of my chocla' cake. I am puts extra pecans on these top. Shore is somthin', I's tellin yous, yea sir, shore is." With that, she waddles out of the dining room, back in the direction of the kitchen.

Asked to give grace, the reverend does so graciously, ending with a personal blessing on the family. "Tis a fine day for sure, but it's gloomy faces I see. There is a problem I take it, care to tell me?" he loafs along with the Irish accent not lost in thirty odd years since leaving Ireland. The wise eyes of the kindly minister glance about the dinner table.

Myra's father makes the first move, explaining the circumstances to his old friend, who listens with furrows across his forehead, indicating the seriousness of this predicament. After the meal, the family and guests retire to the living room where Gerti's daughter, Melinda, serves coffee and brandy. The conversation is grave, and plans discussed center on how best to handle the exorcism of the Dark Spirit from Worthington Manor.

The blessing of the O'Keefe's occurs that night, before the Reverend leaves. He requests two identical amber colored glasses, and a bottle of olive oil to be brought before him.

Melinda retrieves a bottle of holy water from the Reverend's car. Gerti brings in the two glasses and an unopened bottle of olive oil. Mrs. O'Keefe brings in several candles and two incense burners and places them in front of the pastor.

Everyone stands and joins hands, with bowed heads, as the Blessings take place. First, each glass is half filled, one with water, the other with olive oil, and then each glass is individually blessed. With this done, each candle is also blessed individually, and then the two incense burners. They light the candles and place one in each room of the house, with instructions that as they burn down, another is to take its place. They fire up the incense burners and place one at the front door and the other at the back; they must keep these burning at all times. They carry one each of the blessed glasses of oil and water to each room and sprinkle some of the liquid at doors and windows. Each person in the house is also sprinkled and blessed.

A ceremony now takes place on the front lawn to bless the house itself.

Reverend McGregor faces the house, dashes what is left of the oil and water around the door and steps, then bows his head briefly. He then spreads his arms and in an authoritative voice, invokes the resident demon to vacate the O'Keefe's home:

"I exorcise this creature of old: all power of the adversary; all diabolical armies; all hostile attack; eliminating every satanic apparition. And all who use this will have health of mind and body! All those who are sick will be free of all weakness, languor, listlessness, all sickness, freed of any snares of the enemy, and all the opposing powers that separate your creature from you. Begone I demand you. Inhabit these dwellings no longer. In the name of Christ I cast thee out."

Dropping his arms in weariness, the mild minister continues to pray while gazing at the O'Keefe's home. It is now well past midnight, the Blessings are completed, and at the last spoken prayer, a low rumble begins beneath their feet as a terrifying earthquake shakes the home and grounds. There are cries of surprise as they reach out to each other for support, not comprehending just what is taking place. An unearthly shriek erupts from the house as a yellowish green iridescent fog, emulating the hideous face of the demon in agonizing pain, rises skyward and disperses in the air until nothing remains of it.

The little assembly is hypnotized by what has happened. For a minute, they are rooted where they stand. Myra reacts first with sobs, while covering her face with both hands. Adrian puts his arms about her shoulders and talking softly reassures her that for now things are safe. The family and company together go back into the house, but none will be able to sleep this night.

Myra's parents, with the scene they have just witnessed, are now confirmed believers in the evils in this world that most people choose *not to see*.

During this long disturbing night, the little congregation has candid discussions on the episode they have all witnessed, and more prayers are said, this time with extra sincerity and intensity. Everyone is tired, and the events have exhausted Myra, for she finally dozes off, with her head resting on Adrian's shoulder. Myra's mother and Mrs. Grey help her to her room and put her to bed, where she sleeps to the late afternoon. At dawn the rest of the family take to their beds, with Adrian opting for the sofa, so his mother may have his room, and Myra can sleep without being disturbed. They sleep until noon, when Gerti comes in to her job as cook; this awakes the family, all except Myra, who sleeps exhaustedly.

CHAPTER THREE

POSSESSION AND ASTRAL FLIGHT

Mariah's growing friendship with Myra is precious to her, but Myra is losing her strength and endurance. Spiritually she is growing weaker, the many weeks with the incubus have taken its toll, for it has been draining her of her life-force and nothing is stopping it or restoring her weakened spirit. Mariah feels that there is only one thing left that will sustain her until this is over, *Spirit Possession*. With the exorcism of the incubus from the O'Keefe's home, Mariah is now free to come into the house without using telepathic methods. Thus, on one morning early, with the entire family sleeping, Mariah is unseen and unheard as she drifts along the corridor, stopping at Myra's closed door and passing through it.

Myra is alone, which is good. Had Mrs. Grey been in the bed also, Mariah would be unable to achieve this *procedure*. Myra is lying on her back in a deep, sound sleep. Mariah slides above her and turning with her face upward, she lowers herself into Myra's sleeping form.

This is not a *takeover* but instead, a merging of mind and spirit. Unlike a hostile possession, this is done to save the life energies of the possessed person. Mariah and Myra will function as one entity, each will know what the other knows, feel what the other feels, love or hate what the other loves or hates. Myra will now know the spirit world, and Mariah, once more will know the physical.

• • •

Arising at around mid-day, and after a moderate breakfast, Adrian receives permission to work in the study. Bookshelves line three walls, for Myra's father, a lawyer, has his law-books and other academic material here for easy reference in preparation of law cases.

Sitting at the keyboard for hours, he learns a good deal of the O'Keefe's family history. Mr. and Mrs. O'Keefe join him there around two o'clock and both are instrumental in giving information that helps him narrow his search and speed things along. He researches Frances O'Keefe's family, which is where they suspect is the relationship to Mariah. They trace this back for only seven generations, to an abandoned male infant. Someone had left him on the steps of an orphanage (now destroyed) in Charleston, South Carolina, in June of 1869.

The family that took in and raised this orphan, named him *Lewis Mercer*. The period coincides with the dates in the Family Bible of Worthington Manor, just four years after the civil war. However, this does not reveal how the murder took place: the identity of the perpetrator; why he committed the foul deed; who took the infant and why or how the child came to be in South Carolina. Even now, this search is asking more questions than it is answering, such as, why Mariah's body left was at the mansion and what happened to the other family members. The parents of Theodor Worthington were still living at the family home, yet there was no trace or record of them found anywhere. Still, the number one unanswered question is; how has this old southern plantation gone unnoticed or even thought of, for over a hundred and fifty years? All records of the manor stop abruptly in the year 1869! It is as though a shroud of invisibility drapes over the mansion, yet the farmlands surrounding the main house continue in use.

A detailed search of the history of the Worthington Family reveals it to be a well-respected family, owning five hundred or so slaves, and claiming ten thousand prime acres of cotton, tobacco and corn, in eastern North Carolina. This very wealthy and famous family had great influence on the governing body of the county of Nash, but yet no one remembers it. Why wasn't this family missed? They need to have an honest discussion with the Nash County Sheriff Department about their investigation of the crime.

• • •

Upon awaking, Myra feels unusually refreshed and rested, "This is going to be a most glorious day. I can just feel it!" She rises and quickly showers and dresses. Though the day is mostly over, for it is half past four, Myra feels she can still accomplish a few things. She heads for the kitchen for she is ravenous. "Good morning Gerti!" she calls out cheerfully, while taking a stool by the counter.

"Mornin' nothin', child, 'ts pretty near supper time. Y'all done and sleep the whole days 'way. I'm gonna have supper pretty soon now, you wantin' somethin' now or can you wait?" Gerti speaks without turning to see Myra.

"Oh, Gerti, I can wait. Just a cup of coffee, that should hold me," Myra lightly replies.

"Must say y'all shore sound chipper 'day then yours been at. What airs gotten into you anyhow?" Gerti now turns and closely inspects Myra, as if looking for horns or something worse. "Understand you folks had a might' 'citmen here's last' nigh. But yours mammy an' pappy seemed right happy 'bout it all," says Gerti. "How come' y'all wait 'til me an' Melinda done an' left 'before you all start with the fun, hum?"

"Believe me, Gerti, it was no fun," Myra speaks with a bit of irony. "Where's Mother and Father?" she asks after a bit.

"O they is in yer pappy's study, with that fellow from New Yoke. Been in thar most of afternoon, duin' somethin' on that thara 'puter. Shore keep' demseves buzi. Wanner tell'em supper be readi 'bout seven?" Gerti flippantly asks.

"Sure thing, give me a minute to finish my coffee," Myra replies.

Then Myra makes her way to her father's study. She finds Adrian at the computer and both parents seated on either side looking intently at the monitor. "Good evening all, Gerti said that the three of you have been very busy in here, you must have found something important to hold your attention this long. So what have you discovered?"

In unison the three look her way, "Hello dear," her mother greets her. "Did you rest well? You certainly look as though you have. You seem different somehow, more confidant and lively. You no longer have a thing to worry about, except school, and your father and me," she smiles lovingly at her only child, and then kisses her cheek, then a cheek-to-cheek hug. "Come; listen to what Adrian has dug up today. He has worked very hard, I know he must be tired," she pats his back in a motherly fashion.

"Yes, well," breaks in Mr. O'Keefe, "all of this is quite interesting, don't see how any of it can really be of help. Seems to me the best way to solve this murder is to hire a private investigator," he states, as he too leans toward his daughter, kissing her on the brow. "Evening sweetheart, slept well I take it."

"Yes, Father I did, slept like the *dead*," this with a little humor to it, while smiling sheepishly.

Adrian, however, is not fooled. Eyeing Myra intensely, he sees two *auras*. This is no real surprise to him, and he is just as certain that Myra is not aware of what has happened, but he is not going to tell her until, or if the need arises.

Myra's father gives up his seat to his daughter, "Myra, sit here and Adrian will go over everything with you; I'm going to phone the office to see how well things went without me today. Probably fell apart," he adds jokingly.

"You overrate yourself, Jonathan," says his wife with a smile.

Knowing she is joking with him, he kisses her lightly on the lips, "Maybe I do, but *you* don't" and winks significantly.

"Wait, honey, I'll walk with you, must check with Gerti on dinner anyway."

"Oh, Gerti says dinner is at seven," Myra says, as her parents are leaving the room.

She turns her attention to Adrian, who begins to relate all of the information learned on this day. As she listens, Myra is somewhat surprised by how familiar some of it feels, but holds her tongue, for she has no proof to substantiate it. "It's too late today to start much, but we did call Sheriff Flint and he has set an appointment with us first thing tomorrow morning. Think you can be ready by nine?"

"With bells on," she replies perkily. Adrian smiles and shakes his head, not too sure if two women in one body is something a man alone can deal with successfully!

• • •

On Wednesday morning by eight, Adrian, Myra, Mrs. Grey and Mr. O'Keefe (who is taking a few hours off from work again) are ready for the trip to the little township of Nashville, the county seat. This is a very old and historic town, with the courthouse on Main Street and the Sheriffs' Department located at the back of the courthouse.

Arriving in Nashville, you feel as if you have gone back in time; the storefronts date back to the forties and fifties. The constructions of any new businesses are on the outskirts of town. This small town is very different from New York, at least the part from which the Greys come. The town offers a relaxed, even lazy atmosphere, and the inhabitants walk unhurriedly down Main Street, stopping to talk with each other, as though each might be in his own home.

They arrive at their destination and a deputy greets them, "Good morning, may I help you? Oh, hello Mr. O'Keefe, Sheriff Flint is expecting you. Go right in." he motions to a frosted glass door toward the back. The county has just recently constructed this new facility and there is an air of authority surrounding the buildings.

Sheriff Flint greets them and after the introductions, they get down to business. "Okay John, just what kind of information do you need about the old Walton place?" asks the sheriff getting right to the point, for he needs to get out on patrol. Sheriff Flint is a white male of medium height and stocky build. He is in his late forties, has dark hair and a full mustache with streaks of grey running through it.

Mr. O'Keefe turns and looks at Adrian, nods his head, giving Adrian permission to proceed with the interview.

"Sheriff in your investigation of the—did you called it the 'Walton Place' did you find anything that would identify who murdered the victim, if the crime was committed in this date and time?" Adrian asks, as he leans forward.

"You know people; we were as surprised as anyone when this old place turned up with a mummified body in it. You realize it's been over a century since this crime, and the trail is colder than an iceberg floating in the north Atlantic. And it's for damned certain the murderer is long dead, so there's not much point in trying to apprehend him. So I reckon I don't understand just what you are looking for," the sheriff looks from one to the other. "And if weren't for the fact that John here is an old friend I wouldn't be giving this info to anyone 'cept family."

Mr. O'Keefe explains that it is thought that his wife, Frances, is a descendant of the dead woman. With that bit of news, Sheriff Flint tells what they have discovered. The old manor is sitting on land that is rented from an absentee landlord, Charles Walton, living down in Wilmington, North Carolina, and when contacted, he was as surprised as the sheriff at the existence of the old house. As far as he knew when purchasing the lands, there were no dwellings on it, much less an old plantation with a corpse in it. He purchased the land over forty years ago from an agency in Rocky Mount and he did not know who the original owner was. There were over five thousand acres and over the years, the owner sold bits and pieces, except for the thousand areas where the manor is located. Different farmers at one time or another had rented those lands, but never had anyone suspected the existence of the manor.

When checking the interior of the house they discovered it had three stories; the third story could only be reached by the stairs at the back of the house near the kitchen, for this is where the servants had lived. However, they had found no evidence that could help in solving the case and honestly, they aren't trying, due to the case's extreme age. There is no point to it; they are trying to solve cases that are more recent. Their manpower is insufficient to handle all their caseloads.

Thanking the sheriff for the help he has been able to give them, the group leaves Nashville, heading to Mr. O'Keefe's law offices where they leave him and take the car home.

"I guess we need to go back to the manor house sometime today," Adrian suggests.

"We can't today," Myra speaks, "We need another twenty four hours to rest."

Adrian glances at her, she is looking straight ahead as if she has not spoken, and he knows that this is Mariah speaking and not Myra. Mariah is telling him that Myra is still too weak for the task ahead.

"Adrian," Mrs. Grey whispers in his ear, "Is Myra possessed by Mariah?"

"Yes, Mom, she is," he answers with somewhat of a sigh. "I am in the mood for some sunshine and a swim, what do you say?"

"Oh, that sounds fantastic," giggles Myra. "It would certainly cool us off a bit and I could work on my tan."

"Well, you two help yourselves, after lunch I'm taking a long nap," Mrs. Grey replies.

So they spend the afternoon in the O'Keefe swimming pool in the back yard. Myra chooses a black one-piece swimsuit that contrasts strongly with her pale hair and complexion; they expend built up energy swimming long laps.

Adrian cannot help but admire just how beautiful Myra is; very petite, well proportioned and dainty she is, but still with strong muscles and flawless firm skin. As the afternoon whiles away, Adrian finds that Myra is becoming enlightened to the spiritual side of life, no doubt because of Mariah. He feels that, after tonight, Mariah will release her bond with Myra, for they cannot exorcise Worthington Manor while Myra is possessed.

They swim together, racing each other for trifling rewards, and generally just getting acquainted. Gerti sends them a picnic lunch by way of the housekeeper.

Adrian is finding that his feelings for Myra are growing past friendship and this worries him, for he is twelve years her senior and he had never imagined that this would happen. He senses her attraction to him, but wonders maybe, that it is just infatuation. He will not dwell on it now; just enjoy the moment, for there is a rougher road ahead they need to travel together before thinking of a personal relationship. As the sun drops behind the horizon, turning the sky from Carolina blue to hues of lilac and rose, they decide to call it a day and head for the main house. Each has a large beach towel; Myra ties hers at the waist in Tonga fashion and Adrian's is about his shoulders.

Gerti is ready to serve dinner as they enter and she calls to them. "We'll be there as soon as we shower and change," Myra answers. She stops for a moment and looks up at Adrian. "It has been a marvelous afternoon, Adrian, thank you," she then stands up on her toes, for he is a good foot taller than she is, and taking his face in both of her hands kisses him lightly on his cheek. She gazes into his eyes, then Adrian, as if being controlled by an outside force, wraps his arms around her waist, pulls her closer, and presses his mouth firmly to hers. She sighs and parts her lips slightly, allowing the kiss to deepen. She moves her arms up about his neck in an unexpected response. For a brief moment, they forget everything but each other and the closeness of their bodies . . . their spirits.

Adrian, with all the strength that he can muster breaks away, taking her arms from around his neck, "We had better get inside," his voice is husky. Myra nods, and quickly heads for her room.

• • •

He will be sleeping again on the sofa, allowing his mother the guestroom. Later, as he is readying for bed, Adrian considers the events of the day. He can't say he regrets the intimacy with Myra, only he wishes that she had not been under Mariah's influence at the time. Myra may not even remember the incident after Mariah's departure from her. He will have to wait and see.

Later, Myra goes to her parents' room to ask her mother if she has a sedative she can give her. "What's the problem Myra? Don't you feel well?" Mrs. O'Keefe asks with concern.

"I feel fine, Mother, just keyed up from all the swimming this afternoon, just overtired I think," Myra answers wearily. She doesn't want to reflect long on the encounter with Adrian. How could he have any respect for her? After all, she kissed him first and he was the one who stopped it. What must he think of her? Thanking her mother and kissing both of her parents, 'Good night,' she returns to her room.

• • •

Much, much later, at one in the morning, while the household is sleeping soundly, Mariah departs from Myra. Her spirit lifts up and separates from the sleeping girl. While suspended in mid air over the still form, Mariah calls. *"Myra, come with me."* She extends her hand and Myra's astral body reaches out its own hand and takes hold of Mariah's.

Both figures are clothed in fabric as sheer as spider's silk and, with their hair flowing as a colorless scarf in a strong wind, looking down, they both see Myra's physical body asleep in her bed.

"*Am I dead?*" Myra wonders.

"*No,*" answers Mariah, their thoughts being transferred without spoken words, and the two spirits depart Myra's bedroom.

"*Where are we going?*" asks Myra looking at Mariah with a new perceptive; for this Spirit is wonderful and sensitive, unearthly, even heavenly, magnificent and so like Myra in appearance, that it is hard to comprehend.

"*We are going sight-seeing in a lofty way,*" smiles the Spirit, "*but first to visit Adrian.*"

They have no trouble moving about, traversing through walls, doors and other objects as easily as through air. Hovering above the slumbering Adrian, the Spirits, together, call his name, "*Adrian,*" after a second, again, "*Adrian.*"

Startled out of a deep sleep, Adrian awakes, but is paralyzed where he lies.

He is sure he is dreaming with his eyes open, for before him are two identical female beings and surrounding each is a soft bluish-white glow. They are semi-nude and their bodies are shimmering as though they are made of crystal, their hair appears to be of white gold and is rippling as waves in a pond. Their eyes blaze purple fire, and they are drifting in slow motion, side to side, and up and down, five or more feet above the sofa. They both look like Myra!

"*No, Adrian, you are not dreaming, although we can not allow you to move. I am Mariah,*" she communicates to him.

"*I can hear her but she does not seem to be speaking,*" thinks Adrian.

"*Yes, we are using our thoughts to speak with you . . . Yes, we are able to read your mind.*" Mariah informs him. "*I wish to thank you for what you and Myra are doing to save me. It has been an eternity since all this has taken place, but I, at least, now know part of what became of my son. When done, I will reunite with him and his father on the next plane. I am taking Myra on a tour, she will remember this as a dream, but you will know that it is not. I will have her back by dawn. See to it that no one awakes her, for if she is awakened and the astral body has not returned, it will never be able to do so, and Myra's physical body will perish. Wait and let Myra awake on her own.*" With this, the two spirits levitate through the ceiling and Adrian falls back to sleep.

● ● ●

Higher and higher, they soar as eagles on silent wings; time stands still and the earth is surreal. They are able to see where there is no light, hear where there is no sound, feel with their minds and taste the wind. They speed along with the swiftness of light, seeing lifetimes passing before them, seeing the past, and seeing the future. They feel no cold, no heat, no discomforts . . . only the pleasure of being so completely free that there is nothing in the universe to compare with it. They look down at the earth flying beneath their feet, up at the heaven and the stars, each one in its given place in the sky. The sky itself is dark blue velvet and the clouds are puffs of silver cotton. The moon glows white, sending spirals of radiant, silvery moonbeams down to the sleeping earth. They soar even further, leaving the earth behind, taking a tour of the outer-most planets, close to the very sun, where in another form they would have perished. They anticipate its heat but there is none, there are comets roaming the heavens minding their own existence, keeping to their own paths, as with the order of a superior Being. There are other astral bodies traveling here, all with the magnificent glory of Mariah and Myra.

It is time for the return trip to earth and for Myra to her physical self. As promised to Adrian, they arrive just as the sun is peeping over the horizon, turning the sky to crimson. Mariah escorts Myra to her bed. She lowers herself down to her body then back into herself, and immediately she is sleeping soundly. Mariah bids her farewell and retreats to the Manor house.

• • •

Adrian is startled into consciousness, events of the night before quickly returning to his waking mind. Seeing Mariah for the first time is shocking and even more so because Myra is with her and the duplicate pair they present is quite hard to come to terms with. Psychic he is, but Adrian has never witnessed the Astral Body before now. He is aware that this mode of paranormal transformation has been debated but, as yet, he has not been able to accomplish this feat so did have his doubts, until now. He also knows just how dangerous it can be, and for that reason, Mariah came to warn him of the danger of awaking Myra if her astral body had not yet returned to the physical one. Looking at the bedside clock radio he sees it is four forty six am, an hour or so until dawn. He will wait for them.

Pulling on just his jeans, quietly he makes his way down the long narrow corridor to Myra's room. Slowly turning the knob he eases open the door; the obscurity of the room is broken by the glow of the full moon spreading its soft bluish light over Myra's still figure. She is lying on her back, with one hand up around her face and the sheets pulled to just under her arms, so they are resting outside and on top of the covers. Her ashen hair spreads out over the pillow. She lies so perfectly still, that you might think she was in death's grip. However, after a few seconds of watching, Adrian can just make out her breathing; yes, she lives. He takes a seat over in the corner of the room and waits.

As the first rays of the rising sun break through the bedroom window, Mariah and Myra slide in headfirst on the waves of light. Myra lowers herself back into her motionless body and is at once sleeping soundly. The two spirits look as they had when appearing to him the night before, so Adrian is further convinced he has not dreamt the visit. Mariah catches sight of him in the corner and in less than a heartbeat is at his side; he rise to face her.

"*You and your mother come to Worthington Manor today, alone,*" and with that thought, she tilts her face toward the ceiling and effortlessly glides up and out through the roof.

Adrian does not move for a minute. Mariah has something to reveal to him at the Manor, and she does not want Myra or the others to know it yet.

He walks over by Myra's bedside and gazes down on her lovely face. If only he had not fallen in love with her, for it complicates his job and compromises his reasoning and psychic abilities. He leans over her and places a soft kiss on her parted lips, there is a slight twitch of her mouth as if tickled by a feather, but she does not wake. Adrian smiles and noiselessly leaves her room.

CHAPTER FOUR

VISIONS OF THE PAST

A few hours later, he greets the rest of the family in the smaller dining area, where they are having breakfast.

"Morning Adrian," Mrs. O'Keefe is the first to speak, "have a cup of coffee and a cinnamon Danish?" Adrian sits down and greets them, then informs his mother of the need to go to the manor house today. On hearing this, Mr. O'Keefe offers them the loan of his car. Thus with these arrangements made, they set about getting ready to leave. Myra has not yet risen and Adrian wants to leave before she wakens. There are a couple of reasons for this; he doesn't want to have to refuse if she wishes to go with him, and he is not ready to discuss last night's events.

Adrian and his mother are ready to leave at eight fifty and, with the directions given them by Mr. O'Keefe, they set off.

They reach their destination and it is on this road that Myra had her accident; they locate the site, but not the access road. However, Adrian knows there is a hidden path, but it is blocked from view by the thick forest. They park along the edge of the road and get out, then walk a quarter of a mile in both directions and finally locate the path. They maneuver the car carefully down the sloping roadway, across the drainage ditch, through tall grasses until they reached the overgrown path. Although recently used by the Sheriffs' Department, the path has an unused appearance, which is why it is so hard to see, if you do not know of its existence.

After a fifteen-minute drive through thick, blackish green underbrush, and tall swaying pines that block the sun, they arrive at the old plantation. It looks much as Myra had described, with one big difference; a thick white fog shrouds the house. You could be forgiven for thinking there is nothing here, for with the gnarled oaks, dense shrubs and the pine forest growing behind the house, it appears vacant. However, you can plainly see the farmland surrounding the house, with tobacco and corn, two tall plants that help to disguise the manor.

After parking, they stand outside and stare at the looming house. Adrian glances over at his mother then speaks, "Can you sense evil here, Mom?"

"Yes, I am overwhelmed with the immense suffering and grief this house harbors. Are you ready?" Mrs. Grey replies, wondering just what malice dwells in this house.

"As I ever will be, let's go, but stay behind me," Adrian lowers his voice. Thus, they cautiously approach the overbearing mansion, the thick fog swirling around their ankles as they move through it. They come upon the double door, which Adrian pushes forcefully with his full strength; the doors slowly swing open with a groan. "I'm surprised Myra was able to get these heavy doors to budge," he said.

It is dark and Adrian turns on the flashlight he has brought with him, and aims it around the room. This is the reception hall, looking much as expected, "Let's try the back stairs," Adrian is still speaking in low tones. So they enter the door to the left of the staircase; this is the dining area. In here is a rectangular wooden table, which is broken in the middle. To the right of the outside exit is a winding staircase that goes up rather steeply to the third floor. There is only one entryway, a door that is open. Here are three rooms directly connected to each other. As a result, to get to last room it is necessary to go through the first two, which they do. These rooms face the rear of the mansion and each one has two tall windows with darkened panes and tattered curtains. This isolated part of the mansion is where the servant quarters were, with three to four beds per room, but there is nothing here to arouse any suspicion. These rooms have a unique odor, different from from the muskiness that you would expect to find in an old house such as this. Not able to define what it is that they sense, they put it to the back of their minds for now. The usual cobwebs and dust that you would expect here are oddly missing; though not clean, it does not appear as it does downstairs. Not sensing any paranormal activity, they retreat back down.

"I didn't experience any spiritual activity up those stairs," Mrs. Grey said, "Strange, too; you would think that there would be."

"Yes, you would think so, if anything out of the ordinary had happened up there. Let's try the other part of the house. I believe the third room is the only area where anything was found," Adrian adds.

Back at the front staircase, they climb to the second floor. As Myra did, Adrian sees the same six doors with the third one having yellow tape twisted across it, sealing it closed by the Sheriffs' Department. Checking the other rooms first, they find them pretty much as Myra had said, except for the nursery, which sends strange vibes to both Adrian and his mother. "Mom, I feel paranormal activity in this one particular spot, do you?" Adrian turns and studies his mother intensely; she stares back at him, nods her head in the affirmative, but doesn't speak.

Adrian enters the room with reservations; he waits for a few seconds as he watches the chair that is rocking. He places a steadying hand on the back of it, and instantaneously the room changes around them, and they are back in eighteen sixty-nine, Adrian and his mother see the events as though watching a 3D movie.

The lightning and thunder are persistent, but inside things are warm and dry. This room is a typical nursery, done in baby blue and yellow and Mariah is sitting in the chair, with an infant nursing at her breast. She coos to the infant in her arms to calm him from the frightening sounds of the storm. A young black girl is in the small adjoining room softly singing an old Negro spiritual as she goes about her knitting by the glow of a candle; this is Rose, the infant's nanny.

Suddenly in bursts one of the field hands, he is dripping wet from having rushed in from the steady rain outside. "Missus Mariah they's a coming, up the road and yer pappy done and sent me in here to warn y'all. You gotta get ever' body and hide somewhere!" the Negro is shirtless, shoeless, and his breeches rolled up to his knees. His skin glistens from the rain and his clothing is soaked, attesting to his efforts to give warning to the family.

Mariah stands quickly, "Who's coming, Joshua?"

"I's not real sure, Missus Mariah, but they done and killt all the folks on the Jameson's place. It's those rebels that don't think the war is over, and they is raidin' an' burnin' and just plain d'stroyin' ever'thing theys sees. One of his workers done and escape and he come to warn us!"

"Rose!" Mariah calls to the nanny.

"Yes mum," she answers as she comes out of her small bedroom.

"Rose, come here and take Richard," she hands the child over, "go in here," she indicates the nanny's room, "and do *not* come out until I come for you!" With that order Mariah ushers them into the nanny's room and locks the door; she then pockets the key in her bosom. She and the field hand both leave the nursery and rush down the landing to her bedroom where she begins searching through her dresser for a handgun.

"Joshua, get the servants into the hidden chamber!" As Mariah is speaking, she is loading the gun and checking out the window to see if anyone is coming down the path. It is dark but the lightning does not show anything on the path leading up to the mansion.

"But Missus Mariah, I don't knows 'bout no secret room," says Joshua.

"Oh never mind, I forgot you aren't in the household servants. I'll take care of it. But where is my husband?" demands Mariah, remembering she has not heard from him since early morning.

"He's out yonder with his pappy, thay's getting all the field hands together and are going to try and fight them," by now, Joshua is panting, leaning over with his hands on his knees.

• • •

The scene changes, Adrian and his mother are back in the present. Looking to each other, they analyze what they have just seen. "Who do you suppose these bandits were," queries Adrian.

"It could have been any one of the bands of renegades back then, that continued the war for their own profit," declares Mrs. Grey.

They next stop is at the room with the spinning wheel; Adrian places a hand on it and the scene changes.

• • •

There sitting at the wheel is a much older woman, spinning by the light of several oil lamps. Mariah comes to the door, "Mother Abigail, we are under attack, I don't know who, but get the servants and yourself into the chamber with the sliding panel, I'll come and close it."

"Mariah!" calls Mrs. Worthington as Mariah turns to leave.

"Yes, Mother Abigail?"

"Where is the baby?" the older woman asks.

"With Rose locked in the nanny's room, I have the key here," she pats her chest, "I'll let you all out when this is over. I don't think much is going to come of it, the storm is too bad, they are over-reacting and more than likely the band went the other direction," Mariah states with more confidence than she feels.

• • •

THE CURSE

Now they are back in the present; they leave this room, and stop at the third door where they had found Mariah's body. Disregarding the yellow sealing tape, they tear at it and enter the room. Adrian walks over to the sofa where Mariah's mummified corpse was found and places his hand on its back. Again, the scene changes, and they are back in time.

• • •

Mariah is in here alone with a pistol held in one hand and she is looking out into the night. The sound of gunfire is faint, but there is no way of telling what is going on outside. It is still storming and it must be hours later since the scene in the nursery, probably around midnight. There is a ruckus at the door, which is locked. Mariah blows out the one candle on the table next to her and shrinks into the drapes as though trying to hide, the door is violently forced open, and it slams against the wall. There are three vile looking men, they have beards, are rain soaked and have guns in their hands. Mariah panics and fires her pistol killing one of them instantly, that one falls as one of the men attempts to catch him, while the other one rushes her and disarms her. This one man holds her tightly as the other bends over his fallen comrade, "Matt! Matt!" he calls to the dead man. "She's killed my brother! You just wait bitch 'til I'm finish with you."

The other man holds Mariah down and his boss beats her severely and then rapes her. When Cromwell is done, he removes a knife from his boot and plunges it into her semi-conscious body. Adrian removes his hand from the sofa; he did not wish to see more. He no longer sees the events still unfolding.

• • •

"Mom, I need to get out of here!" and with that distressing shriek, Adrian bolts from the room. The horror of what he sees makes his stomach churn; his mother is as shaken as he is. This was too much like seeing Myra raped and murdered, which is a thought that could drive him crazy.

They check the last door where the bats reside. They had returned and are hanging upside down from the three cross beams supporting the ceiling. Only now, they did not leave as they had when Myra had entered. Their droppings cover the floor, while large insects, roaches and spiders and even rats, crawl and scurry about the room. The one window in here is broken, this is the entrance for the bats and the stench on a hot August day is overpowering.

Adrian reaches into his jeans' hip pocket and retrieves a handkerchief, which he places over his nose, and then enters the room, "Mom, if you like you can wait out here" She nods her head in agreement after getting a whiff and stays back.

With the flashlight in one hand and the other covering his face, Adrian picks his way through the filth. He feels an urge to enter the room completely, for he knows that this is where the hidden chamber must be. He crosses the room to the back left wall, places one hand flat against its surface and with sensitive fingers begins searching for an opening that he knows must be here. He finds it and, taking out his pocketknife, he starts trying along the straight edge he has found. With patience, he forces the hidden door, which slides to his right but rather too quickly, so that he stumbles in before he is ready. This hidden chamber is pitch-black; he directs his light about, and a horrific scene greets him. This chamber has a dozen or more corpses lying on the floor. They appear to be mostly women and children, household servants. They had not been murdered, but instead, whoever had placed them in here had been unable to come back to release them. They had succumbed to the lack of fresh air and the stifling heat and died within a few days. Adrian leaves this chamber of horrors; no wonder Mariah's spirit was caught in limbo, she had been unable to come back for the servants and she feels the guilt of them having died at her hands.

Back at the landing again with his mother, Adrian explains just what he has discovered and how Mariah was involved with it. "Let's get out of here, I think I know what we need to do," he tells her.

However, this visit is not finished as they thought, for while passing the nursery, the scene once more changes.

• • •

It is now closer to morning and the storm has stopped. They watch as the door to the nanny's room suddenly falls with a crash to the floor, for someone has taken off the door hinges. Then the young Negro girl, Rose, exits, she picks up the door and leans it against the wall, (where it was when Myra was here.) She goes back inside and gets the baby, thus with the infant wrapped up and in her arms, Rose runs from the nursery but halts at the third door; she stifles screams with her fist to her mouth as she sees Mariah lying on the sofa. Going inside she bends over the body, "O Miss Mariah," is all she can say. The girl, with one hand, straightens Mariah's clothing, for it is obvious what has happened to her. Rose carefully removes the key from

THE CURSE

Mariah's bosom and hastily leaves the room, closing and locking the door, leaving the key in its lock. She hurries down the flight of stairs and out the double doors; she takes the time to close them, but why? It is as though she can shut in the horrors, which occurred here on this day. It is still dark, the dead litter the courtyard and the Master and his family, the entire field hands and household servants are dead, murdered. The young black girl is crying, she looks down on the infant who is also crying and swears, "I's promise you Master Richard, and I's promise Miss Mariah, they will never know that we got away. We, with the help of the Lawd, are going to leave here and never come back. I's not gonna tell no one 'bout what happen here today, 'cause ifun I's do they's shore and try to kill us too." She is last seen running down the oak lined path and then, this scene also vanishes.

• • •

Adrian and his mother are still at the nursery's door, "That is how the baby was saved," states Mrs. Grey. "The girl somehow made it to South Carolina. A black girl with a white baby would have aroused suspicion, which is why she left the child on the steps of the orphanage," she looks at Adrian in amazement.

"I agree with you on that, the thing is we will never know for sure how he got to South Carolina," there is a note of sadness in his voice. "Let go back to the O'Keefe's and let them know what we have learned." With hurried steps, they return to the outside world. But as they are emerging through the double doors, the scene here also changes.

• • •

As they watch, it is near the noon hour, it is the next day, and the bodies are still lying about the courtyard where they had fallen. Flies are buzzing over and on the corpses, vultures are circling in the sky and wild dogs are starting to feast on the human remains. There is no movement outside in the courtyard; no wind disturbing the leaves on the trees or blades of grass in the yard. There is no life moving inside the mansion, all is deathly still and silent.

From around the house come five Negro servants, three grown men and one boy are walking and an old man is driving a cart with a mule harnessed to it and the cart is loaded with pine straw. They had evidently been working out in the pine forest gathering this straw, which they use as mulch around the flowerbeds. They are talking and laughing to themselves but are brought up short as they realize that things are not right. They take in the death scene before them and astonishment fills their faces. They run into the yard, chase off the dogs with sticks, then start checking the bodies; they moan and they cry and the boy screams and runs from this scene, as the men go about this dreadful task. They cannot leave the bodies for the vultures, so they decide to bury them and the grim chore begins. It takes them the better part of the day to dig a mass grave. They take the bodies three and four at a time on the cart to the old cemetery in the back of the house. Their gruesome jobs complete, the servants leave the Manor, walking down the oak lined path, and are never seen again. A thick white fog descends over Worthington Manor obscuring it completely.

• • •

Adrian and his mother are back in the present and each is lost in thought, as they get into the car and head back to Rocky Mount, leaving Worthington Manor again shrouded in the thick white fog.

CHAPTER FIVE

RETURN TO THE MANOR

It is nearly six o'clock when they arrive back at the O'Keefe's home, having picked up Mr. O'Keefe on their way. With a few hours of daylight left, they decide to call Reverend McGregor in order to finish the arrangements started on Monday night. When invited over, he jokingly replies that if they would serve him dinner again he would be more than glad to come. Mrs. O'Keefe laughs heartily and replies, "Yes, certainly come for supper."

Adrian has not seen Myra since the night before and she is not in the main part of the house when they arrive. When questioned as to her whereabouts they inform him that she went out to lunch with a girl friend, then on to the Public Library for a more detailed search. She had called a little while before their arrival to say that she would make it by seven, dinnertime.

Adrian showers and shaves, then lies down in the guestroom for a twenty-minute rest, so that he can decipher the visions that he had witnessed earlier today at Worthington Manor, without interruptions. He rationalizes that Mariah did not want Myra to know the details of her death. She knows also that it was difficult for him to watch, but there had been no choice. No one knows of the bodies in the concealed chamber: or that Mariah had closed the door; or that due to her own death, Mariah had not freed them. Thus, they had died a slow agonizing death by heat and suffocation. These souls are trapped; the Dark Spirit holds them captive on the third floor and that explains the bizarre odor they encountered when there. The demon is feeding off their fears, while they re-live their last days repeatedly, caught up in a kind of time warp from which they are unable to escape!

Horrifying this is, and these poor souls are damned for eternity if this terror goes unrevealed and the Dark Spirit unvanquished. There is so much evil there, that it hides the manor behind a thick, white fog, successfully concealing its existence. Adrian did not think it necessary to re-bury the bodies in the mass grave, but they will pray for them.

A tap on the door, "Adrian . . ." it is Myra, "Dinner is ready and Reverend McGregor has arrived." He did not expect to see her before dinner; going to the door he hesitates a moment, then opens it. Myra is already walking back towards the living room.

"Myra!" he calls. She turns and looks his way, smiles briefly but continues. Adrian follows her to the living room where everyone has gathered awaiting the call for dinner.

"Well, it looks like we all are present, shall we go in?" Mr. O'Keefe glances around the room, everyone agrees and they make their way to the dining area.

Later, after dinner, they return to the living room and everyone settles down and waits for the main reason the reverend is here.

"Adrian, my boy, what have you learned this day?" Reverend McGregor inquires. "I understand you and your mother went back to the mansion."

"This is a case like neither Mom nor I have ever seen. Mariah remains stranded there for more than one reason. It seems there is a hidden chamber, which was used as a safe place for the family if they should come under attack, and this is what happened." Adrian continues with the description of his visions, trying not to give too many details so as to spare Myra the horror of the murders. Even so, it did not take much imagination to know what actually did take place.

"I could be wrong but I feel that it was one of Theodor's brothers who took possession of the property. And instead of living there, he made a good deal of money by renting out the land to sharecroppers. This doesn't mean to say that he, or they, had anything to do with the carnage and they may not have known that Mariah's body was still inside. They just closed up the house. They would not have wanted to live there, and the leasing off the land was the best thing to do." Adrian looks at everyone to see how his speculation was received; they all agree that it would explain a great deal.

"There was a small band of army deserters from both sides that for years after the Civil War continued to create havoc, especially in the South," Mrs. O'Keefe, who is a history teacher, explains to everyone. "There was one bunch in this part of the state, and they called themselves 'Cromwell's Raiders'. Their leader was Rudolf Cromwell, a Union colonel who deserted under fire at Gettysburg, along with fifty or so of his men. They merged with some southern deserters and continued the war for personal greed and profit. It took the Union Government four years or so to capture these renegades, but they never caught the colonel. His men told the authorities that Cromwell was killed, but it was not the Colonel who was killed but his brother, and we now know the authorities never learned of this deception at the time."

Myra surprises everyone when she offers even more information, "Frances and I, as you know, went to the library today, and we searched through old newspapers of that period. They have them scanned onto disk now. The Evening Telegram had an article dated June 3, 1869. What surprises me is that it was not on the front page but back with the obituaries. The paper reports that the Raiders attacked the two plantations. One they burned with everything destroyed and everyone killed, massacred in fact, all members of the family, all of the black servants, absolutely everyone. They first raped the women then murdered them; the children and even babies butchered! Anything of value, they carried off, and as Mother just said, they suspected Cromwell and his outlaws. They were here in this part of the state. It so happened, that one of the members of the gang had family close by, Hardy is the name. That family has relocated somewhere else since then, because of the scandal it brought on them. The plantation that burned was owned by Jules Jameson. The paper never did name the other place, only saying that all were massacred!" Myra pauses for a moment to catch her breath, and then continues, "This event was reported to the authorities by an old man, a servant of the other family. He tells of them having buried the dead at the other plantation. That seems to fit in with what Adrian and his mother saw today, am I right?" Myra, having completed her report, glances around the living room at the rest of them.

Adrian nods his head, all the while staring at Myra. She has really bounced back from her depression of a few days earlier; Mariah's possession had rejuvenated Myra mentally as well as physically. He was so glad to see this improvement in her, for she would definitely need it.

Myra, feeling Adrian's eyes on her, turns his way and smiles, "Are we ready for the next phase, Adrian?" Her question seems to have double meaning and Adrian understands what she really means. So she did remember!

"What do you say Reverend?" asks Mr. O'Keefe.

"I say Friday will be the best day, after the setting of the sun, and before the hour of twelve. Tis the old Hebrew Sabbath, the holiest day of the week. The Sabbath starts at sundown. This is the demon's weakest time, and then again at midnight he grows strong," states McGregor. "I will perform the necessary rituals and the collection of religious aids. Tomorrow, Thursday, we must bless the grave; tis important, for they've lain un-blessed for more than a century now. Tis the freeing of their souls, and their return to the Father," Reverend McGregor explains. "Friday," he draws in a long breath and exhales, "Tis a day to be spent in prayer and fasting. We must bathe ceremoniously in the blessed waters of the baptism vat at the church; we must all be ritually cleansed. Myra, if these be your woman days, this we will postpone, 'til you be clean again."

This causes Myra to blush a bright red, but she answers him, "I am done with that for a few more weeks."

The Reverend smiles at her embarrassment and continues with the instruction. "If we are successful in eradicating this demon from the Manor, then Saturday will be a day of rest and feasting. Which I must say 'tis my favorite part."

"Must Myra go back to that awful place? Why, the beast tried to kill her!" says Mrs. O'Keefe.

"For this deed to be done as it should, go she must," reasoned the Reverend. "We're not certain what role she will play, but it's plain that Myra's part 'tis important."

"I just don't know, we worried all night the night she was missing, and *this* is worse than that was! I know I can't stop her, but it will not have my blessing," Mrs. O'Keefe declares.

"Frances, now you know I wouldn't let a thing happen to our daughter, but this affair must be settled or she may never have any peace," points out Myra's father.

"Well, I guess you've made your case, I just hope we all don't live to regret it," argues Myra's mother as she folds her arms across her chest in defiance.

Myra stands and stretches, raising her arms high over her head as she yawns, "I don't know about the rest of you but I, for one, am beat, it's bed for me," She gives her parents a kiss, each on their forehead, she then crosses the room heading for the hall.

Adrian wasn't about to let her go without talking with her first. "Myra wait up a minute, can I see you in the study? I have more questions on what you've learned today."

"Okay, but I really am quite tired, Adrian," she knows that he suspects that she is avoiding him, and he is right. She is still feeling embarrassment over yesterday, and does not know how to deal with it. Yes, she is eighteen, but not a wise one when it comes to the opposite sex, for experience, she has none.

"I promise this won't take long," he places his arm lightly across her shoulder in a very casual manner, but this does not fool his mother who suspects there is a developing affair between them. She smiles to herself but does not say a word.

Entering the study Adrian closes the door behind them.

"Oh no," thinks Myra and she knows it is not her visit to the library that he wishes to see her about. "Why have you shut the door?" she demands to know.

"Oh, I have my reasons," he replies, and turns to look her in the face. "About last night.... Myra I do apologize for kissing you as I did. I know I took advantage of the little innocent peck on the cheek that you offered as a thank you and I had no right to carry it further. It will not happen again, this I promise—at least not until you grow up a little more," he stares at her and almost smiles.

Myra turns away, "I see—I don't quite know what to say. Here I am thinking how I have made a fool of myself . . . I feel like a child. Don't worry Adrian, it wasn't a big thing, we'll both get over it," with that remark Myra turns to leave the room. But Adrian grabs her by the arm and stops her. As before, there is no plan, as he takes her into his arms and kisses her soundly. She again responds and they both realize that they are fooling no one but themselves. They end the kiss but Adrian does not relinquish his embrace, he continues to hold her close. Myra sighs and lays her head against his chest. For a long time they do not speak, it is enough just to be together. Finally, noise in the hall alerts them to visitors and they break apart, each knowing there will be no turning back now.

Adrian opens the door, for he knows that it is his mother out in the hall and she is warning him not to stay too long in this room alone with Myra.

"Good night, son, I'm off to bed myself. Good night Myra, you best scoot on to your room before your parents get suspicious," Mrs. Grey grins sweetly at the young girl.

Myra blushes for the second time this evening, "Good night Mrs. Grey. Good night Adrian." Myra hurries to her room down the hall.

"All right Mom, I know you suspect something. But nothing has happened, just an innocent kiss. You know Myra is much too young for me, why she's barely more than a child," Adrian is talking much too fast and he knows it.

"Who are you trying to convince, Adrian, me or yourself? Sleep well, son," and she gives him a motherly kiss on the cheek and makes her way down the hall.

• • •

Early, at the crack of dawn, Adrian and his mother are up, plans have been made to meet Reverend McGregor at the Church across town around seven thirty AM. They wish to get an early start to beat the heat of this August day. It had been decided not to take Myra to Worthington Manor on this trip, for it is not known what effect she might have on the *Dark Spirit*.

Mr. and Mrs. O'Keefe and Myra join them a little later for morning coffee and Danish. Myra can't help stealing glances at Adrian and he at her. The older adults do not miss it, but they refrain from commenting. Discussions are kept to the day's agenda and apprehensions over tomorrow.

"What I have trouble understanding is how I was chosen to be the one to free Mariah? Is there something about me that qualifies me among anyone else?" Myra is showing a reasonable amount of apprehension of the unknown.

"Well Myra," Mrs. Grey attempts to explain things. "Sometimes a haunting of this nature can continue for centuries. My guess? Well, the fact that you are a blood descendant of the Worthington Family; you have identical features to Mariah and you are probably the same age as she at her death; all of this will help to confuse the demon. For I feel that this is a *demon* and not a disembodied spirit. When you and Mariah are together, you present a formidable force of positive energy, as opposed to the demon's negative force. These spirits consume the negative energy of lost souls. They cannot sustain themselves any other way: without a constant supply of this negative force, they wither and become immobile. They choose weak or evil people or spirits, for negativity already exists there and it increases their strength. What we have here is not possession of another entity or mortal, but instead, the captivity of spirits who died under unusual circumstances. These spirits are earthbound to start with, due to factors beyond their control. They cannot cross, so the demon takes advantage of these trapped souls and uses them for its own purposes, such as draining their protoplasm. This is why it will take two identical, positive energies to defeat two evils' negative energies. We are not certain who this demon has paired up with, but I do have an idea."

"You do, Mother? You want to enlighten the rest of us?" Adrian is taken by surprise at his mother's announcement, "I can't even guess."

"Well Adrian, after Mariah's murder you broke your connection because the scene was too disturbing, but I did not. I knew there should be more and there was.

My theory is this, because Mariah killed the younger Cromwell brother, the older one has been seeking revenge. But he had already murdered Mariah so he continues his retaliation after his death, leaving both spirits trapped on the Earthly plane. Somehow, this demon and this spirit have formed an alliance. Each one is seeking something different from the other. The demon wants energy, Cromwell wants revenge and that is to keep Mariah from crossing to the next plane. In doing that he also traps himself."

"I believe we might be able to give this demon a challenge by exorcizing him from the hidden chamber. We can ask the Reverend to do more than the blessing he suggested and see what happens," remarks Adrian.

"Yes! That's a thought, might work better than we think," says Mrs. Grey.

"Okay, that seems to be a solution for now. Well, I'm ready if you are, Mother," Adrian looks at his mother to see if there is any more she needs to tell but there isn't.

"I need to gather a few things together to take with us. You go ahead and get the car ready and I will meet you out front," Mrs. Grey replies, as she heads in one direction and Myra and Adrian go in the other. They once again have the use of the family car and Mr. O'Keefe has pulled it into the front yard. While they wait for Mrs. Grey, Adrian and Myra are discussing her role in Friday night's assault on the demon.

With his arm about her shoulder, Adrian says, "You know, Myra, I don't foresee any real difficulty for Mother and me today. But if you don't feel up to this just now, we can wait a little longer. I will need to get back to the hospital after this week because my vacation time ends Sunday. But I can arrange for more vacation in about three months, if you want to put it off."

"No, that won't be necessary, I have all the confidence now that I'm ever going to have and I don't think a day, a week, or even a year would make any difference," she hopes she sounds confident. "I'll admit this frightens me somewhat, I can't help that, but it will not stop me from doing what I feel I must do," she looks in his direction to see if he understands what she really feels.

Adrian gently takes Myra into his arms and cups her chin in one hand so to focus on her violet eyes; he feels he could drown in their depths and his thoughts drift where they shouldn't. He holds her tightly for a few moments then releases her, knowing he needs to concentrate on the job at hand, and being this close to Myra confuses his priorities.

She forces a smile, "I'll be fine, you three take extra care today. You still do not know what to expect, and I will worry until your return."

He kisses her on her forehead in a brotherly fashion not trusting himself for anything more, and then his mother joins them on the front steps.

"We will be very cautious, so you are not to worry," Mrs. Grey smiles at the both of them. "You rest up for tomorrow night, Myra, and we will be back by early afternoon, I'm sure."

Forty-five minutes later, they are picking up the minister and heading back out to Worthington Manor, arriving there at about nine fifteen. During the drive, Reverend McGregor is briefed by Mrs. Grey on her suspicions about the identity of the hostile spirit and of his probable alliance with the demon. Things look the same as before with the thick fog surrounding the estate, filling all of them with apprehension. They park the car and for several minutes just take in the view in front of them. They don't anticipate any difficulty, with Myra left at home.

"First things first," says Reverend McGregor, "tis the graves in the back that need the blessing, then the poor souls in the chamber." As they proceed around to the back of the mansion, the fog is forced out of their way then closes back around them again. Reaching the ancient burial site, they are struck by the bleakness of the landscape. An aged, broken and rusting iron fence surrounds the cemetery, but it does not keep anything living or dead, in or out. Nothing green grows here, no colorful flowers to chase away the dullness, the entire grounds are in drab gray. One tree still stands in its midst, acting as a sentinel, but its uniform of green leaves have long ago blown away, leaving it naked to the elements. Its branches are broken and twisted into grotesque shapes, and a lone crow, perched high in its branches, calls to them. The burial plots are forsaken, no loved ones visit in remembrance, and they are as forgotten as though they never were. The aged scribing on the headstones is the only thing to testify to their once mortal existence.

McGregor has brought more holy water and sanctified olive oil, and his purple ceremonial robe, which he now slips into and proceeds with the blessing. The mass grave is located outside of the main cemetery and is marked by a single decaying, wooden cross. It has words carved on it but most of them illegible, save one,—'MASTER.' He instructs them to kneel and to bow their heads in a prayer.

"Oh most gracious heavenly Father, we request Your holy blessing on these lost souls. Let not their lives to have been in vain. Conduct these souls to the heavenly realm. We ask for justice on the ones who committed this foul deed. We ask forgiveness for our own transgressions. Give us the strength to do what we must and end this terrible demonic possession of the innocents. We do beseech you in Your holy Son's name, Jesus Christ, our Lord and Savior. Amen."

"Amen," they speak as one and rise to witness the reverend walking around the unkempt cemetery, all the while sprinkling the oil and water. The liquids hiss as they come in contact with the ground as though striking a hot surface. With the ceremony completed, all is still and deathly quiet, with no movement of the wind, no song of birds, or whispering of the pines.

They return to the front of the old mansion, and the vast dual door protests strongly at being disturbed yet again, as Adrian forces it to allow their entrance. The inside is even darker than the outside with its heavy mist, but after a moment, their eyes adjust.

Let's go up these stairs first, for it is here that the hidden chamber is located," suggests Adrian, spreading his right hand out in invitation. "We can check out the rest of the mansion afterwards if you would like, Reverend."

"Certainly, I think I would. Never have heard of this place before now, and I've been in the area thirty years or more."

Mounting the staircase with Adrian leading, they trek up to the second level. Stopping at each door, they discuss in detail the events that occurred for that particular room. The reverend is very attentive as he listens to the stories that happened a hundred and fifty years before. The most astonishing thing is that evil can hold the past captive in this manner, and imprison innocent souls.

As she had done before when Myra came, Mariah follows along behind and above them. She feels no need to reveal herself to them just yet. Mariah understands that tomorrow night is set for the exorcism of the demon. Then she, as well as the others, will be released from bondage. She also knows that the *Dark Spirit* has grown stronger and is not ready to release his hostages. The old Hebrew Sabbath presents the perfect time for exorcising demons and evil spirits, for it is then they are at their most vulnerable. However, the ritual must be completed by sun-up, or it will need to be repeated from the beginning, on the next Sabbath. The midnight hour offers a short reprieve for the spirits as they regain some strength for a time, but within an hour, this advantage is lost.

Reaching the room that has the hidden chamber, Mrs. Grey volunteers to wait out on the landing. Adrian eases the door open so as not to frighten the bats and have them swarming all about. This time he is prepared; he has breathing masks with him and hands one to the reverend, and together they enter. As before, they step carefully through the accumulating refuse, quickly reaching the chamber. The door is deliberately left open and McGregor looks inside; before him lie numerous bodies in various states of decay. They are grayed and the skin has shriveled up and dried on the bones, eye sockets are empty with spiders crawling in and out, the lips are drawn back over the teeth giving them permanent grins, noses are two black pits in the center of the skull. Several have their mouths wide open as if screaming in pain, but there was never any relief from their agonies. Clothing is shredded and colorless and shoes are still on the feet of some of the adults.

"Aye, the poor souls, tis children and women, how they must've suffered." The scene is very disturbing; McGregor's hands are shaking and he is sweating profusely both from the stifling heat of this tiny chamber and from the gathering dread and fear of what might happen.

Adrian steps back to allow the reverend to begin the prayers, and, as they pray, the bodies start to stir, as though life is returning. Formless pale shapes can just been seen, rising up from the corpses, and they twist and turn as though being released from shackles. There are moans and cries from the ghosts as they ascend up to the ceiling then out the door over the heads of Adrian and the reverend, who crouch down instinctively as they pass over their heads. They then spread out into all parts of the mansion. Reverend McGregor becomes very distressed, but continues with the rest of the service; he sprinkles the holy water and oil over the dried up bones, in an instant they catch fire and burn rapidly until nothing, but smoldering ashes are left. Nothing else catches fire!

"My son," McGregor begins, "What has happened? No experience have I ever had such as this. Why were we able to see these spirits?" His questions have no answers, at least none that can be easily explained.

"I can't answer you on that one; it surprised me as much as you. I wouldn't have thought that the souls would have remained with the bodies. I damn near lost it myself. I think this is all we can do today, let's go home," having said this much, Adrian and the reverend quickly leave the sixth room.

"Mother, did you see the spirits leave here?" Adrian asks his mother, when back out on the landing.

"Yes Adrian, I did, and we are in much danger if we stay longer. The *Dark Spirit* has temporary released them, so that he can focus his powers on us!" Mrs. Grey's voice has a note of alarm.

Immediately, Mariah becomes visible, and with her thoughts communicates to them, "Adrian that is so, you must leave quickly. Otherwise, he will force you to fight now. Do not worry about me; I have been resisting him for over a century!"

"Let's go!" insists Mrs. Grey.

Down the flight of stairs, they hurry and out through the double doors, which slam shut when they emerge. Adrian helps his mother into the back seat, he and the reverend jump in the front, with Adrian again behind the wheel. He guns the engine and they are quickly leaving the mansion in the dust. Adrian can see in the rear-view mirror the white fog growing dark, with sparks of lightning dancing in the cloud and the low rumble of thunder as they speed away. He knows they have come very close to confronting the evil forces, which were anxious to do battle.

It is only two o'clock in the afternoon when they arrive back to the O'Keefe's, having dropped off Reverend McGregor at the church. He informs them that he will search the church history for more material on formal exorcism.

Myra greets them at the front door as they enter. A look at Adrian tells her that things did not exactly come off as expected. "How did everything go?" she asks.

"We're in for a fearsome battle I'm afraid," replies Mrs. Grey. "It would have happened today, had we remained much longer."

"Okay Mother," interrupts Adrian, "No need in speculating on the matter, we will know the truth soon enough." He had stopped his mother for he does not want to alarm Myra any more than she is already. "Care for a swim?" he asks Myra.

"Sure, that should be relaxing," she replies, feeling the growing tension in the room, for she knows there is more than they are telling her. However, for the afternoon she will ignore it, as they appear to be doing.

She and Adrian, as well as her mother, spend the afternoon lying around the pool, and occasionally making laps in its cool water.

CHAPTER SIX

BATTLE PREPARATIONS

Friday morning comes far too quickly for Myra and she can already feel the butterflies fluttering around her inside. She drives her own car and the three of them head for the First Baptist Church across town.

On this morning, the church is empty except for the Reverend McGregor and a few altar boys who will assist them in the ritual cleansing. The only substance they will ingest today will be water but just before leaving the church, they dine on fish, bread and one small tumbler of red wine.

The day's intensity is straining Myra's nerves and she is finding it hard to cope. For the ritual bathing, which is done at noon, they wear their swimsuits and afterwards each is given a sparkling white robe, trimmed with a wide purple and gold embellishment at the collar. They assemble later in the central arena of the church, where Reverend McGregor conducts sermons.

Here McGregor, in his purple robe, delivers a brief but powerful sermon. He explains the tools they are going to need; they will wear around their necks an amulet of pure gold. Each talisman opens, and, inside are small samples of myrrh and frankincense, the gifts the magi gave the Christ Child. Each will also carry three tiny vials, one of holy water, one of olive oil and a shaker of virgin salt, worn at the waist, suspended from a golden rope; with these, they will fight the demons. A virgin must be at the head of a triangle, to lead them into battle. This virgin will represent the purity of Christ.

• • •

The six o'clock hour brings about more rituals, after which, at seven they are ready to leave for the mansion.

They will travel in one of the church's limousines; Steve, a church deacon, has volunteered to drive them. Myra's father insists on going, although he will not directly take part in the exorcism, but will wait in the car with the chauffeur. Myra's mother calls on Mr. O'Keefe's cell phone, to wish everyone luck and says she will be praying for their success. She tells Myra how much she loves her and to please be careful, but that, if she wants, she can still back out of this. Myra replies she can't or their family's line will never be complete again, and Mariah's soul and salvation will be lost, as well as the souls of the others now being held as hostages. They are ready to leave; they climb into the back seats of the limousine for the thirty-minute drive to the mansion.

As they approach Worthington Manor, the sky grows red and jagged arrows of lightning blast over their heads and run parallel to the path they are traveling. The thunder sounds with deafening shrieks, like the cries of cats, filling them with apprehension and dread. They are expected!

The mansion is no longer shrouded in fog, for it has lifted into the skies and merges with the storm raging around them.

They get out of the car and McGregor starts with his instructions, "Myra, you stand here, Adrian on your left, Mrs. Grey behind, and I will stand to your right." As he speaks, each does as instructed.

Mr. O'Keefe hands each a tall white candle; he lights each one and even though the flames flicker from the wind, they do not go out.

The double doors, which are shut, swing open begrudgingly as they move near, as if inviting them to enter. The black interior is uninviting as they cross the threshold and the meager light from the candles offers little assistance. Myra halts a few feet inside, for the blackness impedes her advancement any further.

"Myra, go to the center of the room," Adrian instructs her.

Cautiously, Myra forges ahead to what she thinks may be its midpoint, with the flickering glow from their candles casting sinister shapes on the walls. The cobwebs dangling from the ceiling take on a life of their own, swaying and pulsating to an unheard melody. Even the dust on the floor takes part in the festivities, swirling in miniature whirlwinds, in an unholy dance.

"Everyone go to your corresponding corners; secure your candle to the floor, then form a circle around yourself with the salt. As long as you are in this circle you will be protected from a direct attack," Adrian's voice is unbelievably calm as he directs them.

Each does as instructed, then takes up a position in the center of their circle. Reverend McGregor and Adrian together go to the center of the room, and with the salt, draw an even larger circle. Then, back-to-back, they pace away from each other; they go around this circle sprinkling the holy water and the sacred olive oil until they meet on the opposite side of the circle. Adrian returns to his corner, while Reverend McGregor remains in the center of the larger one. He begins the exorcism.

"We invoke you fallen angel of Satan and all of your demons, to release your hold on these innocents souls, which have been held by you and your league. We call for your banishment from these grounds, to return to the depths of hell from which you came. You are to remain there until the return of God's own Son with his Army of Angels, for then you will do battle, and you will be cast into Perdition for your eternal damnation!"

The reverend returns to his corner and soon the lost souls are gently flowing into the room from all areas of the manor. They are barely visible, quite pale and shapeless except they have human faces, with their own features, and eyes of glowing yellow. One by one, they glide in on waves of pulsating light and begin to follow each other as they zigzag back and forth, encircling each person in a kind of figure of eight, then back into the center of the room in an ever-decreasing circle. It has the harmonious appearance of a sacred dance, performed to the tune of the beating rain and claps of thunder.

After a while, Mariah drifts in and links with the others in this dance; her form is not shapeless as the others, but she appears to wear a garment of white, which clings to her as a second skin. Her eyes flash blue light and her ashen hair flies about in disarray. She glides up to Myra and reaches out her hand; Myra responds and takes Mariah's hand in hers, then leaves her physical body, which slumps to the floor, and her astral body joins Mariah. She is now clothed in the same kind of silken gown as Mariah. Together they move smoothly to the axis of the room.

Adrian rushes over to Myra's unconscious form but Mariah stops him. "Do not remove her from here; the astral body needs to return to the physical body where it left it!"

As instructed, Adrian lays her back in a more comfortable position and well inside her circle of salt. He is greatly concerned for Myra's safety, for this action has taken him by surprise. What are Mariah's intentions? Reluctantly he returns to his corner.

Mariah, Myra and the spirits are entwining together into one figure, acting as one entity. Together they form a commanding force of positive energy; they are at the pinnacle of the spirits and are clearly distinguishable. The spirits encircle them just below their shoulders, and, as this is completed, they radiate a blinding white light and sparks of electricity emanate from their core. They unite in a song with a poignant melody but the words are neither logical nor clear. The music is shrill and piercing and continues to rise in concerto until the windows are vibrating violently.

Adrian, Mrs. Grey and the reverend are forced to shut their eyes and cover their ears for this is excruciating to their senses.

As this mass is revolving faster and faster, and the light becomes more blinding, the song more shrill, a great roar is heard rising up from the depths of the earth. The wooden floor erupts violently, sending splinters flying like sharp daggers throughout the room, barely missing the occupants.

Mariah and her mass of energy are forced to the outside of the main circle where they encircle the hole and the beast that is emerging from the depths. This is what they have intended, acting as bait and irritating the demon into careless action. The beast is terrible to behold! Two heads emerging from one body, one of a human male and the other of a demon, the one Myra had seen in the back seat of her car. It continues raising itself to the very height of the building; its torso is part snake and part human, yellowish green in color, with dull scales covering the body. Its four arms are those of dragon and of man. There are two huge leathery black wings on its back, and like a bat, it keeps unfurling them, as if preparing to take flight.

"Who dares torment me?" the demon rages in an unearthly growl. "Do none of you answer?" he screams. "We will take you all back to my domain, and feast eternally on your souls!" Then he laughs, hideously.

At that very moment, Mr. O'Keefe rushes through the open door, pausing as he takes in the scene before him. After looking around the room, searching for Myra, he sees her lying on the floor, unmoving. He cries out as he goes to her.

"Mr. O'Keefe," warns Adrian, "You must leave her where she is! Stop before it is too late!"

"Man, are you crazy! What's happened to Myra?" He rushes over to Myra and lifts her up in his arms, just as Adrian leaves the security of his corner to stop him. He steps outside the circle of salt with her, and before anyone can realize it, the demon lunges forward and snatches her from her father's arms, and not a soul can stop it kidnapping Myra's body, as the demon retreats with her, back into the abyss from which it came.

• • •

Myra! They scream together; they rush to the edge of this gaping crevice and focus their attention on its great depth. The upper segment exposes the smashed and torn earth, which is breaking off and tumbling down the sides of the abyss, but there is nothing else but obscurity. McGregor checks the time. It is a little after midnight, when the demons are at their strongest, and they had seized the opportunity when it presented itself to press their bargaining power!

Mr. O'Keefe regains his senses after being flung hard to the floor, and, as would any father having witnessed the horrible abduction of his child, comes up ready to fight whomever they think is to blame. In his eyes, this is Adrian. He rushes for Adrian and lands a punch on his jaw, effectively knocking him to the ground. Adrian is taken by surprise and is unprepared for this attack. "O'Keefe!" he yells at him, "you must wait and let me explain."

Mrs. Grey runs to her son to help him up from the floor. Adrian sits up rubbing the left side of his face; O'Keefe has landed a solid blow. Adrian stands ready to fend off any more blows when Myra's astral body appears.

"Father!" she calls to him, O'Keefe looks about trying to locate where this voice in his mind is coming from, then he sees her hovering just above him. *"Father, look at me, I am Myra, you must not blame anyone here for what has just happened, I knew of this possibility, I was warned of the danger, please let Adrian and Reverend McGregor tell you what has happened, for it is only Adrian who can save me now."*

Adrian stares at Myra, "Myra, do you know where your body was taken?"

Mariah joins Myra and answers this question for her, *"Myra's body is safe for the moment. It is protected by the amulet she wears. The demon can only guard it from our retrieval, they hope to ensnare others by enticing them into a rescue and they want Adrian. They know that the astral body is unable to reunite with the physical body as long as they have possession of it. There is a very limited time frame for the recovery—twenty four hours, after that it will no longer be possible and Myra's physical body will die."* Mariah waits for this to register, then continues, *"Adrian, this is the only entrance to the abode of the demon; it is here you must begin your journey, and you alone. Take all your knowledge of the underworld and apply it here. Do not be deceived into thinking you have rescued Myra's real body, for they can give illusions; do not believe all you see or hear. Rely on your own natural psychic powers. There is nothing that anyone here on the surface will be able to do to assist you. Our prayers go with you, and there might be some assistance from others already trapped."*

"How will I be able to recognize Myra's real body?" Adrian asks anxiously.

"*Check behind her right ear. Myra has the exact same birth mark as I; it is a raspberry mark shaped like a diamond, look for it!*" Mariah has related all the knowledge she has. "*I will keep Myra's astral body safe for as long as possible, but you must hurry, for you only have until midnight tomorrow and you must start now!*" She and Myra then slowly dissipate.

Immediately Adrian removes his white robe, for the length will hinder his movements. He is wearing jeans, a t-shirt, and sneakers, "Mr. O'Keefe will you please get me my satchel from the trunk of the limo?" Mr. O'Keefe goes to the car and returns with it. Inside Adrian removes a long length of golden rope, flashlight, a fedora and goggles. He takes the golden rope with the two remaining vials and ties this around his waist. He stills wears the golden amulet. He asks for and receives all of the sanctified candles, which he also places in his satchel; he then flings the strap over his shoulder and takes a good look about him. Mrs. Grey has tears in her eyes. She holds her son close, but she does not speak, no words can express her feelings of impending disaster. She steps away to allow him to begin his quest. He removes from the bag a two-way radio and hands it to Mr. O'Keefe, "I have no idea if these will work subterranean but I will try to keep in touch for as long I can." He then addresses the minister, "Reverend, I already know that you will pray for our safe return, but if I should fail, take care of my mother for me."

"Indeed my son I will. Distressed am I over this outcome; it would seem more trouble we bring than help we give." The older man is upset and cannot hide his emotions.

Walking over to Adrian, Mr. O'Keefe apologizes, "Sorry son about the . . ." and he indicates where he had struck him.

"Don't worry a minute more over it. I must admit you pack an impressive wallop," Adrian remarks rubbing his jaw again and working it back and forth to check for possible breakage.

Not saying another word, for time is not on his side, he shines the flashlight into the cavernous void. He can see nothing but darkness so, securing the flashlight at his waist, he releases the length of gold rope down the pit, then fastens the other end around the wooden planks of the foyer's floor.

"I don't know how far this rope will take me; I'll just have to do the best I can." Adrian looks about him, taking in his unfamiliar surroundings, and tips his hat in farewell. Everyone looks solemn, but they bid him goodbye, while hoping this will not be the last time they see him or Myra.

Stepping to the edge of the abyss and taking the rope in both hands in the style of a mountain climber, adjusting his satchel behind him, he steps backward and down, lowering himself as he does so. As the minuscule amount of light from above quickly wanes, the cavern grows darker, and the only sustaining light comes from his flashlight. His thoughts turn to the task at hand. He has no plan in mind, just to get to Myra and bring her back before midnight tomorrow! His own weight is getting heavier and his arms are tiring and still no end in sight, it has been at least seventy feet and the rope is only hundred and fifty, something must happen soon. Removing the two-way radio he stops his descent long enough to contact the surface. Myra's father answers.

"O'Keefe here, Adrian where are you, over?" he asks anxiously.

"Right now I'm still descending. There is no way of telling when, or even if, I will reach bottom. It is extremely dark and I feel disoriented. How are things up there, over?"

"Steve, out in the car, has called the Sheriffs' Department. But this storm has gotten a good deal worse since you left and they say that unless we are in immediate danger they won't come out until the storm has passed, over."

"They can't do anything anyway. So it's best maybe if they don't come. I'll radio you when I hit bottom. Over and out." He breaks transmission and continues his descent; the dirt walls have turned to stone and he isn't sure when it happened, but he does notice that it is getting lighter beneath him and by now, the rope has ended. What to do now? There is only one thing so he turns loose of the rope and allows himself to fall. But surprisingly his decent is gradual; he is not plummeting down at a dangerous speed. Well, getting down is one thing but how will he, with Myra's body, ever get back to the surface. This may be a one-way trip after all, but Adrian's inner self takes control, and he reasons that this is not a place of logic and things will not be as they appear. All this time he is without any support and still descending into the void, things are blurred, but then they stop, and Adrian lightly touches down, unharmed. Here is what you would expect, a much larger cavern with stalactites and stalagmites, there is water dripping from the top and it is incredibly bright. The stone walls are of varying shades of oranges, reds, browns, yellows, with a touch green here and there.

Adrian immediately radios the surface, but static is all that comes through, so he is out of touch with the upper world. He won't be able to inform them of his progress or his approximate return, or even if he is able to retrieve Myra's body.

CHAPTER SEVEN

UNDERWORLD

Adrian is confused as to which way he should proceed; he meditates a moment and a mental picture forms in his inner eye. An unpleasant scent erupts in his subconscious, a scent that he can identify as the odor created by the demon; he now knows where he needs to go. At a jog, he begins to follow his senses but soon his progress is halted. There is a tall black iron gate; could this be the gateway to Hades? It is constructed with thick iron poles, which are connected by many slender pikes and twisted cross-lattice scrollwork. At the junction where the two gates meet is a hefty lock of an oddly shaped medallion, with a repulsive face etched in the center. The face is three-dimensional and it comes alive and speaks to him.

"This is the entrance to the underworld. No one may enter without the rite of passage, which you do not have. Be gone you mortal before Cerberus has you for his lunch!" the voice echoes through the cavern, and with a wicked laugh the image freezes again.

This gate is twenty feet high, and the roaring sound of fire and the smell of sulfur are strong. His attempts to open this gate lead him to a confrontation with the Guardian of the Gate to Hades, a huge three-headed dog. This canine is nine feet tall, with burnished brown fur, and each of its heads has three blazing red eyes, with the third one in the center of its forehead. Smoke bellows from its nostrils, the lips snarl back over black fangs that are dripping drool. Its paws are huge with claws ten inches long of black iron and sharp as blades, and its tail is that of a serpent. It charges him, Adrian has no defense, or so he thinks. He sidesteps the first charge and his movement is multiplied threefold, so that he leaps into the air over the head of the beast. This angers

Cerberus and his barks are vociferous, as he rears back on his hind legs and leaps towards Adrian again. Adrian jumps straight up, and as the beast lands on all fours, Adrian is up in the air and lands on the beast's back. The animal's growls are deafening and smoke from the three heads almost blocks out the light. Adrian takes his amulet and buries it into the thick neck, just where the three heads start, it sizzles as it burns a brand into the hide of the beast. Suddenly the monster drops and as it falls, Adrian leaps off. The animal is not dead but paralyzed.

The image on the gate is again animated. "So you have soothed the savage beast, and thus have earned the Rite of Passage. You are allowed entrance. However, a warning, he who enters does not always exit. Cerberus will only sleep for one twenty-four cycle of time. Do what you must by then or you will be our guest for eternity!" it laughs evilly, and again it freezes. The massive black gate clanks open allowing Adrian to enter.

Adrian is very cautious, and halts briefly at the point of entry, he does not believe they will allow him to cross the threshold. So, he waits, then the Gate starts to close and he leaps forward just in time, as the gate catches the heel of his shoe, when it shuts.

"Well that worked out," he says to himself. "Wonder what's next."

He does not have to wait for long, for five naked little devils meet him, just three feet tall, red bodies, red faces, long spiked tails, cloven hoofs for feet, and little horns growing from their foreheads! Their tongues are forked like a snake, eyes like those of a serpent, and each one carries a small pitchfork! They rush towards him and start stabbing at his lower legs with their weapons.

"You've got to be kidding!" he exclaims, but kidding or not the attack is real and genuine pain is being inflicted on his lower extremities. He reaches down, grabs one of the little devils by the nape of his neck, and flings him hard away from him. The creature screams, and lands hard on the stone ground and lies there twitching. So, one by one, Adrian flings the little devils left and right until they are all lying about twisting, squirming and screaming, "Bloody murder!" (Yes, they are actually screaming *bloody murder*.) This proves to Adrian that this is an illusion, but illusion or not his shins are bruised! Adrian steps past the gyrating bodies and as he does so, one by one they dissolve into a puddle of water that flows away!

He takes his first good look around him. There are mountains spurting fire and ash in the far distances, and about his feet are miniature volcanoes throwing out methane gas, which stings his eyes and burns his nose. Soon his eyes are streaming and he dabs at them with his handkerchief.

He presses onward and the landscape swiftly changes around him. He is in a lush green forest, with the sweet scent of honeysuckle, a welcome change from methane gas! There is no undergrowth but there are small birds and animals; squirrels, rabbits, chipmunk, cardinals, bluebirds and yellow finches moving about freely.

There are numerous butterflies, dragonflies, and lighting bugs fluttering about and the soil is spongy under his feet. Nearby are the soothing songs of whippoorwills, bobwhites, and the cooing of mourning doves permeating the air. The distant twitter of a flute sounds as if it is from another place and time; its tune is reminiscent of Myra. Could this be a sign to guide him to her? Or, is it a deception to point him away from her? And how can he be sure?

While debating this in his head one of the lighting bugs leaves the cluster and flies up to him—it is a fairy! She is a dainty three inches high: her garment is made of rose petals; there is a honeysuckle hat atop her head, and she sports a pair of sparkling dragonfly wings! Her small face looks like a three-year-old child, she has pointed ears and she is twinkling.

"I know this is an illusion for these creatures do not exist," Adrian affirms.

"Ha, but Sir you are quite wrong," she speaks in her lovely petite voice. "We do exist, your devils were an illusion . . . we are not. Your world no longer believes in us so we were trapped and brought here to the Underworld to remain until eternity. However, if one true of heart comes in search of a loved one, and should he be successful in rescuing her then we too may return to the world of sunlight. We know of your mission, one not attempted since ancient times, and with our help, you will be triumphant. We know the ways of the inhabitants here and can inform you of truth or lies."

"And how am I to know you yourself, are not an illusion meant to trick me yet again?" demands Adrian.

"Close your eyes," she orders; Adrian does as she instructs him, "Now imagine you are somewhere else. When I say so, open your eyes, and if you are no longer in this place but another, then you will know that this is an illusion!"

After a brief interval, "Now Sir, open your eyes!" Adrian does as bid; he remains in this picturesque forest with this miniature lass nearby. "You see? You are still here. I am no illusion, and I will accompany you on your journey. I will be of great help, you can be sure."

"Well, thank you kind Miss, and I welcome your companionship," Adrian is still not a hundred per-cent certain, but for now, he believes.

"You may call me Sleyvia, my parents are King and Queen of the pixies and the fairies and . . . you are Adrian," she offers this tid-bit of information. She flutters around his head a few times then alights on the brim of his fedora and snuggles down for a ride.

Adrian is alarmed for she is abruptly gone, "Sleyvia; where did you get to?" His call echoes back to him. She is nowhere in sight, "Just as I thought, an illusion."

Then suddenly her tiny face appears before him upside down as she leans over the brim to speak, "I am here Sir." Adrian is startled so badly, he jumps. Sleyvia giggles and returns to her spot at the pinnacle of his hat. "I see no need for the both of us to be walking," she clarifies for him.

Adrian recovers and laughs at himself, "Sleyvia," she leans over the brim again waiting for him to speak, "the sound of the flute, it plays a tune that Myra loves, will the sound conduct us to her?"

"The flute is played by the sirens on the shore where the ferry carries passengers across the river to the *Isle of the Dead*. You may find Myra there or you may not," Sleyvia informs him.

"Well, will I or won't I!" he demands. This was infuriating; she tells him she will help him with the truth but when he asks for an answer, she responds with riddles. "This is going to be a long twenty-four hours!" he proclaims and looks at his watch. He finds that it has stopped at twenty minutes past midnight, the time he left the surface. "That settles that," he mumbles. He reasons he has been here an hour or so.

"Sleyvia."

"Yes Sir," she answers, leaning over the brim again.

"How long has it been since I left the surface?"

"You Sir have been here for six hours," she replies in her fairy voice.

"Six hours!" he exclaims, "How can that be?"

"I am not sure Sir, would you like me to ask?"

"Who would you ask?"

"Why the leprechauns of course, they have been following us for awhile now," Sleyvia is surprised that he has not been aware of them.

Adrian quickly turns and looks, "There is no one there!"

"Ah, you must see with your heart and not your eyes," she teases him.

"And just what is that supposed to mean?" he demands.

"Close your eyes and look with your heart," she instructs him.

This statement makes no sense, but he closes his eyes and then opens them and there they are; half a dozen leprechauns, they are a foot and a half tall and dressed in varying shades of green.

They sweep off their caps and bow low, simultaneously, and in squeaky little voices, together they speak, "Adrian dear lad, to our home you are welcome, and may you be successful in your quest for fair maiden. Of help we may be!"

Adrian bends to touch the elf closest to him, squeezes his arm firmly until the little fellow lets out a yelp, "Hey laddie, don't bruise the flesh, delicate am I!"

"Oh, you seem real enough but how can I be certain?" Adrian does not believe in these creatures either and is in need of proof. "So how do you think you can help? And what is your price?"

"We leprechauns, like the fairies, are a forgotten species in your world, there be few left in the homeland that still believe, but when the last of these are gone, so we be, too. Sad tis, but true nevertheless, and our kind will be banished to the underworld for eternity!"

"And your price for your services?" Adrian insists on knowing.

"Ah . . . . Laddie, you wound me to the heart," and he takes his little cap and covers his heart with it, then turns up his wrinkled face to look mournfully at Adrian. "To think that we leprechauns would seek monetary wealth in our wish to aid a lost soul such as yourself!" The little man pauses and draws a deep breath, then carries on with his monologue. "No, no, dear laddie, if fair sweet maiden be saved from the perils of this dastardly place, then our reward will be to return to the sunlit world above." With that statement, he bows his bald head in silence.

Sleyvia lifts up from the brim of Adrian's fedora and flutters about his face, "You see Sir, you must see with your heart and not your eyes. All of us, fairies and leprechauns alike, have as much to gain or lose as yourself. We get to return with you at that very same moment, if we do not leave then, our chance will be lost." She returns to her place on his fedora.

"I, for one, am lost. My time is wasting. I now have less than eighteen hours to locate Myra's body and return with it to the surface. Will the tune of the flute guide me to Myra?" Adrian scrutinizes the leprechauns. They are curious little guys, although around a foot and a half tall, their ages could be from twenty to a hundred. They are all similarly attired, with black shiny pointed-toed shoes, either white or striped stockings, knee pants, little vests, shirts, and the quaint elfin caps, to which a few of them have attached a feather plume.

The most distinguished of the group steps forward and bows, "Allow I to introduce meself, I be Haghery, I lead this small band of wee folks. Your question is answered by this, believe I that this be a guide to your lady, but tis also a trap. The chances of your recognizing it are quite slim, only we will know it. Shall away we be?"

"Yes, away we *be*," mocks Adrian. Any help in this unrealistic world can only improve his situation.

• • •

Reverend McGregor, Mrs. Grey and Mr. O'Keefe gaze into the abyss long after Adrian's flashlight has faded away and there is nothing but blackness! Reverend McGregor decides that they should call the sheriffs' department just in case this cannot be resolved in twenty-four hours.

O'Keefe looks at the two remaining people with him, "Which of you care to fill me in on what has happened, and why is it that I see my daughter snatched and carried away, yet again I am confronted with what looks like her 'ghost'?"

Mrs. Grey comes closer to him and places a calming hand on his shoulder, "Let us move nearer to the door and I will see if I can make all of this clear to you."

Outside, the storm is ongoing with lightning striking close by and often hitting the ground, and the thunder clashes nonstop, sounding much like a train running down the tracks. The black clouds are venting their anger by discharging their stores of water on the defenseless landscape. Rain puddles are growing in size, turning into torrents, creating little streams rushing to nowhere. The night has grown chilly making the situation miserable for everyone involved. The headlights from the limousine are focused on the front of the mansion offering a steady supply of light; it is here that the events of the last week are unfolded for Myra's father.

"Do you really expect an educated person to believe all of this rubbish?" he exclaims.

Mrs. Grey is a little surprised by his reaction, following everything that he has witnessed for himself in the past few days. "Mr. O'Keefe do you really think that? Have you not seen with your own eyes much of what I have just told you? I don't believe you have forgotten it all."

O'Keefe wipes his face with his hand, from forehead to chin, "I guess you're right. It's just that seeing Myra in that way, two of her, and then seeing this Mariah looking identical to her, I don't understand it all. And someone please tell me how am I supposed to explain all this to her mother. The woman will never get over it if Myra . . . well, she is our only child. We were never able to have any more." He places his right hand over his eyes, as if to hide the fact that he is about to break down.

The deacon, who has been waiting in the limo, makes a mad dash for the mansion and races into the open door, "It's not a fit night for man or beast," he exclaims as he enters!

Reverend McGregor meets him, "What's up, Steve?"

"The Sheriff just called on the car phone, he and another cruiser is block out on old sixty-four. Seem that this is a gully-washer, and they can't make it across the drainage ditch. He says that severe thunderstorms and flash flood warnings are out until four o'clock this morning and so is a tornado watch, 'till noon tomorrow. He wants to know if we are in danger out here, I told him 'no.' He says to stay put until this is over, that is the safest thing to do right now. I said I would let the rest of you know." Steve is out of breath after his run.

The two-way radio buzzes at that moment, and O'Keefe hurriedly activates it. Adrian informs them of the latest, which isn't much, for he hasn't touched bottom yet, but that he will keep them posted. O'Keefe lets him know that the reverend has called in the authorities but they can't get through due to the severity of the storm. They end their conversation and nothing more is heard from Adrian.

"Thank ye, Steve," McGregor takes his arm and leads him further inside out of the rain.

"Gracious sakes alive, what the devil happen in here?" Steve removes his baseball cap, and shakes the moisture off it. "Y'all have an earthquake or something?" he asks.

"Something likes that," O'Keefe remarks. "It seems that about all we can do now is wait. I won't bother to call Frances 'till daylight, maybe we'll know more by then." He walks across the room and sits down on the broken couch that his daughter slept on so many weeks ago.

The hours drag by; O'Keefe tries the two-way radio several more times but there is never an answer, only static. By four in the morning, the rain is still coming down in sheets of water, with no let up in sight, and everyone is more than a little worried. By daylight, nothing has changed and still no word from the subterranean world. They have about decided that they are stuck here for the full twenty-four hours. It is obvious that they will not be allowed to leave these grounds and no-one else will be able to come in.

• • •

Adrian and his entourage have left the forest behind; the faint sound of the flute is the only thing they have to guide them and its refrain is disturbing. The terrain has gotten rougher: it is rocky but level and wide, spreading like a desert; there is strangely shaped vegetation growing sparsely about, with unnatural coloration; orange leafless trees, blue tufts of grass, yellow sky with pink clouds racing swiftly overhead. This locality has a dream-like quality that they can't wake from, making it all too real. As far as the eye can see, there is nothing but land and sky. Menacing dragons soar overhead, occasionally swooping down to capture large jackrabbits, and carrying them off to feast on them. Pea-green and purple striped snakes slither out from stones, then back again when seeing the group nearby. Blue and white polka-dotted lizards dart here and there, and an old gray warty toad stays put as if challenging the intruders' right to be here. Scorpions and tarantulas meander about looking for prey.

Then there, in the distance, a human figure is silhouetted against the yellow sky; as they draw nearer, it is clearly a female form, it is Myra! The leprechauns hasten to greet her. She is awake, and wearing the white robe. She recognizes Adrian. She strolls up to him and without saying a word, takes his face in both her hands and kisses him full on the mouth. Adrian pushes her roughly away from him, for he knows that this is not Myra, just another trick hurled his way to confuse him and waste what time he has left.

"Adrian," she calls to him, holding out her arms in invitation, "don't you know me?"

"Leave me, you she-devil," he cries at this shade, "Did you think I could be fooled this easily? Go back to the fiend that sent you and tell him I will save the true Myra and commit his unnatural existence to perdition!"

"But Adrian," pleads the impostor, "please take me with you, for I am also a prisoner held here for centuries. I can be just like your Myra and no one would ever know the difference!"

"I would know!" shouts Adrian; he is getting frustrated with this wasting of precious time.

Sleyvia wings her way up to the shade, "Be gone, you old hag, before we hurl you to the troll under yon bridge!" She indicates ahead of them a brook appearing out of the bleak landscape, with a rickety bridge over it, and there, a troll looking out from beneath, wringing his hands together in delight at the prospect of getting his hands on supper. The shade, furious, transforms back into its true shape, an old hag of unknown age. She looks like a typical Halloween witch, with green skin and black eyes, a hooked nose with a hairy wart growing from it, and many lines on her face; the tall pointed witch's hat, black frock and cape, and her favorite mode of transportation, a broom. She hurls insults at the band, then mounts her broom and zooms into the yellow sky, far out of sight in less than a minute.

One of the leprechauns takes the lead, "Laddie, we need this way to go." He starts for the bridge and all the others follow suit, in line behind each other, with Adrian and Sleyvia, who is sitting on his fedora, bringing up the rear. Suddenly, without warning, the troll leaps out and challenges them.

"He that crosses my bridge must pay . . . my toll that I seek on this day . . . if he cannot pay my toll . . . then to be sure his head will roll!" This ugly dwarf is three feet tall, has a huge head, a protruding hooknose, beady yellow eyes with one heavy brow, and slack swollen lips over yellow broken teeth, and no chin.

"Oh kind Sir," Sleyvia takes the lead, "What price do you ask?"

"My price will be . . . gems of high quality!" He sniggers and all the while, he is circling the little troupe, sneaking to see what he might be able to steal.

Adrian comes forward, "Little man, I have this excellent time-piece that I will trade for clear passage across this fine bridge." He takes it off to show to the troll, since it is useless for timekeeping, maybe it can serve another purpose.

The troll snatches it from Adrian's hand and turns the watch front over back inspecting it very closely, "This has no value that I can see, of what use will it be to me?"

"Oh you wise one, this fine watch is from the Upper World. It is a lucky charm and will keep you on time," this said without a smile, by the tiny sprite.

"For my fee, this watch I take; you swear to me, it's not a fake. Then over my bridge, you may pass, in your search, for fair lass. For over yonder hill I say, in the demon lair she lay. In a spider's web is she, only you can set her free. But do not attempt too soon, for you must wait until the noon. Then the demon takes his rest, only then will you have success. Your time you mustn't waste, for if you do and don't make haste, in Hades you will be, for the rest of eternity!" Having said his piece the troll slips the watch onto his right arm and while admiring it retreats back to his cave under the bridge.

Adrian turns to his companions; "Can we believe what a troll tells us?"

The leader of the leprechauns stepped forward, "Once a troll accepts a fee, he's obliged to tell the truth, yes he should be believed." Then Haghery marches across the wooden planks of the troll's bridge, and, in step behind him, the others follow.

Now on the other side of the brook, things are quite different from whence they came. The sky is blue, with puffy cotton clouds, and they are so low that you can reach out and touch them. The ground is now covered in velvet green grass, the music from the flute increases in volume, and sounds much closer than ever before. Adrian insists they follow this first clue and heads in that direction. Sleyvia flutters along beside him, "You will see Sir that it will be the sirens making this music. I assure you this will be a deception, what kind I cannot say. You must promise me to be extra cautious."

"Aye Laddie," Haghery tugs on his pants' leg, "believe I too that a lie this be. But insist you do, only this remember, the sirens song a spell will cast, and your name you will forget and why to this place you came."

"I heard there is a protection from the sirens' song. If I plug my ears and am unable to hear them directly then I should be safe," Adrian looks dubiously at his companions.

"Aye, true enough" replies Haghery, "Do you have such a thing?"

Adrian reaches into his satchel, produces a pair of earplugs, and displays them to Haghery, "Aye work they should, your ears we will be, the sirens' song has no affect on us, only mortals do they harm."

Adrian inserts the plugs and follows the leprechauns in search of the magic flute. Not long after this, they hear the mesmerizing voices of the sirens, and soon they see them. They have come upon an enormous river, its surface is smooth like pure crystal, for there is no movement and the water is murky and dark. The shore is of the finest white sand and sitting on rocks at the water's edge are three mermaids. Incredibly beautiful, these women have fish tails with shimmering sea-green scales: their upper bodies are nude, their hair streams down to past their flippers; one has hair of pink, another blue, and the third is purple. The one with the pink hair is playing a flute while the other two are singing.

Adrian goes up to the mermaid with the pink hair, "Pardon me, ma'am, but you were playing a melody that a dear friend of mine enjoyed, can you tell me where you heard this song?"

"This melody drifted to us on the wind. It came from the direction of the Thanatos' tower across the river." Her voice was supple and mellow, and had not Adrian had on his plugs he instantly would have been under her magic spell.

"Is there a way across this river?" Adrian asks.

"Charon, the ferry driver will row you across for a golden coin, but why do you need to go the Isle of the Dead. You are not dead are you and you have not a corpse with you. Is there one on the Isle you wish to visit?"

"A dear friend of mine has been abducted and brought to the underworld by a demon. She is without her mortal soul and he may have passed her off as a corpse, but she is not truly dead, only sleeping, until her soul can reunite with her body. She is a very beautiful mortal with long straight colorless hair. Have you seen a woman that this describes?"

"Indeed master we have, this very morn, Thanatos came with such a body as you describe, and was rowed across by Charon then back again. We though this most unusual, for he usually wings across."

"Where is the ferry man now?" asks Adrian

"He has a regular time schedule he must keep, morning, noon and evening," replies the mermaid. "It is almost time for his noon crossing now."

They decide to wait, and some twenty minutes later, can distinguish the shape of a small ferry approaching the shore. When it finally lands, it is strange to see a hooded figure in a black robe standing at the stern of this boat, with a push rod held in both hands to power the ferry.

Adrian speaks to the ferryman, "Will you take us across the river?"

The ferryman's face is not visible for the hood is covering it completely, but he nods his head twice, does not speak, and holds out an aged blue-veined hand that trembles.

"Sir," Sleyvia removes the plug from Adrian ears and whispers, "He wishes a gold coin for this voyage."

"I have no gold coin, will he take something else," Adrian asks.

"Not to worry, Laddie," Haghery speaks up, "Where would a leprechaun be without his pot of gold," and deftly produces a gold coin, which he hands to Adrian.

Adrian in turns gives it to Charon who takes the coin and drops it into a brass urn at his feet, then Adrian climbs into the boat and motions for the rest of his entourage to do likewise. They are stopped by Charon holding up his hand and pointing one bony finger.

"He will only allow you and one other to cross at a time," the pink-haired mermaid tells them.

So it is decided that Adrian and Sleyvia will be the ones to go; the leprechauns will wait here for their return. Charon, in deathly silence rows them to the other side, a trip that takes a full thirty minutes. Adrian disembarks, while Sleyvia rides on the brim of his fedora, her favorite place. Charon indicates that he will wait for thirty minutes for them to be taken back to the side they just came from.

Sleyvia shows Adrian a small mortuary, slightly up a low hill. It is only a roof supported by four columns and a wooden casket is plainly seen in the center. Adrian's heart skips a beat when he thinks that Myra could be in it. He starts running, hardly believing that he may have found her. The casket is closed, and Adrian lifts up the top half of the cover. There lies Myra, looking as though she is sleeping. Adrian is so sure she is real that he lifts her up by the shoulders and holds her close to him. Unchecked tears start to run down his cheeks, he is so relieved to have found her; he kisses her motionless lips . . . but something is not right. Holding his breath in anticipation, he looks behind her right ear. It is not Myra, and, at the moment of this discovery, the body starts to decay while still in his arms. In horror, he drops it back down into the coffin, for the flesh is turning to mush and falling from the skull. The eyeballs liquefy and gush from their sockets, then the whole body dissolves and turns to dust, which is taken away by a rush of wind, and only dried up bones remain.

This happens so quickly that Adrian has no time to turn away and this memory will haunt him for a long time.

Sleyvia tugs on his ear and whispers, "We must go Sir, the others wait for us." She takes a hold of his earlobe and pulls.

Adrian is struggling to regain his composure and heads back from where they came. Charon is waiting for them. Sleyvia does not speak on the way back, for it is obvious that Adrian is in deep, emotional pain, and no words will soothe him at this moment. Haghery recognizes that this has been as predicted and was another deception, about which they had warned Adrian.

Arriving back on the opposite shore, Adrian replaces the plugs in his ears, and deftly leaps from the ferry to the bank of the river. Haghery comes near, "Laddie, tis plain this be a lie, sorry am I for the trouble you saw. But there be a longer way to the Turret of Thanatos, underground the river will go, walk across we will on dry land."

"Then that is the way we will proceed," declares Adrian. "Sleyvia how long have I been here now?"

"Oh Sir; you have been here thirteen hours, an hour past noon, an hour later than when Thanatos takes his mid-day nap. And if we take the long way, it will be two more hours by foot before we reach his Turret!" Sleyvia points out. "We must get there and save Myra and leave without his knowing about it. It will be hard, but it can be done."

● ● ●

Above at the Manor the storm rages on, although the noon hour has come and gone. The sky is ominous; the grounds are flooding, the wind is howling, and the lightning and thunder are unceasing. There is no way to leave and it would seem that they are trapped for the duration of the storm. All agree that a hurricane must have moved inland, but no one can remember any watches or warning being issued before coming to the manor. August is a prime month for hurricanes, and there is always a system forming, or growing stronger out in the Atlantic but even with today's technology, they are still difficult to predict precisely.

Whatever is happening; it seems to be in connection with the exorcism of Worthington Manor. They are all exhausted, and a few of them have taken catnaps. The picnic lunch that the church had packed is getting low and with no word from Adrian, they are beginning to lose hope. Myra's mother has not been told everything that has happened about Myra's abduction, or that Adrian is at that very moment searching for her. She has only been told partial truths and, since then, no contact to the outside has been made; it seems that all means of communications have been lost. There are no paranormal activities going on at the mansion, though no one has done any exploring in the house. Either they are not curious about what lies beyond this large front room, or fear of the unknown keeps them together.

"Do you have any idea what could be going on down there?" O'Keefe is standing close to the door checking for the hundredth time the worsening conditions outside.

"I know a little of what the underworld may be like," Mrs. Grey informs him, "there are so many interpretations; from the Greek Myths to today's Roman Catholic Church; from the three-headed dog that guards the gate of Hades, to the Romans' purgatory. Which one you actually believe, is for the most part a matter of choice. Very possibly none of what we believe is true and there may be no hell fire, or a Red Devil, that most of us are taught in Sunday School. How many people have been to the underworld and returned from it? We will simply have to wait and see." Mrs. Grey hopes she is reassuring him and lessening his worries and doubts.

Reverend McGregor and Steve are playing with a deck of cards that Mrs. Grey had in her handbag, everyone is looking for something to occupy his time.

• • •

So, the small brigade proceeds in the direction that the troll had originally advised them. Haghery takes the lead and they begin their trek up the narrow path over a mound, to a nearby grove of trees that beckons enticingly with their shade, with fresh fruit hanging heavily from their branches. Adrian is starting to feel very fatigued. He knows that he needs to press on, but without rest and food, it is uncertain he will complete the task. "We can take a break here beneath these trees, Sir, if you like," Sleyvia, as if reading his mind, leans over the brim of Adrian's fedora to speak to him. "We all are tired and hungry and can better achieve our goal if rested and fed."

"I agree with your logic, but can we afford to take the time?" he responds to her, with weariness obvious in his voice.

"Aye Laddie, indeed we must, it will not take long, a few minutes is all that's needed," Haghery insists.

So, they settle in the midst of this tiny forest, where it is cool; the green grass is soft and fragrant, with sweet clover and wild violets, and a small brook hums at their feet as it meanders down the hill towards the river. Adrian begins to pick apples, pears and peaches from the trees, and grapes from the vines, which he distributes to the leprechauns, and then cuts up his share into small pieces to share with Sleyvia. After this refreshing and reviving feast, Adrian reclines against the trunk of a tree and asks, "Will you all be able to watch over things, if I take forty winks?"

Sleyvia wings her way to face him, "Indeed we shall, Sir, you sleep and I will wake you in one and a half time cycles."

Adrian says nothing more but closes his eyes and pulls his fedora down over his face and is soon in a deep sleep. Sleyvia settles down in her familiar spot and prepares to stand guard, while the leprechauns do the same. After Adrian is sound asleep, the leprechauns form a circle around him; they each remove from their pouches a hand full of gold dust, which they toss into the air, while Sleyvia with her little wand casts a magic spell, and supernaturally, the dust forms a solid globe over Adrian, shielding him from view.

Much too soon Sleyvia is bouncing up and down on the brim of his fedora calling, "Wake up Sir, wake up Sir, we must be on our way! Our time is here to seek out the demon's lair and to save Myra!"

The mention of Myra's name rouses him quicker than the dance Sleyvia is doing on his hat. He rises up and looks around, and thankfully, nothing has changed as he might have expected. The leprechauns gather around him, "Sleep well, did you, Laddie? A spell we did cast to shield you from detection by Thanatos while you slept. All is well and forward we must go, for just over the next rise is what we seek."

With the leprechauns once again taking the lead they continue down this path, which is getting dustier by the minute, until the small troop is obscured by it. With the wind picking up in strength, they are soon in a blinding dust storm.

"How can it be that this storm has come upon us so quickly? Everything was so calm a few minutes ago?" Adrian is forced to shout so that he is heard over the roar and whistling of the wind. The wind is so dynamic that they must hold onto their hats and coats or else lose them to the wind. Adrian tucks Sleyvia inside his shirt pocket to keep her safe, for with only her tiny wings she will not have a chance against the blustery weather.

"Laddie, tis to force us back and it is one of the barriers set up to stop intruders, but hold on we must, for it soon will stop," Haghery shouts back at Adrian. "We have been this way before, this is where the river goes underground, and after crossing here, we will be at Thanatos' Turret."

"We must continue on then," agrees Adrian, "It must be nearly six o'clock and maybe we can catch them by surprise." Taking the lead Adrian leans into the wind and strives forward with Sleyvia safely tucked in his shirt pocket.

Gradually the dust cloud lifts and they are in close proximity to the *Turret of Thanatos,* it is no more than a few hundred yards from them. Built to be a deterrent to invaders was this battlement, for there is a narrow moat surrounding it, with only the one drawbridge to gain entrance to the tower. Constructed of glass bricks, the tower has marble columns, embedded in the limestone to support it beneath the murky water. The only other way into the tower is by boat, which they do not have, and also there are bizarre creatures swimming and diving in the depths of the black water. The terrain surrounding the tower is barren, offering no hiding places that they can use to approach the tower unseen.

"What are we to do now?" Adrian asks in exasperation, feeling hindered at every turn and that there is no momentum to his crusade. "There must be a way to get inside. I will need a weapon; I have nothing in my bag that I can use. Where can I get help?"

"You Sir," Sleyvia speaks excitedly, "Will have the help you request. But you must see with your heart and not your eyes. You have more power than you realize. Close your eyes and open your heart and reveal to us what it is you seek." Adrian closes his eyes as asked, while Sleyvia darts around his head showering him with twinkling stardust. Then, with a wave of her wand, she strikes him smartly on the crown of his head. "There you be Sir Adrian, open your eyes and see more clearly than you ever have before!"

At the strike of her wand, Adrian feel a surge of energy shoot through his entire being, from the crown of his head, to the tingling soles of his feet, down both arms to the tips of his fingers. He is invigorated and rejuvenated. He opens his eyes to see things in sharp contrast; everything is more defined and detailed, and his hearing is clearer and more distinct, even from miles away.

He feels the power intensify in his muscles, increasing his agility, flexibility and endurance; he is confident in his own knowledge and abilities.

Adrian stretches his arms and flexes his hands into fists feeling the surge of power, "What'd happen to me, am I different? Did you cast a spell over me, Sleyvia?"

"You have done this yourself, Sir Adrian, you had this power already. I only made you release it," explains Sleyvia. "But, before this moment, you would not have accepted your own natural ability; you had to be encouraged in mind and spirit before this change could take effect in you."

"Aye Laddie true this be," pipes up Haghery, bouncing around in a display of joyful delight. "Had you been told before, believe us you would not. Now you can defeat the Evil Duo. Time is wasting and onward we must go."

They step out into the domain of Thanatos. Adrian looks at his small companions, "Little ones, you can do no more, wait at the edge of the glen and I will go alone to meet this malevolent spirit."

Having said this to his little friends and certain that they are safe, he begins to run across this open wasteland, then from nowhere a figure materializes; it is the specter of Cromwell. Although dead for well over a century and a half, Thanatos has resurrected his body. This is not the face of a living person, for he has purple shadows around his opaque eyes, and pasty white skin, which peels from the muscle and bone, sunken hollows at his cheeks, blue split lips and a scruffy brown and green beard. He has pale hands with bony fingers, and claws for nails. He is attired in the tattered uniform of a Civil War Union Colonel, a *zombie*!

As he starts walking toward Adrian, a black stallion, snorting fire, gallops up to him, and in one fluid movement Cromwell mounts the black beast. He pulls his saber from its scabbard and holds it high over his head; he whips the animal into a full gallop and makes a charge directly at Adrian. As he rides by, he sweeps the saber violently; it cuts the air with a swish as Adrian sidesteps the attack.

With a raspy voice Cromwell speaks, "I know why you are here, you foolish mortal, and, I say, you will fail in your efforts to reclaim this girl. I intend to keep her worthless body until it perishes, then I will capture its spirit and drain the energy from it to fuel my own soul! You will never defeat me for I will destroy your body and drain your essence. They denied me this power in my lifetime. I am determined to have it now, and I will, with the bargain I have made with Thanatos, for he will gain the soul of the other one. So fight me you mortal, if you dare, then *die*!"

Adrian responds with, "The girl's body is all you have, her spirit is not there. When the body dies, you will only have a decaying corpse and nothing else. The girl's spirit is safe."

While Adrian is speaking, Cromwell reins his horse around for another frontal attack on Adrian. Then a fiery red stallion is released from the vicinity of the leprechauns. This is a magnificent animal with a coat the color of flaming fire. He is saddled up ready to ride. He gallops up to Adrian and nudges him in the back to get his attention. Amazed at seeing this splendid charger, Adrian mounts the horse as if he has done so all his life. The roan rears up and beats the air with his hoofs, and whinnies to let everyone know that he is ready for battle. Then in a powerful leap, the animal is in the air and soaring into the sky! He climbs higher until he is amidst the clouds, he is soon joined there by the black stallion and his rider, and then in a ballet of death they pivot around each other, seeking opportunities to force the other's hand.

Adrian observes the terrain below him, all is vast and flat, there is the grove of trees where the small band had taken its rest, and the dust storm in which they were caught is raging still. The tower is one tall column of glass bricks with large open windows placed at intervals up the tower's walls. One of those windows, about ten feet square, has a gigantic spider's web filling the entire opening, and plainly seen is a huge black spider. It is guarding what appears to be a silken cocoon, and closer inspection reveals it to be holding Myra's body! When Adrian sees this, his anger is increased, knowing he is within feet of her but unable to affect a rescue. With his blood red-hot from rage, Adrian draws the saber that is on the saddle, but no, this is not a saber but a sword. He recognizes it as an English sword from medieval times. He has not the time to dwell on this and urges his mount into a steady gallop in a calculated charge at his opponent.

Cromwell makes ready for this attack. Whipping his horse into action, he moves toward Adrian, and laughing cruelly, meets Adrian's furious assault with one of his own. With the horses face-to-face, then neck-to-neck, they cross blows with the weapons; sparks fly from the steel blades, for it has drawn dark since the challenge was issued. The horses hold their position in this aerial battle seemingly without effort, repeatedly the sabers clash with the clang of metal against metal. They veer off, then come around again for another attack. So far, no injury has been inflicted on either one; they fight a battle of defense as well as offence! Each is aware that this is a physical battle of strength and endurance, and not one of magic or spells. Each must rely on his own merits and abilities, not good against evil but man against man, and horse against horse.

With another charge at each other, a slight misjudgment on Adrian's part turns into painful reality, as Cromwell's saber catches him across his upper left arm slashing a gash and drawing blood. Adrian has no time to feel the pain just inflicted on him; he chases it from his mind and prepares to return in like fashion. He reins his mount to a halt, blood is running down his arm and sweat down his face; the twilight offers barely enough light to see effectively for aerial combat, but Adrian, with his new found vision, is seeing better than is his rival, and he must use this to his advantage. He urges his horse to climb even higher into the darkening night, until he is well over the head of Cromwell. Then, in a dive, horse and man plunge downward to engage Cromwell, who is caught in an awkward position, which is nearly impossible to defend. He is not quick enough to make the adjustment in his defensive tactics and is now wide open to this maneuver. Adrian's sword cuts into Cromwell's back laying it open, exposing the ribs, and green pus oozes from this death wound instead of red blood. Cromwell's agonizing screams are numbing to hear as he loses his grip on the reins, his feet slip from the stirrups and he slides from the saddle. In a headlong descent, he plummets down to earth!

Moments later, his body crashes with a dull thud to the ground, where it splatters into pieces. The water in the moat begins to agitate and foam, as hideous lizard-like creatures emerge to start devouring the fleshy parts lying all around. They feast until there is nothing left but bone, and then quickly retreat back into the murky depths of the moat.

Adrian views this from his vantage point aloft. The black stallion, knowing defeat, retires back into the night. Taking a moment to bind his wound with his pocket-handkerchief, Adrian forms a tourniquet to halt the bleeding. He spurs his big horse downward and reins him over to the second highest window, for he must now get Myra. The battle has used precious time and it is well past the ninth hour. In less than three hours, it will be too late to save her!

He removes from his satchel, and lights one of the consecrated candles. Steering the horse to one side of the window, he allows a few drops of melting wax to fall onto the ledge, then secures the candle into it, and repeats this action on the other side. Then, lighting a third candle he dismounts onto the ledge, hoping the horse will wait for him, for without the animal he has no safe way down from this tower. He is careful to keep his balance, for a fall now would be disastrous for them all. Holding the candle high he peers into the darkness, and many red eyes stare back at him. From out of the gloom, long hairy spider's legs are carefully picking their way across the web to challenge this intruder. In the far corner of the web is the still form of Myra, living, though in a deep sleep.

Adrian squares off opposite the giant spider, not knowing exactly how he is going to defeat this arachnid; he cautiously places his foot on the web, testing its strength; it sags under the pressure he exerts; it does not break however, but bounces. At this intrusion into its domain, the spider springs at Adrian, catching him with its two front legs. Adrian is off-balanced, but manages not to be pulled from his precarious perch on the last run of the web. He is still holding the candle and now begins to use it as a weapon. Burning the hairs on the spider's legs makes the spider release him long enough for Adrian to take the burning end of the candle and thrust it into several of its many eyes. The spider shrieks as these eyes are blinded, it backs off in Myra's direction as though it plans to fight for this treasure! Adrian knows he does not have time to destroy the arachnid, but maybe he can keep it at bay long enough to retrieve Myra and make his escape with her.

Taking the olive oil and using his fingertips, Adrian disperses a spray in the direction of the spider, all the while inching his way across the web toward Myra. The olive oil does the trick, even if it were not sacred oil the spider would still retreat from it, for oil on its body would cause the spider to suffocate. Adrian continues to work his way around the web, knowing that these runs of the web are not the sticky type that entrap, but the supporting runs, the threads running vertical being the ones to avoid. At last, he is next to Myra; there is not enough time to remove the cocoon that holds her fast and so he burns the holding filaments with the candle's fire, extinguishing it when finished and placing the candle back into his satchel. The first thing he does is to check for the birthmark behind her right ear; if it isn't Myra, then there is no time left for them and everything will be lost! Nevertheless, it is she, and now she is freed from the spider's web; he gently hoists her up and over his right shoulder, ignoring the burning pain in his left arm. They now begin the perilous trip back to the window where the big red horse is still patiently waiting. The spider has retreated to the farthest corner of its web, intensely preoccupied with the cleaning of the oil from its body. Adrian dares not breathe for fear that his luck may not last, and at the last possible second, he might be prohibited from leaving here with Myra. Their time is fast running out!

Finally, they are at the window, and the roan whinnies an acknowledgment at their arrival. With great difficulty, Adrian first sits sidesaddle, then swings his right leg over the saddle horn, and carefully lowers Myra's body from his shoulder to the narrow space in front of him. Gathering the reins in his right hand he "clicks" to this magnificent animal and the roan deftly soars downward and skillfully lands.

Back on the ground, Adrian does not take time to undo the cocoon, but instead heads back to the glen where his entourage is worriedly waiting for him, for they have much to lose if Adrian is not victorious!

Adrian urges his horse in the direction he came from earlier in the afternoon, intending to pick up Sleyvia and the leprechauns. Arriving at the glen it is strangely empty; but then he sees a tiny flickering light coming towards him; it is Sleyvia. "Very glad to see you Sir Adrian," she greets him, "no time have we to waste, the Band of Leprechauns has gone ahead to clear obstacles from your path so all we need do is take this fine animal and hurry to the only exit there is." She wings her way to his fedora and settles on its brim, then leaning over it to speak once again, "Adrian, Sir, I will be your guide. For I know the way and will hasten our escape from here. We absolutely must quicken for we have only one time cycle and a half left to us, then Thanatos will start his pursuit!"

With this warning, Adrian lightly spurs the stallion into action; the phenomenal steed mounts to the sky like an enormous eagle, and as if knowing the course, proceeds without further guidance from Adrian. The night, with a persona of its own, has taken over and is preventing any light from entering its domain, making it nearly impossible to discern the route they are taking, Adrian does the only thing he can, trust the animal and the fairy to get them out of Hades on time!

Sleyvia again leans over the hat's brim, with her tiny self glowing profusely, thus highlighting Myra's face, "How be she, Sir Adrian?" She scrutinizes Myra to see if she is indeed Myra, "Did you check behind her ear Sir?"

"Yes, before leaving the web, it is she, but I'm getting worried that we might not make it in time. If we don't, Myra's hope is gone!" his voice is troubled and furrows crease his forehead in profound anxiety.

Sleyvia comprehends that Adrian is captivated with this girl, "Indeed Sir Adrian we shall succeed in our quest; for this I do feel in my heart."

For the first time since exiting the site of the web, Adrian gazes at Myra's stunning features and her comeliness effectively quickens his heartbeat. Life without Myra in it is now hard to envisage, although it has been less than a week since their first meeting. She has won a place in his heart that he will never be able to fill if she is lost. Adrian takes an oath to be her protector and to start a new life together. Will she remember what she has been through after her astral body reunites with her physical one? Will this exploit seem to be a dream to Myra, or will she have no memory of these events at all? These questions remain unanswered until the impending future.

From aloft he sees the troll's bridge, and everything looks normal, "It isn't far now," he thinks aloud, "We must be very near where I arrived some twenty three hours ago." They travel a few more miles and there is the gate of Hades, and sleeping on the outside of the fence is Cerberus, the three headed dog,—the gate's guardian. They swoosh over the gate with barely a sound and without a challenge to their exit. Thus far, their luck remains with them, or could it be the unseen hand of their unknown benefactor. Arriving at his original site of entering the Underworld, the mighty stallion glides safely to the ground. Now at a gallop they head for the cavity that he can now see. Anxiously waiting for them are the leprechauns and the fairies. This is their chance to return to the world of sunlight and of the living. Haghery rushes to meet them, "Aye Laddie, hurry you must, behind you we will be. Tranquill, the stallion that you ride, will take you to the surface. Taken up with you also are all of the wee folks. In less than a quarter time cycle, Thanatos will be arriving at this very place, and we must escape now."

The mighty red stallion whinnies at his recognition of the leprechauns, and then leaps upward into the blackness, carrying Adrian, the sleeping Myra, and tiny Sleyvia with him, back to the normal world; a world without glowing fairies, mischievous leprechauns, sneaky trolls, or wicked witches. Neither does this world have flying horses, red devils, singing sirens, nor terrifying demons! Nor will there be three-headed dogs, talking gatekeepers, large hairy spiders and mysterious ferrymen. It seems that time has stopped, for there is no way of knowing just how far they have come, or how much further they need go. Carry on they do until at last the magnificent red steed breaks into the upper world—in the middle of the hall at Worthington Manor!

CHAPTER EIGHT

RETURN TO THE SURFACE

The vicious storm still rages at Worthington Manor; the storm has been perpetual for twenty-eight hours or so, ever since they first arrived at the mansion, Friday night at seven thirty. Now it is eleven forty five pm on Saturday and still there is no let up from the ferociousness of the storm. There has been no relief from the pounding rain, the incessant lightning's strikes or rolling thunder, and now the grounds are flooded and the exit road impassable. There has been no communication from the outside world or from the abyss for more than a day. The situation has grown extremely dismal, with only fifteen minutes left before it will be too late to save Myra, and all they can do is wait and pray!

Mrs. Grey and Reverend McGregor are quietly talking while sitting on the floor close to the double door, which has been shut against the storm, while O'Keefe and Steve sit in different areas of the room. Mr. O'Keefe is next to Myra's circle of salt, feeling somehow that he is closer to her here. Steve's head has dropped down on his chest in a deep sleep. Neither Mariah's nor Myra's spirits have communicated with them since before Adrian's descent into the underworld. Their hope is fading and the time for a successful rescue is rapidly running out.

"Reverend, what time do you have now," Mrs. Grey asks for the tenth time. She is watching the crevasse in the floor, hoping that she can facilitate Adrian's return by using the influences of her mind.

"Tis a few minutes 'till midnight, give or take a minute or two. Take heart my dear lady, for sure am I that make it they will," Reverend McGregor hopes he sounds optimistic, for he too has become disheartened at their prospects of a triumphant outcome. Reverend McGregor has barely finished speaking when a rumble emanates from the abyss, and in a blinding light a huge red horse flies up from the depths of the crevasse, then lightly touches down on the wooden planks of the entrance hall of Worthington Manor. Upon his back is Adrian, with a figure wrapped in a silken lucent material, sitting in front of him. Could this be Myra? Indeed, it is Myra! Mr. O'Keefe rushes to them and Adrian hands her over, "Quickly place her in her circle!" Without a word, Mr. O'Keefe does as instructed, laying her carefully onto the dusty floor within the circle of salt.

Adrian quickly dismounts from the stallion and follows O'Keefe; he squats down beside Myra and lifts her head into the crook of his right arm. Her head falls limply back over his arm indicating that no physical activity has yet returned; then, at that precise moment Myra's astral body materializes and with hardly a second to spare enters her physical body.

Even so, she remains motionless and lifeless, "Why doesn't she move?" Mr. O'Keefe shakes her, "Myra . . . wake up." There is no response; is it too late, have they lost her after all?

Hastily removing his hat, Adrian lowers his face close to Myra's; he is unable to hear or feel her breath, he checks for a heartbeat, none is detected. He lays her flat on her back and starts CPR knowing that in a case like this, it is probably for naught, for there is no physically injury, only her missing soul. The astral spirit did not enter the body in time. After several frantic minutes of trying, he knows that it is useless, and with tears rising up in his eyes, he raises his head skyward and screams, "Noooo!" It resounds throughout the mansion and the agony that is expressed in this one word is more than a soul should bear. For he cannot bring himself to even consider that she is gone, when he has done all in his power to save her, and yet it is not enough.

Mr. O'Keefe takes her hand in his and bows his head in silence, while great sobs shake his whole body, for he feels more to blame then anyone here, or so he imagines. "Why didn't I listen to her mother? She will never get over this, and how will she ever forgive me, when I can't even forgive myself."

Mrs. Grey stands behind her son, her hands on his shoulders with tears running down her cheeks, but she tries to console him.

Reverend McGregor places his hands on the heads of Adrian and Mr. O'Keefe and in a low voice, he whispers a prayer:

"Most gracious heavenly Father, we know that in *You* all things are possible. With just *Your* voice, *You* can defeat armies; there is none in Heaven or on Earth that can be compared with *Your* mercy and *Your* might, or the love You give us poor sinners. We ask in the name of *Your* most holy Son to return our daughter to us, in Christ's name, Amen."

Sleyvia wings her way over to Myra's unresponsive form and with her tiny wand taps her sharply on her nose, a shower of twinkling stars discharges from the point of contact, and Myra inhales deeply as though she has been holding her breath. "Adrian Sir, your prayers are answered. Call to her, she is but sleeping."

Adrian gently shakes her shoulder and softly calls her name three times. Myra slowly opens her eyes. She stares up into Adrian's face and then at her father, she struggles to sit up and becomes conscious of the fact that she is bound. "What is all of this?" she exclaims, with rising panic, fighting the restraints around her. "And what is that?" she is speaking of Sleyvia, the fairy.

Adrian exhales the breath he has not realized he is holding. She is all right, she is alive, and obviously does not remember a thing that has happened. "How much can you recall, Myra?"

"I last remember being in the corner, here inside this circle of salt. I remember Mariah coming toward me and reaching for my hand; then I am floating and everything is moving in slow motion. I am with Mariah and others like her in a very distant place, far from here. It is very bizarre and nature's laws are broken. I can fly without wings; things are brilliant and fantastically unreal. I feel as though I am missing time. Then . . . the next thing I know I am here with you."

Myra glances around herself in wonderment, then questioningly at her companions, as if hardly believing what she has experienced.

While she speaks, Adrian and O'Keefe set about hastily undoing the silken cocoon, with assistance from Mrs. Grey who uses a pair of scissors from her handbag. Myra helps the best she can and finally she is free of the spider's silk. Adrian helps her to stand; she is weak and her legs are trembling, "Why do I feel so stiff, and so weak in my legs . . . and so hungry?" She looks around the room, "Is that a fairy? Are those leprechauns? Where did the horse come from?" she asks these questions and each time she looks at Adrian.

Adrian lifts her into his arms, carries her to the broken sofa and sits her down, "I'll tell you everything later when we get back to town, but for now you are safe, and that is the only thing that concerns me." Adrian wraps her tightly in his embrace, so relieved that she is alive and safe. Myra cannot quite understand why everyone is so upset, but for now, she takes pleasure in the warmth and security she is feeling in his arms and, without reservation, lies her head on his shoulder.

Myra's safe return is foremost in everyone's minds. The fairies and leprechauns, except for Sleyvia and Haghery, all make haste and leave the premises to begin their new lives in the upper world. So far, the only one who had been able to see them when they came up from the depths with Adrian is Myra, and they need to keep it that way. For actual living proof that leprechauns and fairies truly live would be detrimental to their causes here on Earth. They must remain alive only in the minds of the innocents and the virtuous. A crusade will be started to increase the believability in the fairy folk, but without definite proof. It must be taken on faith alone, so that they can be of service to man, but lessen the chance of abuse by unscrupulous people.

Thus, while all are absorbed in Myra's welfare, they do not take notice of what is occurring around them.

• • •

Their relief that this episode at Worthington Manor is over and that they will soon leave for home, causes them to forget that the demon, as of yet, has not been exorcized from these premises. They do not notice that the huge gap in the center of the foyer's floor is closing up, the dirt is reassembling into a compact hard surface and the wooden planks have reconstructed themselves into an undamaged whole.

Myra's safe return is foremost in everyone's minds. Sleyvia is becoming very friendly with Myra, who thinks that this little sprite is the most charming creature she has ever seen and they speak of plans for her to come live at Myra's home when things here are settled. Haghery and the Reverend McGregor are discussing the home land of Ireland and that in today's modern world most people no longer believe in fairies or leprechauns. This resulted in their being trapped and carried to the Underworld. Adrian's exploits in the Underworld are divulged to everyone; from the soothing of Cerberus, the three headed dog, to the final defeat of Cromwell; and how the stallion Tranquill helped save the day by bringing them all back to the Upper World. Tranquill is led outside by Steve, to stand on the porch of the Manor; here he can wait out the storm without being in danger.

The mostly dismal ingredient of this celebration is that the storm has not abated in intensity, if anything it is worse. Adrian takes this as a sign that only the battle has been won, not the war; there is more to come but at the present, he says nothing to the others, sensing they need to replenish their morale and strength. Thus, the lightning assaults are as frequent as ever, the accompanying thunder is deafening and the downpour is coming in torrents.

"Adrian, thank you. You have done much more than anyone has the right to expect. I bet you didn't think you would get involved in such a complicated exploit as this when you answered my e-mail, did you?" Myra looks at him in admiration. "You got yourself wounded and dirty and I know you must be worn out from dragging me around like a limp dishrag. I don't know if I would have done as much for a person I've only known less than a week. But this injury, just how bad is it?" Myra had noticed his wound right away but until now did not have the chance to ask about it. Myra inspects his injury and then stares at him, "Adrian, your wound . . . it's healed. See for yourself."

"Well it's only a scratch," replies Adrian, trying hard to get the attention off his injury, "It doesn't even hurt anymore." He removes the handkerchief and although his shirtsleeve is stained with blood, his cut has disappeared. "Like I said, it was only a scratch, must've had a little help from a certain fairy we know," Adrian smiles and looks at Sleyvia, sure that she has used a little fairy magic to cure him. He then removes the bloodstained shirt and tosses it across the room.

"Not I Sir, you did this yourself with your own natural abilities, I only help you recognize them. If you have faith in yourself, there's much, much more you are capable of achieving. Just give yourself a chance, see with your heart and not your eyes," Sleyvia spreads her little glistening dragonfly-like wings and darts about spreading sparkling fairy dust as she speaks.

"Adrian, you are going to catch a chill without a shirt on," his mother scolds him.

"No, I'm warm enough, I'll be just fine, after all it is August, Mother," he grins back at her.

"Everything you tell me is incredible," says Myra in wonderment, "I don't remember things too clearly, only being with Mariah and the others in a marvelous place which I thought I dreamt . . . but I know now I didn't. I find this very astounding. But where is Mariah? Shouldn't she be with us? Maybe she has passed to the next level already."

"No, I don't believe so," answers Adrian. "We would have been aware of it. No, the storm hasn't stopped yet, there's more to come."

"I have Mariah!" This supernatural voice bellows abruptly into the arena and they are so startled by this incursion on their conversation that they literally flinch, for it is so unexpected. Now the room becomes deathly silent as all heads turn toward the source of this raspy voice. It is Thanatos, the Demon, in his full repulsive glory, standing twenty feet tall with leathery bat-like wings that he extends twenty feet out into the foyer, nearly wrapping the group in their shadow. Ambling on two goat-like legs, with hoofs instead of feet, his naked body resembling a man's, but with reptilian scales, he is an awesome spectacle indeed. His blazing, red eyes focus on the terrified mortals, calculating their size and strength. Atop of his head are ram-like horns, three feet long and curving up and in. He exhibits himself at the foyer rear door leading to the back of the house and the entrance to the third floor. In his right claw is a six foot long crystalline capsule that is pulsating with a bluish light . . . it is Mariah! She is trapped and in his demonic power!

"She is mine, now! I seized this spirit whilst you fought that coward Cromwell; you will all belong to me before this night is over. You will not defeat me nor stop my possession of this manor. Fight me, you fools, if you dare!" He laughs cruelly and then in a puff of black smoke he vanishes, returning to the third floor, where he has been residing all along, sustaining his existence from the energy of the lost souls. He is the *Dark Spirit* that occupies the third floor and the one holding the others hostage, making them repeatedly relive their last days on Earth. In this manner, he has kept up his own power with no need for other resources.

"What are we to do now," Myra and the rest seek Adrian's guidance in this new development.

"We must unite and fight him for the possession of Mariah and Worthington Manor," Adrian states emphatically, standing and glaring in the direction of the now departed demon. "Reverend, you must do the exorcism of the house. He will not vacate the Manor as easily as the O'Keefe's home, but it can be done." Adrian helps Myra to her feet and places his arm about her small shoulders in a defiant stance against the demon, more or less saying he is her protector.

"Aye my son, we will proceed with the exorcism. We need more holy water and oil. I usually conduct this on the outside, but with this heavy rain it will be most uncomfortable," McGregor is anxious to get started. This has been a long thirty six hours, and now the advantage that they had on the Sabbath is gone, and they are under the demon's terms, which is why he has issued the challenge to them at this precise time.

"No, Laddie, we need not to go out in the rain," Haghery pipes up, "I've been here awhile and I know a few secrets. The exorcism can be done at the main entrance of a house. Most effective it will be."

"Adrian Sir," Sleyvia flutters to a point in front of Adrian and Myra, "Haghery is right. We must form a half-circle in front of this big door on the inside. Light again your candles, sprinkle the holy water and oil at the door. This will create a barrier that neither the demon nor we can cross. Only victory in battle will open this door. Be it the demon or be it us."

"Aye People," Haghery completes the instructions started by Sleyvia, "Reverend McGregor will cite the invocation. After which we must go to the third floor to confront Thanatos in his own territory, surprised he will be, for this he will not expect. Be us ready? We must get started, time is wasting."

Not waiting another second, they perform the requirements for the exorcism; each taking their former position they had held in the first ceremony. Sleyvia balances her tiny self on the brim of Adrian's fedora and Haghery perches on his shoulder. They stand back from the doors about four feet; together Adrian and Myra shower the oil and water at the base of the doors, where the liquids hiss, forming smoke and steam indicating the demonic possession of Worthington Manor.

Reverend McGregor opens a prayer book and begins to recite, "May the Holy Cross be my light. Let not the dragon be my guide. Be gone, Satan! Suggest not vain things to me. Evil is the cup thou offer. Drink thou thine own poison. We order Thanatos, to vacate these premises. Possess not this house any longer. Release your hold on the innocent. Return you to Hades, and there remain until the second coming. We command you this in the name of Jesus Christ, your Master and mine!"

An earth-shaking howl issues forth from the upper levels of the house. Thanatos is demonstrating his displeasure at the exorcism, trying their nerves. They go to the only entrance to the third floor, halt at the bottom of the back staircase and Adrian takes the lead. Down here things look normal, but as they approach the one door, which is closed, it transforms into decaying flesh. Pea green pus oozes from the abscesses on this rotting carcass. The stench is overwhelming, making the entire entourage nauseous.

"We can't let this bit of abhorrent pulp dissuade us," Adrian encourages them; "This is just another illusion which he thinks we will believe. He will be defeated and exiled to *Perdition*, where he will never be able return to Worthington Manor."

Spreading wide his arms Adrian forces everyone behind him; closing his eyes he conjures an image in his mind and the decaying flesh bursts into flame, burns until it is blackened carbon, when it disintegrates into a pile at their feet. This shocks everyone, except Adrian. "Just one thing I've learned from being in the Underworld. I've learned their tricks and their ways and how to use them. Alright, if everyone is ready, let's get started."

Upon entering, the room is obscured by the same white fog that has shrouded Worthington Manor all these decades. An evil presence resides in this vapor and it is perceive by Adrian. This incubus is lying in wait for its first opportunity to deploy its evil scheme, which is to capture and hold them in bondage for eternity.

"Thanatos!" shouts Adrian, "YOU COWARD! BRING YOURSELF BEFORE ME. You do not have the courage of an earthworm; you foul, perverted, deplorable debris. You are not worthy to be in the company of the benevolent spirit known as Mariah!"

"There's Mariah!" shouts Myra, and there, entombed in a crystal capsule is the spirit; she is in a state of collapse, being slowly drained of her energy. The lost souls are also imprisoned but are not in capsules as is Mariah. They are desperately trying to free her but millions of electrical sparks, keeping anything or anyone from approaching too close, bombard her capsule. Mariah's beauty is still vibrant, but she is obviously very weak.

Impetuously, Thanatos charges out of the gloom in a fit of rage, annoyed at the audacity of Adrian's challenge. He is snorting fire and roaring like a beast in torment, stomping rapidly towards Adrian.

"Myra, transform into your Astral body," Adrian orders, "You must save Mariah, and you can only do it in spirit. I will deal with Thanatos." The determination in his voice invites no arguments from her. "O'Keefe, you hold onto Myra, so when she falls you can catch and protect her body, and that is the only thing you do. If she should be injured in the astral body she must return to her physical body immediately."

"I have never done this without Mariah's help," Myra is willing but is not sure she can.

Sleyvia flies in front of Myra, "Miss, I will help you." With her wand showering sparks, Sleyvia circles it in front of Myra's eyes, "Myra, come hither!" Forthwith the astral body separates and is free, it is semi-nude, and, as before, is scanty clad in the silken garment; the physical body falls back into her father's arms, he carries her just outside the door and sits to guard her. Myra's astral body soars toward Mariah but Thanatos sees her and spreading his bat-like wings flies in front of her, stopping her advancement toward the spirit.

"And what are you up to?" challenges Thanatos, and grabs out toward her, barely missing capturing her.

Myra halts in mid dive, avoiding physical contact with the incubus. Adrian takes the initiative and once again closes his eyes, concentrating deeply and in his hands appears the sword he had used in battle against Cromwell. He now recognizes it as the sword, Excalibur, the sword of legend and of power. Then a suit of armor, forged of platinum assembles one layer at a time on his body.

The demon reacts violently, roaring and thrashing about in his attempt to stop Myra from getting any closer; he bellows and fire rushes out from his gaping mouth. Moving quickly in his armor, Adrian takes hold of Excalibur's hilt with both hands, then brandishes the mighty sword and, with a fearsome blow strikes the demon in the breast. Aiming true, the sword attains its target, inflicting on the demon pain he has never had to endure. "Myra, release Mariah!" Adrian shouts to her, this time Myra reaches Mariah.

Meantime, McGregor, Mrs. Grey and Steve, with Sleyvia and Haghery, have joined hands and proceed towards the demon while McGregor recites the exorcism again. This further enrages the incubus and he shrieks insults at them.

"You inferior nuisances, you dare to invoke me from here. I will show you who is god," and he hurls balls of fire towards the little group, but they do no harm for Haghery throws a handful of gold dust into the air as Sleyvia waves her wand and a clear golden dome forms over them.

Myra manipulates the fog to clear an opening, through which she propels herself across this vast arena. An intense laser pulse, like invisible shackles, detains the lost souls and pins them against the walls. There are a dozen of these captured spirits, all struggling to get free, and begging for help. Myra calls to them, for she will need their help to save them as well as Mariah. In agonizing wails, they respond. She must release them, but how. An inspiration occurs; she will neutralize the pulses by presenting a positive charge. Without hesitation, Myra creates the positive energy field with her own body; she starts a counter clockwise spin, steadily increasing her momentum until she feels the force building up inside her. She then surges into the pulses, taking the charge and breaking the circuit. It is enough to free the spirits and they float away, freed of their shackles and out into the room. The next thing Myra knows, she is out in the hall with her father, and he is gently calling her name and shaking her awake. The astral body was injured by taking the full charge of the laser pulse, but it worked; and now to free Mariah. Her father insists, however, that she rest a few minutes first.

McGregor, Mrs. Grey and Steve are still shielded from attack by the transparent golden dome created by Sleyvia and Haghery and in here, the Reverend continues with the exorcism, repeating it again and again. This had the desired effect on the demon, for it drew his attention long enough for Myra to free the lost souls.

With the mighty sword in his possession and knowing that it is instilled with supernatural power, Adrian is confident enough to do combat with this obnoxious fiend. He advances on the demon, wielding Excalibur as if he has always used this glorious weapon of kings. Thanatos is greatly angered and is determined to destroy this imperious mortal; he spews forth from his mouth large ugly toads, the size of dogs. They are poisonous and hop lazily toward Adrian; they hurl their long sticky tongues out into space in an effort to entangle Adrian and pull him into their wide-open mouths. The first toad lashes out toward Adrian, encircles his waist with its pale pink sticky tongue and begins pulling him toward its oral cavity. Adrian struggles furiously against the strength exerted by this warty toad, but finds himself being tugged into its cavernous orifice. His right arm is free and with Excalibur, he hacks down on the amphibian's tongue, severing it. The toad croaks as blood gushes from this deadly wound.

There are seven of theses gigantic toads and Adrian tackles and defeats each one by slicing off their heads with the powerful sword. As he defeats each one, they vanish, and soon they are all eradicated. Seeing this infuriates Thanatos into a paroxysm; this time he spews out an even deadlier reptile, snakes. They are of different species and very poisonous and they immediately start slithering toward Adrian. Covering the floor are hundreds of interweaving bodies all bearing down on their intended victim. These creatures move faster than did the toads. Soon they surround him, and strike savagely at him, but the protective shimmering armor inhibits their attacks; Adrian wielding Excalibur, as one with a true and faithful heart, demolishes them, and soon the ground is covered with bloody, squirming, dying snakes, which soon disappear, as did the toads. Again, the demon bellows his scorn at this mortal's victories. Disgusting bile is disgorged next, a green slimy sludge meant to entrap Adrian and hold him fast. True enough it covers his body but the magic charm on the silvery armor repels this substance as if it were nothing more than water.

Realizing that these plagues are not defeating this human, Thanatos angrily stomps the floor shaking the whole structure. Howling a piercing roar, he recklessly charges at Adrian who meets this charge head-on with the sword raised high over his head and, with both hands on the hilt, thrusts down into the calf muscle and cuts deep into the flesh. Each thrust of the blade draws not blood but the negative energy from the demon; with each slash, the sword opens a gaping wound that releases waves of energy, effectively draining the beast.

Mariah's strength is leaving her, for the more energy the demon loses, the more he draws from her to replenish his own. She is slowly fading in and out of their range of vision, soon she will disappear for good, her spirit forever captured in Perdition, from which there is no return. Before he can be defeated, Mariah must be set free to deprive him of her precious energy. For this reason, it is crucial that she be released promptly. Myra knows that it is urgent that she re-enter her astral body now. This time she is able to accomplish it on her own, and, as she transfers, she gives her father a tiny smile, *"I'll be fine, Father, please do not worry, there is another presence here that is rendering aid. I'm not sure who it is, but it is the same force that guided me to Worthington Manor the first time."*

Myra's astral body rises into the air and gracefully sweeps across the room in a headfirst posture, reaching Mariah in her clear cell. The electrical impulses emitting from the capsule prevent her from touching it, so Myra calls for help from the lost souls and they issue forth. As before, they move smoothly about the room, performing their ritual dance. Their translucent bodies shimmer in the low light; they are clothed in flowing colorless shrouds as they fluidly encircle Myra to begin their ballet.

This differs slightly from their previous dance, in that it is to call forth a stronger force of unity needed to release a captive spirit from bondage. They revolve around Myra in ever-increasing velocity and singing yet another song, without melody, but with rising tempo and timbre. Myra is the lone apex of this encirclement and she must do this alone. The electrical charges begin to fly out from this swirling mound to penetrate deep into the gloom of the thickening fog, which is growing dark from the anger discharging from the demon. As the musical sérénade continues, the windows in the entire mansion start vibrating and then exploding with earsplitting crashes, until Worthington Manor is trembling with the intense concerto coming from the gracefully rotating cluster. Eventually the crystal starts cracking, beginning at the bottom, slowly traveling up the sides of the capsule and splitting off in many directions, as lightning splits.

Inside the capsule, Mariah hovers, seemingly unaware to what is happening around her. Myra only hopes that they are not too late and that Mariah has enough strength left to survive. Their persistent efforts produce the desired results, the capsule finally breaks open, and the pieces fly out into the room. Mariah is free! Slowly she shows signs of recovering, as Myra goes to her and wraps her arms around the spirit to boost her draining energy level.

"Myra," Mariah's thought patterns are weak, *"Thank you, I could not have held on much longer."* Mariah and Myra float back to the hall and Myra lowers herself back into her physical self, she sits up and this time she remembers all that has happened. Together she and her father face Mariah, *"I will be truly free once the Dark Spirit is defeated,"* Mariah informs them, *"After which, I and the others will be allowed to pass to the next level."*

Mariah's release from the capsule has denied Thanatos of his energy reserves and he is steadily losing his battle with Adrian. He has massive injuries and exerts one last effort; he discharges a vile smelling acid. Frothy foam that is so thick that it adheres where it lands. It covers Adrian's suit of armor, adheres to the platinum and somehow breaks through the charm placed on the armor. The acids start eating away at the metal, giving off obnoxious fumes, choking Adrian, so that he begins coughing, and gagging. He knows that his time is short; he must extend his strength and psychic abilities for his one last chance at warding off this latest assault.

Adrian holds Excalibur across the palms of his hands, and closes his eyes to concentrate; the sword's silver blade grows brilliant, so vivid is it, that soon there is a blinding light enclosing Adrian. He can begin to feel the heat coming from the acid that is slowly penetrating his armor. He must act now, so, in a last attempt, he concentrates intensely. The Sword of Power rises from Adrian's hands, then rotates into an angle perpendicular to the incubus and flies true toward its mark; it strikes Thanatos in the center of his forehead, dealing him the deathblow.

The demon's screech is spine chilling; any who hears this unholy scream will never forget the unearthly sound of it. His skull splits and rays of energy forcefully escape, deflating the demon like a balloon; the empty shell collapses in on itself and a black vapor impregnated with the demon's spirit rises toward the ceiling. Thanatos' spirit is damned to Perdition; it ascends through the white fog and out the ceiling. The demon is defeated!

CHAPTER NINE

GAURDIAN DISCLOSEUR

The storm no longer rages at Worthington Manor, for, with the demon vanquished, the storm subsides. Thanatos is no more; no longer can he inflict harm on Mariah or the lost souls, and hold them captive for the purpose of utilizing their energy for his own selfish needs. To Perdition, he has been damned until the judgment. Mariah and the lost souls have gathered together in the center of this large upper room. They stand upright instead of floating, looking as they did immediately before death. Their appearances now have grown extremely luminous and they are wearing the semblance of the clothing in which they died. Even the household servants are recognizable, as well as Mrs. Worthington, Mariah's mother-in-law. There are also three very young children from a year old to four. It is most unusual for such young children to be held in limbo, because of their innocence, but when a demonic spirit becomes involved; all sorts of rules are often broken. With the teaming of a human and a demonic spirit, forces are released that never should be, with unimaginable powers.

"We are deeply in your debt for your assistance in releasing us from our state of limbo, soon now we will pass on to the next level," Mariah can now speak with her own voice. "We will no longer be able to have contact with living beings, but we will see you in your dreams," Mariah expresses the feelings of all the spirits as they expressively nod in agreement. "We have not long before the corridor to the next realm will return for us. There is only enough time for us to express our enduring thanks and say good-bye. Myra, you *are* my descendant by the only child Theodor and I had; Richard, as you will know, is his name. He is waiting along with his father at the end of this passage. We wish you and Adrian a happy marriage and many children, one of whom will be a girl. She will have our identical looks, which, just for this one time, will not skip a generation as in the past."

"Mariah," Myra approaches guardedly toward the group, "It has been an honor to have met you and, of course, the others. I will never forget all that you have taught me, and your demonstration of unending love. Maybe you and I can have future astral flights together."

Mariah smiles at her great, great, great, great, granddaughter, "Yes, that we will do. It is time now."

There is a hint of celestial music drifting in from all directions, permeating the Manor. It is a haunting tune filling each spirit and living soul with great expectations of what is yet to come, a dazzling beam drops down through the ceiling; it is rotating slowly as a whirlwind. This brilliant corridor is leading up into infinity; each soul eagerly steps into the beam and ascends into the vortex. Soon only Mariah is left, and now she too, with a smile and a wave, lifts up into the glorious light. With a rushing sound, the tunnel is pulled back into the dark animated clouds and out of sight, and the Manor's roof reappears.

While their eyes are still fixed on the exiting spirits, the fog starts churning as it folds away, creating a path through which a tall lean figure emerges. This mysterious being is wearing a full, violet, hooded mantle, with a golden cord tied at the waist. In one hand he holds a long staff with a crystal orb on its tip, while the other hand is tucked inside his robe. A golden aura defines this figure as he seemingly drifts to where the assembly waits. His face is in shadow.

Adrian steps boldly forward, speculating if this might be an evil being, "Who are you?" he asks as he bends a little, trying to see what is under the hood. At this moment, it falls away from the face and they can see it is a man of indeterminable age. His hair is long and white, as is his beard and mustache; his eyebrows are bushy and low on the brow. He has piercing light-blue eyes, a long straight nose, a very distinguished face but with a look that chills you to your core. Across his forehead is a silver band encrusted with many diamonds, on the index finger of his right hand a huge ruby gleams fire.

"Merlin!" Haghery erupts into a happy dance, as he recognizes this famous wizard and rushes out to greet him.

Sleyvia also knows him as she wings her way beside Haghery toward him, "Yes, Sir Merlin, I knew it was you the whole time, especially when Excalibur appeared to help Adrian defeat the demon."

"Only Excalibur could defeat the demon, and only one with a true heart could wield it." The wizard's echoing voice is deep and compelling; it is tinged with an English accent, "Greetings . . . Adrian, Myra . . . I am Merlin." Merlin lowers his head in an informal bow acknowledging the rest of the assembly. "For many centuries I have been entombed by Morgana, the half sister of Arthur. She was my protégée in the mystical arts, and quite jealous of her brother's kingdom, as well as of my power. She wanted both. She schemed and connived to get what was not hers. She tricked me into revealing the art of charm making, and in so doing, ensnared my being into the very bedrock beneath the kingdom of Camelot. I was only able to converse with mortals in their dreams. My release came with the defeat of the demon known as Thanatos. Because of Morgana, Arthur and their son killed each other. The demon drained her of her life force, and she now awaits judgment in Perdition. I was imprisoned for centuries, awaiting the one who could free me and all the others held in limbo by this demon. Mariah is a direct descendant of my family line by my mother's sister, Eileen. She had the same characteristics as Mariah. Adrian, you are Arthur reincarnated. You possess his wisdom and psychic ability, which is why you received the Sword of Power and the charmed suit of white armor. Excalibur was also waiting, guarded by the Lady of the Lake, until Arthur's return to this Earth. When Thanatos joined with another evil human spirit, I saw my chance to act. It was only a matter of time. I am the one who guided Myra through that storm-besieged night, to enter this manor. I also influenced you, Adrian to take part. All was resolved, as I had hoped. Myra and Adrian, with your actions you have freed not only the spirits in this house but thousands of others throughout the centuries. They have now all crossed to the next plane. I entreat the both of you to continue with the crusade started so many centuries ago by Arthur and his court. There will be many opportunities for you, with the aid of Sleyvia the fairy and Haghery the leprechaun and of course, myself, to fight the injustice in this and the next world. The powers you have gained in your endeavors, you will retain and they will grow stronger."

Myra and Adrian look at each other and together they draw near to Merlin. They are in awe of him, for everyone has heard of the legends of King Arthur and of Merlin the Sorcerer.

"I would find this hard to believe had I not experienced the things that I have," speaks up Adrian, "But is it possible to carry on with the legend?"

"My dear boy . . . indeed you may . . . you are Arthur . . . the King. Remember if you fail, so this great land will fail. At your side this time is a true love; she will not betray you as Guinevere once did. This is an age of marvelous happenings, miraculous even, but which are now commonplace. What a wonderful time for me to return to this great world. A stay I will most appreciate," says Merlin with a slight twitch of his mustache, revealing his humorous side. Adrian and Myra come together in an embrace that makes them all smile.

"I have one more unpleasant task to perform before the end of this crusade; this manor must be demolished. There is too much evil here to allow it to remain." Merlin motions for them to step back to give him working room, raising the staff high and gazing toward the ceiling, he chants in Latin a curse that only Adrian can understand.

"I call forth the dragon, the keeper of all earthly elements that influence the earth, wind, fire and water. Cleanse this house, these grounds. Destroy the evils that once flourished here. Allow them no further existence on this Earth. Destroy . . . Destroy . . . Burn . . . Burn . . . Now . . . Now . . . !"

With these commands the orb lights up, and glows brilliant. Sparks discharge from its center and strike the manor in all directions, creating fires at each contact point, outside is a terrible crash, something ultimate is happening.

"I think we need to leave," suggests McGregor.

Adrian takes Myra and his mother by their arms and directs them in front of him, ushering them out through the door. O'Keefe and Steve help Reverend McGregor down the stairs and out. Merlin seems unaware of their leaving as he continues with the charm. Sleyvia and Haghery stay with him to ensure the incantation's success. By the time the mortals reach the big double doors, the house is trembling and swaying and windows are flying apart with deafening crashes. An unearthly groan erupts from the walls as they start to splinter and collapse in all directions. Green slime is dripping from the ceiling and the walls. The bats from the second floor are swarming inside the great foyer, trying to escape the damned Manor. The large doors are forcefully opening and slamming shut, and with each incident, some bats fly through. Taking their cue from the bats, the humans do likewise. None too soon it would seem, for as they rush toward the car, the house is collapsing and fire is erupting. The thick black smoke billows up and the intensity of the fire increases.

"Adrian! Merlin and the little ones are still inside!" shouts Myra fearing for their lives.

"No, look Myra, can you see?" asks Adrian.

"No, I see nothing but black smoke."

At that instant a figure emerges from the flames, Merlin, and with him are Sleyvia inside his robe and Haghery on his shoulder, they are safe. The fire sends chilling sounds out from its center, and the flames leap leagues into the sky. They all are forced back from the increasing heat and overpowering smoke. This continues until the manor collapses and smolders into gray ash, in only a matter of an hour.

The cemetery at the back of the house is now visible; one grave explodes, throwing out soil and stones, revealing the skeleton buried there. The bones take on a temporary life as they jiggle and dance eerily about the cemetery, then burst into flame while the skeleton carries on with this spooky performance. It falls back into the ground and the grave sinks deep into the earth, leaving no sign of it once being there. This is consecrated ground and the others buried here are pure and innocent souls. This one occupant is evil and satanic and has no right for burial here on holy ground. This is Cromwell's younger brother's grave and the others have banished it from their burial site.

Merlin and the little ones have joined the rest at the car. "What just happened?" Myra speaks. But there is no answer from any of them; there is no need, they all know the reason for the destruction of the Manor. Looking toward the East the sun is making its appearance for the day; it is Sunday, a new day and a new week. The nightmare is over. Where the house stood is blackened soil, like a scorched scar, forever identifying the place where good conquered evil. No foliage will ever grow on this site.

The soil around them has dried after the thirty-six hour storm; no water stands in puddles and the sky is brightening with the kiss of the dawn. The musical repertoire of birds welcomes this new day and new a start. It is now safe to return home.

CHAPTER TEN

THE WEDDING

The brisk North Wind is ushering in the chilly days of autumn; summer, with her lingering scorching days has long since retired, giving way to the shorter days and cooler nights of her sibling.

October bedecks herself in her most colorful finery. Vivid oranges decorate the oaks and vibrant reds grace the maples, the birch adorns itself in brilliant yellow but the stubborn pines refuse to give up their uniform of evergreen, thus standing out significantly among the riot of fall colors.

Golden leaves drift leisurely by the cave's entrance, occasionally picked up by a gust of wind and tossed persistently into the air in graceful swirls, until the mischievous breezes tire and allow the leaves to continue their journey to the forest floor, which is rapidly being carpeted with the multi-hued tiles.

Overhead, a V-shaped formation of Canadian geese wings its way south, racing Ole Man Winter who is progressively forthcoming, with his freezing temperatures and gloomy days. Their honks, heard for miles, are informing the entire region of their journey, and with a warning that others, too, should do likewise. A flock of crows perched high in the pines caw in reply, stating frankly, that they will stay right here, thank you!

The croaking frogs and chirping crickets are gone; in their place are the hoots of owls and the barks of squirrels as they go about gathering nuts for the winter.

The forsaken little brook gurgles forlornly, as it continues its never-ending meandering toward the river, leaving the worry of winter's preparation to the forest inhabitants. In the distance, the cries of bobcats permeate the forest, as they seek out their winter's lodgings.

Even now the air has a bit of a bite; while the afternoons can be pleasantly warm, the nights are steadily growing colder and longer. The fall harvest has been abundant, bright orange pumpkins grow chaotically amongst the neat rows of cornstalks and haystacks. A lone scarecrow still keeps his daily vigil over this isolated meadow, enduring the ever-declining temperatures and the whipping by the North Wind on his defenseless form, provoking his arms and legs to flap frantically.

Autumn, in all her splendor, is welcome by the inhabitants of this land, even though when her visit draws to a close, she will leave the trees stripped and bare, the meadow brown and lifeless, while the forest residents struggle to survive the long winter months.

Autumn wears the cleverest of disguises, for one would not believe that all the beauty this one season brings belies the hidden truth, that this is the most deceptive of the seasons.

• • •

Merlin sits alone, for the moment, inside of an isolated cave located somewhere in the Smokey Mountains of North Carolina. He has taken refuge here after the liberation of Mariah and the lost souls. Needing to revive his mental faculties and to catch up on what has happened in the world all these many centuries now passed, he prefers solitude. Mr. O'Keefe provides Merlin with generous reading material, and being the great wizard that he is, Merlin reads these quickly. He is not surprised that many of his prophecies are now realities. Although imprisoned in the crystal for all these centuries, he was not in a state of unconsciousness, he was fully aware of the passage of time. Through the visions reflected back to him by the mirror-like walls of his crystalline prison, he saw history as it occurred. As he had helped Myra and Adrian in the real world, through the power of his mind, so he had done throughout time, influencing man in his struggles for survival. Locked fast in the crystal and unable to move his arms, legs or body, Merlin used his mind power to help sustain his mortal life and in so doing, he became immortal; no longer is he flesh and blood, or spirit, for his life is self-sustaining. His mental ability increased fifty fold; he became able to see into the future and even influence its outcome.

It was a hard fought battle after the decline of Camelot, and the final fight between Arthur and Mordred, which ended in both their deaths. At the time, he experienced the greatest sorrow of his long life, by the death of his best friend, who was more like a son. With the influence of his inner strength, he called forth the soul of Arthur from Limbo and reincarnated it into the body of an unborn boy just hours before his birth; this occurred exactly 1535 years after the death of Arthur, on the true date of Arthur's birth.

Thus began the struggle to return to the world of light, the world of the living. Merlin had recognized an opportunity to achieve his freedom when Thanatos formed another unholy alliance with a depraved and greedy human. The partnership between Thanatos and Morgana was such that it allowed his imprisonment in the first place. Thanatos deceived Morgana by allowing the dragon to defeat her, leaving him to reap the rewards of their foul plan. Thanatos had, for millennia, survived by draining the positive energy from the trapped souls here on the earthly plane. He had never fulfilled his part of any bargain he made with mortals, while relishing in their agonies when taken to Hades. Merlin knew that if a willing mortal would participate in an exorcism and be willing to sacrifice everything held dear, to help another soul, that Thanatos' power would break and release all whom he held captive, Merlin included. Thus with Mariah and Myra being identical mortal beings and blood related, it was enough to trick Thanatos and break the hold. So, with this battle won, Merlin readies himself for more conflict, for he knows that as long as humans exist, there will be a need for further battles against the forces of evil.

• • •

There are none of the modern amenities in this humble habitat, for they cook by an open fire; there are multitudes of candles placed randomly on the floor and in nooks on the cave's walls, which lend an air of ancient times and give warmth to an otherwise dismal abode. An old wooden table and two straight-backed chairs sit at the back of the cave, where the temperature is a constant sixty-eight degrees Fahrenheit. Merlin sleeps on a hammock swung between two poles driven into the soft sandstone. Many tapestries hang here and there on the rocky walls, softening and stopping resounding echoes.

Adrian had returned to New York and resigned his position at John Hopkins Hospital, which meant he was working out a two-month notice. Myra had returned to college, and the little ones, Sleyvia and Haghery are living with Merlin in this mountain sanctuary. Mr. O'Keefe did try to persuade Merlin to stay with him and his wife but Merlin refused, citing the reason already given.

Merlin sits in one of these chairs at the small table, he has pen in hand taking notes. There is a thick three-wick candle illuminating his working space and creating shadows that dance across his stern features as he concentrates on the book before him. So, here he sits, when down the long corridor of the cave comes Sleyvia, fluttering her sparking dragonfly wings, with Haghery jogging close on her heels.

"Oh, Merlin," gushes Sleyvia, "There are such marvelous things out in the world. Man can now fly with the help of machines, and they no longer have to use horses and carts to travel."

"Oh, mercy, to be sure," joins in Haghery. "Automobiles they be called, and huts fit for King Arthur himself."

"Ah, little ones, I am aware already of this progress. And you will witness much more. You know I am the one who whispered in da Vinci's ear about some of the inventions he designed; and was it not I who persuaded Edison to continue with his experiments, when all others were mocking his efforts? The world was not prepared for some of the wonders that they put to paper and so many remained hidden for eons. Most have only now in the last century been made reality."

"Being trapped in Hades prevented us from witnessing all of this. You were so lucky, Merlin, to see all as you did," says Haghery.

"Believe me, my little friend, at the time it did not seem so," Merlin sighs. "But I made the most of my situation, and now I am more powerful than I would have been, had I stayed completely 'human.'

"And I feel no animosity toward Morgana; she reaped what she had sown, as is often said." Merlin slowly shakes his head, as a great sadness overtakes his otherwise sunny disposition.

"Oh Merlin, please do not be sad," pleads Sleyvia in her musical little voice. She flaps her wings and fairy dust showers all about her, which brings a weak smile to Merlin's face. "Ah! That is so very much more like the wizard I remember." Sleyvia wrinkles her nose as she speaks.

"I have been in contact with Mr. O'Keefe and according to him, Adrian will be joining us here this weekend," the wise wizard informs them.

"Oh good," squeaks Sleyvia, "My dear friend Adrian. Be such a treat to see him again. You do know that it is because of me that he became so powerful. I helped him realize his full potential as a psychic."

"Glory be nothing," piped in Haghery, "Our cherished friend. Without my gold coin and gold dust that helped protect him, with us to this day he might not be. Ah, and without the use of the leprechauns' mighty stallion, Tranquill, he would have never defeated Cromwell. That's a special beast that I am proud to inform the likes of all. Nice it was of O'Keefe to keep him in the pasture behind his home."

THE CURSE

"Indeed," agrees Merlin. "Mr. O'Keefe even had a horse stable built for him; And Mrs. O'Keefe rides him daily to exercise him. Myra did this until returning to school. They have become very attached to him."

"HELLO! Is anyone here?" a familiar male voice called.

"It is us," another familiar, more feminine one.

"Adrian! Myra!" Haghery and Sleyvia shout together.

"Oh children, enter, please!" Merlin offers a warm welcome.

Two very bright lights come bobbing up the cave corridor as their unexpected guests make their way toward the small group, carrying battery-powered lanterns. "We've come to see you now," Myra is speaking as they come into view. "I couldn't wait until the holidays."

As they step in, Sleyvia flies first to Myra giving her a pixie kiss on the tip of her nose, then to Adrian doing likewise. "I'm just so pleased that you have come early."

Not to be outdone, Haghery skips up to the pair, blows a tune on his harmonica, and dances a little jig. "Glad am I, to be sure, welcome! Welcome! Welcome!"

Merlin steps up to Myra and gives her a fatherly embrace. "Welcome my child. It is indeed good to see you. And Adrian," he shakes hands with his young protégé. "How are you? Have you completed your work at the hospital?"

"Yes," answers Adrian, "I'm all through with that. That will always be an important part of my life, but I am not too sad to leave it behind me now. I know that what lies ahead will bring more assistance to far more people." Adrian half smiles as he places his arm around Myra's slender shoulder. He looks down on her and she up at him, returning his smile.

"You two have a secret," states Merlin, "and I think I am aware of its nature. Do you wish to verify my suspicions?"

"Okay I will," grins Adrian. "Myra has agreed to marry me. And we are going to do it this weekend. Her parents will drive up tomorrow and we wonder if we can spend the night here with you?"

Haghery let out a whoop and a holler and proceeded to belt out another tune on his harmonica while dancing another jig around Myra and Adrian. Meanwhile Sleyvia showers them with twinkling fairy dust with her magical wand. Merlin just beams on them, as if it was all his idea in the first place.

"Of course, of course you may stay here tonight," says Merlin. "It is unnecessary to ask, as you must know. You have brought your sleeping equipment, I assume. Come in and we will have a feast tonight. Mr. O'Keefe has ensured us a plentiful supply of food, so we may start immediately!"

That afternoon they spend preparing an evening meal. They decide on a freshly slaughtered lamb, roasted over the open fire on a steel rod run through the body cavity. Sleyvia receives the task of tending the roast; she casts a spell to keep the meat slowly rotating. Haghery peels potatoes and dices onions to fry in a large pan. Myra mixes up dough for biscuits, places them in a closed pan and sets it on hot stones beside of the fire to bake. For dessert, they stew freshly picked apples with sugar and cinnamon. This completes their glorious banquet.

Much later, they sit around the open fire, eating their meal. Stories are exchanged on the happenings in their lives since their last meeting.

"Well, my stretch at the hospital is done. They said that should I at any time wish to return, that my position will always be waiting for me," Adrian states.

"I hastened my studies at the University, and have no need to return any more this year," says Myra. "I knew I could do it long before now, but Mother and Father didn't want me to take that route. They said it could be too taxing on my physical health. 'Enjoy being young,' is what they tell me. So I've done as they wished, and stretched out my education. But I see a need to complete it now, so I will take my final exams this spring, with no need to return until then." Myra smiles with an air of being set free from monotonous tasks.

"Well, Adrian, Myra," begins Merlin, "if we wish an early start tomorrow, we must go to our beds now. Sleyvia, perform a little magic and clear away our dishes!"

Sleyvia, ever anxious to carry out magic, giggles and begins whizzing around the group grateful for the chance to practice more spells. Merlin will seldom allow magic, citing that mortals might not understand it. She begins by swishing her wand at the piles of dirty dishes, pots and pans. At the command of, "Swish and wash, wash and swish. Soon we will clean every dish!" All of the dishes along with the forks, spoons and knives, hurl themselves into the air, while a bucket of soapy water jumps onto the fire and starts to boil. Then, one by one, the dishes plunge down into the bucket, where each dish is vigorously scrubbed, then dipped in another bucket of clear water for the rinse, and dried with a towel suspended in mid-air. After which they settle themselves in neat piles on the table. All the while Sleyvia hovers above, orchestrating this with her wand, and sending sparks flying in complete disorder.

As the dishes are cleaning themselves, the leftovers rise slowly up and are enclosed in a clear membrane, which is hoisted up the cave's wall and hangs there on invisible hooks. In a matter of minutes, all is done, Sleyvia then sinks down onto the table, leans against a book, wipes her tiny brow with her forearm, and lets out a, 'whew!' as if she had physically done all the work herself.

Adrian and Myra stand and clap exultantly as the little fairy takes an immodest bow. Merlin tosses back his head in a hearty laugh at the antics of the little nymph.

"Ah, showing off she is," states Haghery, showing jealousy at Sleyvia getting all of the attention.

"You'll get your turn, old boy," soothes Adrian as he pats the leprechaun sympathetically on his back.

• • •

Much later that evening, all is quiet except for the snores of the male sleepers. Myra snuggles down in her soft sleeping bag, while Sleyvia curls up on her pillow using Myra's hair as her cover. Next to Myra, Adrian is in his own sleeping bag and Haghery stretches out at his feet. Merlin slumbers away in his hammock, his white beard lying atop his covers, rippling with each breath. The night is cool and silent.

Abruptly at midnight, the cave is illuminated by an eerie yellow glow. This luminosity moves along the walls of the cave until it reaches the one person it seems to be searching for, and that is Merlin, who sits straight up in his hammock staring out into the open void. This radiance gathers from all corners of the cave until it materializes into a flaming figure standing upright directly in front of him.

"Merlin!" The voices seem to come from all directions at once, all speaking as one.

"Who calls me?" Merlin directs this at the entity.

"I am the Keeper of Time." The response comes from the being, whose body is flickering like a fire.

"Why do you seek me out?" questions Merlin.

"It is said that the greatest wizard of all time has survived an attack and imprisonment by an evil demon, and that he is now immortal."

"If you are referring to me, that is so," he states. "I repeat, why do you seek me?"

"I am the Keeper of Time . . ."

"Yes, yes, so you say, tell me more and what type of being are you?"

"I am a Time Traveler, I keep time synchronized and on schedule," the voice replies.

Adrian is first to awake and quickly takes in the scene before him. He rises slowly to a sitting position waking Haghery; Adrian then reaches toward Myra and gently shakes her shoulder until she too awakes, "What's going on?" she asks. Sleyvia is also awakened by the whispers.

"Shh! We don't know yet," whispers Adrian. "Something or someone has come looking for Merlin, and he is now trying to find out what it is they want."

"I keep Time in balance," the voice continues, "Time is out of synchronization; the Universe will reverse, and all will collapse back through Time to what is known as, 'The big bang', by humans, causing total annihilation."

"That is terrible," cries Myra, "What can be done to stop this?"

"I come to the greatest wizard of all time to seek his much-needed wisdom. He has spent centuries watching time move from one eon to another. He even helps change events to fulfill prophecies. This collapse of the Universe is not scheduled for another twelve billion years. There are things that must be reversed to set history straight and give the Universe back its future. Although this collapsing will take a million years to happen, and it is not apparent just now, when it does become noticeable, it will be too late to stop. That is why the correction must be instigated now!"

As the being speaks, the blaze withdraws into its body, revealing a dazzling woman. Her skin shimmers with the purest gold dust; her hair is as flame, and her eyes flash like white diamonds. She wears a form fitting, one-piece, footed crimson metallic suit. The suit gleams as if on fire and around her waist is a belt made of small twinkling stars; on the first finger of her right hand is a ring with a setting of a miniature flaring sun, and on a rope of small round pale moonstones, hangs the white crescent moon.

"I am known as Eydasi, the Time Keeper," her voice now sounds as one and comes from this being instead of the surrounding space. "I am akin to what you consider an angel. My appointment was given to me before Time itself existed. Before the creation of any other angelic being, Yahweh appointed me to keep Time synchronized."

"I am instructed to give you full authority over the four elements, Earth, Wind, Fire, and Water." As she speaks, she withdraws from thin air a sphere. It is crystal, and churning inside can be seen the four element, all together but each recognizable. "These elements will be at your disposal to use as you see fit to modify what is invalid." She hands over the sphere to Merlin. "You need to replace your crystal at the end of your staff with this one. Should you need me, gaze into this globe and call my name, Eydasi. For I must approve of any episode you deal with before it can change history. As you suspect, this will not be an easy task."

"Where do you suggest we begin?" asks Merlin as he studies this magnificent orb, "Where did Time go awry?" He realizes that here on Earth, there could be billions of time cycles where any number of incidents could have inflicted this type of damage.

"King Arthur's death was out of synchronization; with your imprisonment, you were unable to render aid when it was needed. You have made a start by reincarnating Arthur's soul; he must now win back his crown. In order to do that, you must return to Camelot. BUT a strong warning, do not undo your imprisonment, for if you do you will once again become a mortal human, and will die in your due course. The rightful heirs are not on the throne of England. Throughout the centuries, battles were fought to regain the English throne, but Time could not rectify the true monarchy, for Arthur had died with no heirs. When you replace the monarchy and change history, then Adrian will no longer house Arthur's soul, he will have his own soul and bloodline. And Arthur will have a descendant on the throne."

With that, Eydasi, the Keeper of Time, blazes fire again, spreads herself into the yellow glow and silently retreats from the cave. For a long moment, not a word is spoken, as they try to take in all that they have just heard and seen. Was it to be believed? Could it be accomplished? Who would be needed to carry out this plan? At this point, there was no answer.

Merlin turns and scrutinizes his companions, "It would seem that the wedding plans must be postponed."

"Do you have a plan already, Merlin?" asks Adrian. He draws Myra close to his side for he does not want to delay their wedding.

"Why must we delay our plans, Merlin?" asks Myra. "We already have the license and arrangements made. After Mother and Father arrive tomorrow, we can carry on with our plans and then do what we need to do to settle this affair."

"Adrian, sir," Sleyvia has an idea, "If you be willing, Merlin can conduct the ceremony now and you will not have to wait. What say you?"

"But my parents won't be here. I am their only child; you know they will want to see me wed."

"Myra, Adrian, we must move tonight to travel back to old Camelot, and you two must accompany me. Either I marry the two of you now, or you must wait indefinitely."

Adrian draws Myra to one side and they have an in-depth discussion. When they face the others, they know that now will be their wedding day. "So be it," said Myra, "We will be married now. But will it be legal?"

"I have the power to make it official!" states Merlin. "Just a little magic and your parents will witness it in their dreams. They will think they are actually here. I can arrange for that to be so, but it would serve no good purpose."

"I will make all the decorations, and deliver you your gown," Sleyvia springs to life and excitedly begins. First things first, Adrian and Myra are separated so that Adrian cannot see the bride before the ceremony. So, as the bride and groom sit in different sections of the cave, the magic begins.

Sleyvia flicks her wand, and sparks fly, as long-stemmed, yellow, dark-faced sunflowers appear and start to form a wide circle at the back of the cave, where white daisies, small pearl mushrooms, bright orange pumpkins, cattails, golden twigs and dragonflies join them. Small forest creatures, such as squirrels, rabbits and chipmunks appear for the festivities. They begin dancing, swaying back and forth in time with the music coming from Haghery's harmonica.

Next Sleyvia touches the floor with her wand and as she flies up and over in an arch, she is followed by a trail of bright orange, yellow, and red autumn leaves that twist and flutter, while creating the wedding arch. Here and there amongst the leaves are golden nuts of pecans, acorns and walnuts. Small goldfinches and bluebirds reside among the foliage of this colorful garland. Haghery offers up his bag of gold, which Sleyvia transforms into two golden wedding bells and hangs them from the arch. A bright copper-colored massive ribbon appears and gracefully ties itself into a very large bow at the base of the bells, which start to chime the wedding march.

A pedestal that creates itself, of quartz crystal, follows these and swimming inside the crystal are living goldfish. This lies beneath the arch of fall flora; while suspended in time and space, are shimmering raindrops and metallic autumn leaves. The sparkling drops of water reflect the lights of the candles that are placed about the cave, and the leaves of gold, silver, and copper; each slowly twirl, catching the light and distributing it back throughout the cave.

Now for Adrian's tuxedo; Haghery takes on this job with relish, glad that Sleyvia is not getting all the glory. "Rise up, Sir Adrian," and Adrian comes to an upright position. Haghery reaches into his bag of gold dust and tosses two handfuls into the air, where it completely covers Adrian. When the dust clears, Adrian is wearing an antique gold tuxedo, with ruby lapels and cummerbund, there is a large white topaz daisy pinned to his lapel, and his boots are of bronze.

"Well, this is a suit fit for a king," declares Adrian. He runs his hands down the side of his trouser leg, and it feels smoother than satin. He reaches into the jacket pocket and feels an object there. There's a strange look on Adrian's face as he withdraws a burgundy velvet ring box. He opens it, and there is a set of his and hers wedding bands and an engagement ring. The bands are a matching set of entwined yellow, rose, and white gold. The engagement ring is also of matching colored gold, and in its center is a modest one-carat white diamond, surrounded by smaller pink and yellow diamonds.

"Give the pair to Myra during the ceremony," instructs Haghery. "The engagement ring goes on first, then the wedding band. Not 'til the morrow will they be switched, with the wedding band beneath the engagement ring."

"I don't quite know what to say," says Adrian, "we had decided to just have plain gold bands."

"My dear boy, believe you this, she will love it," says Haghery emphatically.

Meanwhile Sleyvia begins the glorious task of creating Myra's wedding gown.

"You must stand Maid Myra," says Sleyvia.

Myra stands as instructed. Sleyvia waves her wand in a circular motion, fairy dust showers and Myra's clothes disappear, all but her undies. Before Myra can hide herself from embarrassment, she is quickly covered by layers of white lacy petticoats. They are very full and stand out in a three-foot diameter all around her. Again, Sleyvia waves her wand and a beautiful wedding gown grows onto Myra, starting at the shoulder and working its way down to her feet. The gown is of a slightly off-white satin, trimmed in old creamy lace. The bodice is off the shoulders, and low on the breast, showing Myra's golden skin and cleavage. The sleeves are puffed from the shoulder to the elbow, and tight fitting down to the wrist, where they form a V on the top of her hand. Tiny seed pearls are stitched around the neckline, and small diamonds speckle the bodice and forearms of the gown. At her waist, the bodice narrows into a V at the front of the skirt. The skirt billows out over the petticoats in layers of first satin, then old creamy lace, and over that, another layer of transparent organdy. The organdy is studded with thousands of miniature diamonds. Trailing from the waist at the back of the gown, is more organdy, forming a train six feet long, also dotted with small diamonds.

On Myra's feet is a pair of cream-colored satin slippers, trimmed with copper wire.

Myra's colorless hair is gathered up from the temples, braided, then twisted into a knot atop of her head, and the rest is left to drape down to her waist. A tiara of diamonds sits atop of the braids, with a three-foot veil falling over her face, and at the back is a twelve-foot train trailing onto the floor behind her.

A bouquet constructs itself, floating above the floor of the cave. A layer of vibrant autumn leaves tuck themselves into the foundation, while miniature sunflowers and tiny daisies do the same. A copper-colored ribbon entwines amongst the flowers, leaving several pieces dangling. Fireflies wing around the bouquet, blinking, as they become part of it.

More fireflies fly around within the circle, but closer inspection reveals them to be fairies! Now leprechauns are dancing a jig, having appeared from nowhere.

"Haghery, Sleyvia!" call the leprechauns and fairies. "We have heard your call for us to come participate in the wedding ceremony."

Merlin approaches the fairies and leprechauns, "Welcome, it gladdens us to have you fairy people amongst us."

"You know, we would not for a king's ransom miss the wedding of our liberator, Sir Adrian. If not for him, we would still be trapped in Hades," says one of the leprechauns.

"Ah, but Haghery and Sleyvia have outdone themselves, the decorations are the most unusual we have ever seen. I wager not a couple alive nor dead had such glorious arrangements!" says Adrian.

Yes, it is like a fairytale come true. Everything is animated, even the plants dance in place.

"It is time to begin," says Merlin, "Everyone, take your places. Haghery, you will be Adrian's best man, Sleyvia is Maid of Honor, and will attend to Myra's veil. Rudy," he speaks to the youngest leprechaun, "You are 'Ring Bearer'. I require three fairies to be flower girls." Three fly forward. "The rest will be our guests and witnesses. I will escort Myra down the 'aisle' in addition to conducting the ceremony. Yes, I can do both," he smiles.

Haghery conducts Adrian to the podium, where they wait along with the ring bearer. He carries a rust colored velvet pillow where all three rings are carefully laid.

Myra has appeared at the center of the cave's corridor, with Merlin at her side. He takes her right arm and guides it through the crook of his left arm.

The Wedding March begins. The three fairy flower girls fly down the aisle first, scattering the petals of daises and red maple leaves. They are followed by Sleyvia; as Maid of Honor, she carries a bouquet of red maple leaves, which is larger than she is.

Now in step with the beat of the drum, Merlin, in his emerald green robe, escorts Myra toward the podium and Adrian. The veil, which covers her face, is two layers thick, obscuring Myra's delicate features.

She is a heavenly sight, as she slowly approaches her groom. Adrian's heartbeat increases as he watches this vision coming toward him. Behind Myra, half a dozen fairies are carrying her train to keep it from snagging on objects that may be in the way. The music of bells and flutes accompany the organ, which is heard but unseen.

At last, Merlin gives Myra's hand over to Adrian, who takes it in his own, and faintly smiles into the veiled face. He tucks her arm into his, and both turn to face Merlin, who has already stepped behind the podium. The music dies away, not a whisper is heard, as Merlin begins to speak.

Merlin gives instructions to the wedding couple of the expectations from them; the cave inhabitants are beaming, actually glowing, as Myra and Adrian in turn repeat their vows of love and devotion.

When asked to place the wedding band on Myra finger, Adrian glides on both rings at once. Myra does the same for Adrian, then Merlin pronounces them husband and wife.

"You may kiss your Bride," Sleyvia swoops down and raises Myra's veil, up and over her head. Then with a modest kiss, their vows are sealed.

"May I introduce Mr. and Mrs. Adrian Grey?" As Merlin makes this announcement, he guides the couple to turn and face the audience, where cheers and applauds are boisterously given.

Above is a hologram depicting an image of Myra's parents' bedroom, where they are obviously sleeping. In this image is a large cloud-like space, showing in real time the wedding ceremony, so this is what the O'Keefe's are dreaming.

CHAPTER ELEVEN

EYDASI'S RETURN

Things have returned to normal, the beautiful decorations disappear as fast as they came. Adrian and Myra are back in their everyday clothing. The five of them are sitting around the open fire, some cross-legged on the cave's floor; the others sitting on large stones.

"We should be contacted by Eydasi very soon now," says Merlin.

At the mention of her name, the cave fills with a blue mist; it travels along the cave's wall until it materializes into a watery being.

"I have heard your call, Merlin!" The many voices are once again coming from all directions. Now Eydasi appears in human form. This time her skin is platinum, her garment a flowing watery blue, her eyes flashing sapphires, and her hair is a spouting water fountain. She still wears the stars, moon and sun jewelry.

"You are ready for your trip back through Time." It is not a question so much as a statement of fact.

Merlin, Adrian and Myra stand to face this divine being.

"Who is to regress? Just I?" Merlin speaks.

"You must take your protégé and his wife, they will be fundamental in your success. The fairy people have the ability to traverse through Time at will. They will be your connection with History's future."

Adrian places his arm around his new wife's waist; they have only been married for one hour. It is three o'clock on the morning of 'All Saints' Day', November 1st.

"It looks as if we must go," says Adrian.

"Yes, indeed," agrees Myra.

"I wish you both to realize," says Merlin, "that you may not be able to return. I am willing to make this sacrifice. But are you? You cannot be forced to do this. It must be your own decision or we shall not succeed."

The newlyweds look at each other intensely, and without speaking, they each nod their heads.

"Then it is settled," states Eydasi. "Stand to one side."

The five rest against the wall. Eydasi spreads her arms wide. The cave's interior expands, until the whole mountain is hollowed out. It lights up with natural daylight; the interior is immense, and in the center is an enormous hourglass. It is very ornate, antique gold, with the red Sands of Time flowing from the top of the hourglass to the bottom.

"When I reverse this hourglass, the complete Universe will also reverse. There will be no present. The only present that will exist is the one you experience. It will be history as the present; history that has not yet happened. Everything here today will no longer exist."

With that, Eydasi again spreads wide her arms, and the Sands of Time stop, they do not flow, neither down into the future nor up into the past. There is a deathly quiet throughout the Universe as Time is frozen, then the Sands of Time start flowing up, back into the upper part of the hourglass, from which they had just streamed. Slowly at first, as if shifting gears, but now picking up speed and as they flow, the past is reflected on the inside walls of the mountain. Each image shows an outstanding episode in that century's history.

The twentieth century has the first Gulf War, the Vietnam War, two World Wars, man's advances in flight, the explosion of the first atomic bomb, and the moon landings. The nineteen century has the Civil War of the United States, the slavery of thousands of Africans, the conquering of the wild west of the United States, and so forth back through Time. The images are moving so fast now that it is impossible to keep track of the events that appear.

Abruptly Times halts and the reflections on the wall are of medieval times. The picture now is of Camelot in all its glory.

"Are we there?" asks Myra.

"So it would seem," replies Adrian. "There are thousands of pictures. How do we get to England when we are still in the United States?"

"You will go through the picture of the Time period you wish to visit. When you do, you will be in England and Camelot," replies Eydasi.

"How?" asks Myra.

"I am aware how this may be accomplished," replies Merlin. "Just remain close to me and copy my actions."

Merlin first takes the orb that Eydasi gave to him, and removes the old one from the tip of his staff, replacing it with the globe of the Four Elements. The globe glows a white light, as the Four Elements churn inside the crystal. Merlin holds the staff at arm's length and high over his head as though testing its power. As he does, on the surface of the wall showing Camelot, the scene begins to waver. It is like waves of heat rising from the ground on a hot day.

"Follow me," he instructs Adrian and Myra. Merlin moves toward the image, to an area of deserted pasture, Myra next and then Adrian. "We will enter at this point. We would not wish to startle the populace of this time, when we would seem to appear out of nowhere."

At first, it looks to be a barrier, like a two-dimensional photograph, but Merlin puts forth first his staff, and then steps forward into the picture. Suddenly he is there, they can see him, but he looks years younger. His long white beard is brown and shorter. He cannot see them, but he knows they are there, "Come through, Adrian, Myra."

"Take my hand, and do not let go," Adrian tells Myra as he reaches for her hand. Together they walk into the picture. They meet no resistance, and it is as if they had simply taken a single step.

"Ah! Here you are. I knew you would not fail. Welcome to my world. Over the rise is the castle, Camelot. I am suitably attired, but you both appear strange for these times, especially Myra. We will borrow some clothing from the little hut over yonder. Come, let us proceed."

"Merlin, you are so much younger?" says Adrian.

"I expect I am," replies Merlin, as he touches his face with his hand. "It must be Eydasi's magic."

"You are right, Merlin," her voice is behind them. They turn to face her; she is still in the watery guise. "You must look like your counterpart."

"You mean to say there are two Merlins?" asks Adrian in surprise.

"Indeed, and they must not make contact. Merlin, you should allow your 'other self' to follow history the way it happened. This will free you to work without being particularly noticed by anyone. Go your way, and remember to call me when needed." With that, she vanishes into a cool pool of water, which the dark earth absorbs.

• • •

They had entered this time frame just before sunrise; the man of the house is already out and about with the morning chores. The three of them reach the little hut in a matter of minutes; the woman is out in the back feeding the chickens. Merlin goes around to the back door, instructing Adrian and Myra to wait at the front. After a time the front door opens; there is Merlin and a young woman of about twenty-one or two.

"Good morning. Please do come in," her greeting is warm and friendly. "Any friends of Merlin, the Sorcerer, are more than welcome in our humble home. Come in, come in and get yourselves warm by the fire, for it is a bitter day out today."

"Thank you ma'am," replies Myra as she and Adrian cross over the threshold into the modest hut. There are only three rooms, and an infant lies asleep in its cradle close to the huge fireplace, where a fire is roaring.

"Please come and warm yourselves," she invites again.

"Let me introduce every one," says Merlin. "This lady," he indicates the peasant girl "is married to a cousin of Sir Hector, King Arthur's foster father. You remember that it was he who raised Arthur from an infant. Her name is Jean. Jean, this is Myra." Merlin draws Myra forward.

"Good morning, Jean."

"And this is her husband, Adrian."

"A pleasure ma'am."

A small boy of about three, wearing a white sleep gown and no shoes, enters the room. On seeing these strangers he rushes over to his mother and hides behind her skirts, then peeks out.

"Hello," Myra speaks to the child who is beginning to look frightened. "And what is your name?"

The blond tot looks sleepy and yawns, "Are you a man or a woman?"

"Why, can't you tell?" Myra squats down beside him.

"Well, you sound like a girl. And you look like a girl. But you dress like a man."

"Well, I am a girl. I just feel like wearing these today."

"Oh," the little boy accepts her explanation.

"So, what is your name?"

"Quisten," he replies. "What's yours?"

"I'm Myra."

Merlin begins explaining things to Jean, though not completely truthfully about where he had been or exactly who Myra and Adrian are. He asks to borrow clothing for Myra. He just said they had left home quickly and had no time to collect their possessions.

"But why does the girl wear men's clothing?" Jean whispers to Merlin, "You know that it is unheard of."

"Whence they come, it is a common thing. Do not worry, she will be attired as a lady from now on," he whispers back.

• • •

Later, the three of them are riding in a two-wheeled cart pulled by a mule. Myra is not at all comfortable in the woolen peasant frock that she wears. She has kept on her own underwear and boots, so that is something, but the woolen hose she is now wearing, feel very rough on her skin. The petticoats are of linen, the skirt and bodice of the dress are a muted gray, un-dyed lamb's wool; she wears a red linen scarf to cover her white tresses, and Jean has loaned her a dark blue woolen cloak.

"We think you look quite attractive, dear child," says Merlin, when he sees Myra squirming on the seat beside him. Adrian sits in the back of the cart giving Myra the more comfortable front seat.

"To be truthful, I really don't care what I look like, if only I could scratch," complains Myra.

Both Adrian and Merlin laugh at her discomfort.

"When we reach Camelot, you will be treated like a princess," promises Merlin.

"I don't want to be treated 'like a princess'. I just want something smooth and silky against my skin. Something that won't drive me crazy with this mad itch!"

• • •

Soon enough they reach the moat surrounding the castle, and the drawbridge is down. Four men in armor stand guard and one approaches them as they stop at the bridge.

"Ah, it's you Merlin," he recognizes Merlin immediately, "And who might your companions be?"

"They are friends of Sir Hector's first cousin's wife, Jean," replies Merlin.

"Oh yes, James. Well Arthur has asked that you see him as soon as you arrive."

"I will do so."

The knight motions them through.

With a flick of the reins, the mule plods on, clumping its hooves across the wooden planks of the drawbridge.

"I should wish to know the exact date and time," thinks Merlin aloud. "The first thing I shall do is to consult the charts."

"Do you have any idea?" asks Adrian.

"Well, I am certain we are at the beginning of Arthur's reign. But I am uncertain if he has met Guinevere yet. If you remember, he sent Lancelot to bring her to the castle, and she falls in love with Lancelot immediately. I am considering preventing this meeting now. It serves no purpose for Arthur and ruins the kingdom. I gave Arthur fair warning even before he became King, that a trusted friend and a deeply loved one would betray him. But he disregarded my warnings and, as he watched Guinevere dancing for the soldiers, after the battle that would give him the throne, he became captivated by her. He had received a slight wound, which Guinevere bound up for him, and that was the beginning of his infatuation."

Merlin guides the mule to the back of the castle, deciding to enter through the kitchen. He knows his counterpart is not here from what the guard has told him at the front gate. But he wants time to get Adrian and Myra into the castle without any more questions, so that he can help them to dress in the proper attire.

All shout greetings to Merlin as he passes through; Merlin acknowledges their greetings as he leads Adrian and Myra up the steps to the third floor of the palace, where his rooms are located. He pushes on a very heavy oak door that opens into the first room. This is a sitting area, with several large chairs, wooden benches, a huge armoire, and a sturdy wooden table with an inlaid top showing astrological signs. Several straight back chairs are placed randomly around the room, and from the ceiling hangs a branched iron candleholder. A large candelabrum is standing in the middle of the table. There are tapestries hanging on the walls, several small windows, and very heavy dark green hangings. There is a door leading out to the other rooms.

"I require you both to wait here. I will go to Arthur now, and send servants to help you change clothes, and fetch water for you to bathe. I will return shortly."

• • •

Hours pass before Merlin returns. When he does, he has much to tell them.

"Arthur wishes to meet both of you. As I told the guard, he believes you are relatives of Sir Hector. We are too late to intervene with Guinevere. Lancelot is at this very moment bringing her to the castle, so the damage has started. My counterpart has gone to the country to heal a friend and probably will not return for some weeks now. Arthur wondered why I had returned so soon. He thought that possibly our friend had died. At this moment, I cannot remember the episode, so I think he must be alive. I know I would recall if someone had died."

"Well, Myra, are you pleased with your new garments?"

Myra is wearing a light pink cotehardie, a one-piece dress of silk with long sleeves and high neckline. It is straight and close fitting to her knees, where it flares slightly and drags onto the floor.

"Oh I feel wonderful," says Myra. "We have both washed and had time for a nap. Do you realize we've been up since midnight? But the best part was getting into something softer!" The servants had created a simple hairstyle for Myra, leaving it down and adding a silver filigree decoration, held in place by a pink crystal headband.

"You look beautiful, my dear," says Merlin, "I am afraid Arthur may forget Guinevere when he sees you."

"If he does, he'll just have to get over it," cuts in Adrian. "I'm afraid the lady is spoken for."

Adrian is also in period clothing; he wears dark blue tights, and over these a pair of loose gray leg-breeches, called breccias. Then comes the tunic of deep dark blue, embellished with silver studs around the throat, the elbow, and randomly around the shoulders, front and back. The tunic has half sleeves, and, from underneath these appear longer sleeves, called coudières, that flare out wide and hang nearly to the floor. At the moment, he wears no headgear and has opted to keep on his own boots.

"I had forgotten that you two are newlywed and, as of yet, not had your wedding night," injects Merlin.

Myra's face becomes pinker than the dress she wears. The consummation of their marriage is weighing on her mind; after all, she is still a virgin. Of course, she knows what's done, even how it's done, but she has never done it before, and frankly, she's not too sure if she wants to.

"Let me see, it is three o'clock in the afternoon, and we dine with Arthur at the round table, at seven. Yes, there is indeed a round table; a hundred can sit at it at one time. I have arranged for you to share my rooms; I will sleep out here and you will have the bedroom."

"We don't wish to take your bed, Merlin," exclaims Myra.

"Do not worry, my child," says Merlin, "I shall be quite comfortable in here."

"That's very kind of you," says Adrian, "We both thank you."

• • •

At six thirty, they make their way down the winding stone steps to the dining hall. There are hundreds of people milling about; house servants bent on serving their guests, knights in full armor, beautiful ladies in stunning gowns, and more men dressed similarly to Adrian. There are no children here, for bedtime comes early for the younger generations. Hundred of wall sconces and candles light up the hall; from the ceiling hang many tapestries that bear the Coats of Arms for the different reigning families. All are in high spirits, for Lancelot has returned with Guinevere, and her wedding to the King will take place in two days. Many are introduced to Adrian and Myra, men openly admiring Myra while the women give her looks of envy and jealousy. Adrian gets his share of admiring glances as well. Merlin makes the same explanations about them and where they are from, and no-one questions them.

The call comes that summons them to dine, "Just follow me and copy my actions," instructs Merlin. "Do not talk too much; I am afraid they may have questions about your speech."

"Are you trying to say that we have an accent," asks Myra.

Merlin laughs, "That is exactly what I am saying. Jean questioned it, but I told her you are from a foreign land across an ocean, and this she accepted."

Merlin goes to his usual seating position, which is to the right of Arthur, but tonight someone else sits there. It is Guinevere. Arthur stands as the three arrive.

"Good eve, Merlin; and are these your guests?"

"Yes, may I present Myra and her new husband, Adrian of America."

"America? I do not believe I have heard of that house before. From where do you hail?"

"From across the great ocean," Merlin answers for them.

"The great ocean? May I ask, 'How'?"

Myra and Adrian look at each other, then at Merlin.

"It is a long story, which I will explain anon," Merlin replies.

Arthur bows toward Myra, takes her right hand in his and all but touches his lips to her skin, "How lovely you are, my lady."

Myra is a little discomfited with all of this formality, she curtsies as she has been instructed, and mumbles, "Thank you, sire."

"Merlin, you remember Guinevere?"

"Yes and how are you my lady?" Merlin bows over her gloved hand when she offers it to him.

"Myra, Adrian, I wish you to meet Guinevere, my wife to be."

"Pleasure, ma'am," says Adrian as he follow Merlin's action and brushes her hand with his lips.

"Myra, a most unusual name I must say, will you do me the honor of sitting here next to me. Merlin beside her, please, and Adrian, it would honor Guinevere greatly if you will sit next to her."

"Indeed it will," agrees Guinevere. Guinevere wears a teal blue velvet gown, much in the style of Myra's gown. The sleeves are short, almost at the shoulder and long white gloves nearly meet the sleeves of her dress. Guinevere wears her dark hair in one long braid on her left shoulder, down the front of her gown and a tiara of diamonds sparkles on her brow. Adrian takes the seat next to her.

A few minutes later a young blond man enters the dining area. It is Lancelot of Laik. He takes his usual seat just one chair apart from Adrian, and a bit later, a robust redheaded woman takes the seat between Adrian and Lancelot; this is Arthur's half sister, Morgana.

The conversation this evening centers on the upcoming marriage of Arthur and Guinevere. Midpoint of the meal, the announcement is made of the marriage in two days time. Sagremor, one of Arthur's Knights of the Round Table, offers a toast to the bridal couple, and cheers erupt from the diners.

• • •

After the meal is over and the servants have cleared the dishes, the entertainment starts. There are jesters, in their block colored costumes wearing the double pointed caps. They leap around in foolish postures, juggling oddly shaped items, and acting the buffoon to gales of laughter from the audience. Lovely young dancing girls gyrate and twirl in time to the music coming from a small minstrel band. This continues into the wee hours of the morning. Long before the revelry ends, Adrian makes his excuses and he and Myra, with guidance from a maidservant, head for bed. Just as they are about to leave, Arthur hails them and hurries to catch up.

"Most sorry," he begins as he places his right hand on Adrian's left shoulder. At the moment of contact, a sizzling lightning bolt shocks the both of them. Arthur lurches backwards and stumbles, but does not fall. Guards rush over to aid their King. Merlin, as well as the rest of the throng of people, see this and dash over.

"I am not harmed," Arthur assures them, "you may go. Quite a shock there, my good fellow," Arthur addresses Adrian.

"Your Majesty, my most earnest apologies, I do not know what happened."

"Not another thought about it, it was strange but neither of us is hurt. But you will forgive me if I do not lay hands on you again."

The tension eases and laughter fills the hall.

"I was just about to bid you 'good night' and ask that you join us for a late breakfast tomorrow at noon."

"We would be honored, Sire," Myra finds her voice and speaks.

"I will escort you up," says Merlin, excusing the maidservant.

When they are out of hearing range, Merlin speaks. "I should have known that something like this would happen if physical contact between you and Arthur occurred. Remember you *are* Arthur reincarnated! The two of you cannot occupy the same space at the same time, but in the space-time continuum, there would be devastating repercussions should you do so. It would cause the merging of your physical selves and thus your destruction, and maybe even the destruction of the Universe itself. My counterpart and I must also ensure we do not make physical contact. It could happen that closer proximity would not repel as it did this time. So you must avoid contact at all costs!"

"We understand," they say, in a state of astounded comprehension.

They have arrived at Merlin's rooms, "Here is where I leave you. Remember it is your wedding night! I will stay downstairs until the party ends, and then I will take my rest in one of the servants' chambers."

Adrian starts to protest but Merlin stops him. "You cannot persuade me to change my mind. Goodnight to you both and I will send a servant up to help you dress, by eleven o'clock tomorrow morning."

With that statement, Merlin turns and leaves.

The two of them look at each other; Adrian cups Myra's small face in both of his hands, and gazes deeply into her eyes. He knows of her fears and wishes to alleviate them, he leans down, and kisses her gently on her soft and yielding lips, "Myra, do you trust me?"

Myra blinks her eyes as she nods.

Adrian opens the door, Myra enters. He follows. Adrian eases the door shut.

CHAPTER TWELVE

THE CONCEPTION

The next morning at first light, Myra wakes. Always an early riser, she rises from the massive bed where she has consummated her marriage. She glances at Adrian and the love she feels for him swells up in her most secret places. He had been a most considerate lover, not rushing her into anything, just letting nature take its course. Her fear of this act had proved unfounded, and she relishes in the awakening of her new womanhood.

She walks over to the window; it is very cold and she longs for a fire. She pulls the top cover from the bed, careful not to awaken Adrian, and wraps it about her. She would like a drink but does not know how to summon the servants. So she goes into the front room and sits down, pulling up and wrapping her feet in the cover.

Then a faint sparkle comes towards her, what is it? Sleyvia!

"Most glorious morning Lady Myra," the little fairy shimmers in the morning twilight.

"Sleyvia, yes it is very good to see you, is Haghery with you?"

"No, in a bit he will join us. He is with Merlin just now. Merlin summoned us last night. He wishes me to stay with you at all times."

"I welcome your company, Sleyvia. But how can you keep with me? I am sure people will notice. I'll be fine. Only I would love a cup of coffee, but it hasn't been discovered yet!"

The next thing Myra knows, she is holding a cup of hot coffee! With cream and sugar. It appears in her hand so fast that she almost drops it. Then a fire comes to life in the fireplace, sending its welcoming warmth throughout the room.

"Oh thank you, Sleyvia. You are just what I need in this prehistoric place. I never knew how much I'd miss a bathroom. Hot and cold running water. A toilet! The twentieth century has a lot to be said for it. And of course, the twenty-first century as well. I keep forgetting that we have entered a new century," Myra laughs.

"You are especially welcome. We must keep you well and comfortable. I will return in a moment. Merlin wishes that I inform him if either of you are up." The little fairy glistens as she slips beneath the door and out into the hall.

• • •

Minutes later, there is a knock on the door.
"Who is it?"
"Merlin."
"Come in, Merlin," Myra hurries to the door, as it swings open.
"Ah, I see Sleyvia has tended to your needs. We want you well taken care of," he remarks as he and Haghery both enter.
"Yes, a cup of coffee and a warm fire," says Myra. "Haghery, it is so good to see you too. I know that it's only been one day, but somehow it seems longer. In any case it is good to have familiar faces around once more."
"Tis good sure enough, Lady Myra," said the little leprechaun as he picks out a familiar tune on his harmonica. "Forgotten have I at how dreary the dark ages really were. Warm enough are you. Can't have you getting sick, you know."
"Why all of this concern for my welfare? Sleyvia said something, and now you and Merlin. What is going on? You know something I don't. Am I getting a cold or the flu?"
"Who's getting sick," this from the bedroom door. "A man can't sleep with this ruckus going on out here, Good morning darling." Adrian sits down next to Myra and places his arm about her shoulder. Myra returned his greeting as he kisses her brow. Then he is also holding a cup of coffee.
"Well now, this is room service for you."
"I'm wondering if maybe I am getting sick," Myra answers. "They keep saying 'to take care of me'."
"Merlinnn!" Adrian drags out the sorcerer's name. "Spill the beans. What are you cooking?"
"It is not 'what I am cooking', as you put it. It is my privilege to inform you both that Myra has conceived and is with child. My congratulations to you.

"What?" gasps Myra. "You don't mean last night? But it was my first experience. How can you know so soon?"

"The same way I knew of Arthur's conception. I am, after all, the greatest sorcerer of all time. I am Merlin. Yes, you have conceived, and it is a son."

Blank expressions come over Myra and Adrian's faces, as it take a moment for things to sink in.

"If this is so, then I must return to the future," Myra worries. "I will need proper prenatal care. I don't know just how I will tell my parents, especially after they missed the wedding, but I am sure they will be thrilled." Myra quits speaking for a second as her look focuses on her abdomen. She places a trembling hand there, "A baby?" She speaks in wonder, "I am going to be a mother?" A short pause, then she turns to Adrian, "Do you believe this Adrian? We are going to be parents."

"Yes; I can believe, knowing Merlin as well as I do. But I am also very worried. I already know we cannot return to the future until the rip in the fabric of Time mends. And who knows how long that will be. We did not plan on anything like this happening. But we must make the most of this bad situation."

"No, no, this is not a bad situation, it is perfect," interjects Merlin. "Myra, you will have wonderful care. Is not your husband a doctor? Am I not the greatest sorcerer you know? This is a very special child. He will be an heir of King Arthur. The bloodline will not die out when Arthur dies. We have our King."

"No, no! Never!" shouts Adrian as he rises from his seat. "My son will not be raised here in the past. There must be another way." Adrian's stance is of one ready to fight for his newfound family against all who threaten them. "You need to come up with another solution to this problem, for this is not it."

"Well, we need not make a decision just now, time is with us," Merlin relents for the moment, for there is no need to upset Myra. News such as this could cause undue stress and bring about a spontaneous abortion.

Merlin paces the floor and at an odd sound turns, it is Myra. She is weeping. He is reminded of another mother's cries. The day he took Arthur. Ygraine had cried and begged him not to take her son. But Uther had made a vow to Merlin and Merlin held him to it. Merlin took the babe and left him where no one would find him, for he knew the child's life was in danger. Uther would be killed leaving the family no protection from would-be assassins, for the throne was in jeopardy. He had had to secure it for the baby Arthur, who was destined to be its next king. And now the future of the Universe is in jeopardy. He sees a way to safeguard it. But can he once again take another child from its mother's arms? If he does not, the World is lost. He will consult with Eydasi.

"Myra, my child, shed no more tears," he tries to console her. "I will seek another opinion."

Myra raises her face from Adrian's shoulder and turns tearful violet eyes toward Merlin.

"Please," is all she says.

Merlin walks to the window and peers out. Holding his staff up and at arms length, he calls, "Eydasi!"

The temperature drops and icicles form on the windowsills and frost collects on the walls; a white mist rises up from the floor obscuring everything, then it churns until it condenses into a figure of ice. An ice stature of a woman, only partially clad in a thigh length gown of twisting snowflakes. On her head is a crown of icicles and her face is breathtakingly magnificent; the ring of the sun is on her finger, the belt of stars is around her waist, and the crescent moon hangs from her neck. She is a depiction of a living sculpture. The fire goes out, unable to compete with the sudden drop in temperature.

"You call me, Merlin?" as before, many voices come from all directions.

"Eydasi?" queries Merlin.

"Yes! Do you wish to change Time?"

"I do have a plan."

"And it is?"

"Myra has conceived a son, just last night. He is of Arthur's bloodline. Should he take the throne after Arthur's death and thus continue the bloodline on down through time, to place a rightful heir on England's throne."

"Is King Arthur his father?"

"Not directly. Adrian sired the child, but Adrian is Arthur reincarnated. So this embryo is his progeny!"

Both Myra and Adrian rise and approach The Keeper of Time. "Please Eydasi," pleads Myra, "Can you tell us why it is so important for a king of Arthur's bloodline to sit on the throne. Can't you find another way; we are not willing to give up our son. We have years yet before Arthur's death, to be sure by that time another child can be born of this Arthur."

"Mordred will be born to Morgana. Guinevere is barren. There will never be a child born to her. And even I cannot change that. I will tell you what I will do, for now we will wait. I too would prefer a son born directly from Arthur. But if this is not accomplished, then I will sanction your child as legitimate heir to the throne.

"The throne of England is the Throne of King David. Arthur is of David's lineage, as is Christ. There must be unbroken lines of kings from David until Christ's return. When Christ returns to Earth it will be to occupy this Throne from which he will rule the Universe, not just Earth. Without a true and pure heir on it, Christ will not return to liberate Man, the Universe will collapse and God will begin again.

"When Morgana made a pact with the demon, it was Lucifer's way of destroying what God created. He lost the war in Heaven and was cast down to Earth, and ever since, he has been trying to undermine God's creation. He even construed the death of Mordred. Father and son killing each other served his purpose, for neither father nor son then ruled, and Satan could put his servants on the throne, thus the rip in Time.

"You have until the time of Arthur's death to bring this about. I suggest you move about in this time frame. Do not linger long in one, for there is a greater chance of discovery and of failure."

"Thank you, Eydasi. This shall be done," says Merlin.

Before Myra and Adrian can thank her also, the ice statue melts into a pool of water that drains away through the cracks and crevices in the floor. Suddenly the fireplace comes alive with a roaring fire, and for the moment, Adrian and Myra breathe a sigh of relief.

"Merlin, I know we can do it. We can find another maiden to bear Arthur a son. It will not be of his marriage, but neither was Mordred and he was trying to take the throne," Adrian stresses this fact.

"Yes, I understand you. We will trust that might be possible. But you must be prepared if the worst should happen. Then your son will be the only hope for the Universe."

• • •

Today is Arthur's wedding, Merlin decides to stay inside the palace this time until it is concluded. He tries several more times to dissuade Arthur from marrying Guinevere, reminding him he knows for a certainty that she will betray him. Arthur refutes this and commands Merlin to be silent or accept banishment from the castle until after the wedding.

The morning of the wedding, Merlin's counterpart arrives at the castle, further complicating things. Merlin from the future has plenty of warning and after discussion with Adrian decides to confront his counterpart with the truth of what is happening.

"I know myself well enough," Merlin the future is saying, "that should I learn of something of this nature, I would be most open-minded. I think my counter-part will be willing to help us. We will wait until he comes up here, and have speech with him then."

They do not have long to wait, for the first thing Merlin of the past does, is retire to his room. He is tired and dusty from his journey and wishes to bathe and rest before the ceremony. The door swings open. Merlin of the past enters without noticing much at first. The room is dark and he waits for his eyes to adjust. When they do, he makes out a human shape in the room. He sees Myra, for they chose her for their first encounter, feeling he will not feel danger from her. He believes she is the maidservant.

"You may go, girl. Have hot water sent up and food," he instructs her.

Myra comes nearer to him, "Excuse me, my lord, but I am not the maidservant."

"Well, who are you then and why are you in my rooms? What are you trying to steal?" Merlin of the past walks around her, but still he does not sense any danger from her.

"Merlin," Adrian enters from the other room. "I am Adrian and this is my wife Myra."

Merlin of the past feels anger and opens the door to summon the guard. Adrian rushes over to him and takes his upper arm, "No! Wait! Hear me out. We really do not mean you any harm. We are very close friends of yours . . . ah . . . friends of a friend of yours."

Merlin of the past stops, turns, and looks at him, "And who would that be?"

"He is here with us, shall I bring him out?"

"By all means, let us find out how much of a lie all of this is."

"You may come in," Adrian calls.

"What kind of wizardry is this?" exclaims Merlin of the past, for he is face to face with himself.

"No wizardry I assure you," replies Merlin from the future. "I am indeed who I appear to be."

Merlin of the past walks over to Merlin from the future and reaches out as to touch him, Merlin from the future steps back hastily, "No, you cannot lay hands on me. That will destroy both of us instantly."

"I think you need to explain yourself. And should you fail to do so . . . , then I will call the guard."

"Let me introduce myself; I am Merlin."

"What kind of foolishness is this . . ." begins Merlin of the past, and turns for the door.

"I am from the future."

Merlin of the past stops and for a moment does not move. It is as if he is wondering if he has heard accurately.

"Yes, you did hear correctly, I . . . we come from the year two thousand and three, fifteen hundred years into the future."

Merlin of the past turns and faces the three of them. "I believe you. The explanation is too outrageous to be untrue. As a seer, I should have seen this. How did you accomplish it? And how is it that I am face to face with myself? How can there be two of us?"

"I did not bring this about. I am not so powerful. No, the Keeper of Time contacted me . . . ," begins Merlin from the future.

"You are from two thousand and three, correct?" interrupts Merlin of the past.

"Yes."

"I lived for that length of time?"

"Yes, in a way you did. I did. Would you care to sit? And I will explain it all. It will take awhile."

Merlin from the future unfolds the story, leaving no stone unturned. It was even necessary to tell of Merlin's imprisonment and Morgana's role, stressing the fact that they must allow for this incarceration, or the Merlin of the future would not gain immortality, nor could he correct Time. Therefore, the rightful king would never sit on England's throne, creating this rip in time and bringing about the premature collapse of the Universe.

"You say this unborn child is of Arthur's bloodline, how is this?" asks Merlin of the past.

"Adrian is Arthur reincarnated," explains Merlin from the future.

"Ah, so now we have two Arthurs?"

"So it would seem."

"And two Merlins?"

"Yes."

"And Morgana will have a child by her half brother, named Mordred. The dragon will destroy Morgana, using her own son. Mordred, in fact, will kill both of his parents and he in turn will die at the hand of his father. This will leave no true heir to the throne. So the throne will be seized by the strongest. Because of this, a tear in time will bring an early collapse of the Universe."

"I understand perfectly," Merlin of the past nods his head, walks over to the table and sits down.

"Do you really believe us," asks Adrian.

"But of course. No one could create such a fallacy. So it must be true," states Merlin of the past. "My next question is; how is it possible for us to change Time and save the Universe?" Merlin of the past spread his hands wide and looks from one to the other.

CHAPTER THIRTEEN

THE FIRST CHALLENGE

The festivities are on. As promised, Sleyvia never leaves Myra's side. She easily hides in Myra's headdress. Haghery stays close as well; being the leprechaun that he is, he hides quite easily amongst the everyday items in the castle and the gardens. Myra's pregnancy must not be disclosed just now, if ever. There are too many who possess powers enough to destroy the unborn child, should they learn that he could become King, after Arthur's death. Morgana is their biggest concern, for it is already known that, in a few years time, she conceives a child with her half brother, in order to win the throne.

● ● ●

No expense is spared to implement the most splendid wedding ceremony ever. They speak their vows in the abbey of Glastonbury. This in itself is quite humble, only their garments are elaborate and just a few of their closest friends are at the actual ceremony. This includes Merlin of the past, but not Adrian and Myra, but they do go to the feast afterwards.

It is here that their crusade for a rightful heir of the King undergoes it first trial. Merlin from the future goes to the banquet with Adrian and Myra, while Merlin of the past sleeps.

Morgana hails Merlin from the future, "Oh Merlin," she calls, "Wait. I wish to speak with you."

Merlin from the future waits, while contemplating what he knows is on Morgana's evil mind. The ambition for Arthur's throne develops within

Morgana here. He also knows he cannot deny her, to do so would twist time in the wrong direction.

After a brief discussion, for she wishes to study the magical arts with him, she asks if she might become his student, and learn his secrets.

"Ah, you do know something of the arts," says Merlin from the future.

"Yes, I have the sight; my mother passed it to me."

"Meet me tomorrow and we will begin your studies."

As they are strolling and conversing, they happen upon Adrian and Myra sitting off to one side. Merlin from the future attempts to guide Morgana away from them. Morgana's talents are strong enough that she just might sense Myra's condition.

"Wait a while, Merlin," Morgana takes his arm to stop their further advancement away from Adrian and Myra. "Are not these your companions that I have seen with you? I yearn to meet them. The girl is quite lovely, but that hair color is extraordinary."

Merlin from the future is worried, for Morgana has far too many questions. "Indeed, it is a family trait, I understand," he says and steers her in another direction; he needs to get her further away from Adrian and Myra. So he keeps his answers short, he does not want to discuss anything about either of them.

But Morgana is insistent that she meet Adrian and Myra and so Merlin from the future cannot refuse and they approach Adrian and Myra, "Myra, Adrian, I wish you to meet Morgana, Arthur's half sister."

Adrian stands and takes the hand Morgana offers, bending over it as he says, "Greetings, Morgana."

"Please excuse me for being so forward," begins Morgana, "but you look very familiar to me, Adrian. Have we met somewhere before? No, I suppose not. I would remember. But still it is as if I know you. I shall remember later, I am sure."

Morgana reaches out her hand towards Myra, and takes her hand in her own, "Lady Myra. You do realize that you turn the head of every male here. Not that I blame them. You are a most striking lady."

Morgana halts her monolog in mid-sentence as she senses another presence, an unseen being. Her eyes grow wide and her mouth drops open. "You, my dear, are with child. You do not realize it just yet, for it is only just begat. But a babe is on its way, you must be surprised!"

Myra successfully hides her foreknowledge of this event, and gasps, "NO, I cannot be. Why I've only been married two days. No one can tell that soon.

I have no symptoms of pending motherhood. NO, no, you must be wrong. I am not with child."

"Well, maybe not. As you say, it is indeed early. I may be wrong." With that, Morgana excuses herself and heads back in the opposite direction.

"She is not convinced," says Merlin from the future. "But for now she attaches no great importance to your condition. Let us keep it that way."

"I was about to zap her," says Sleyvia, as she peeps from under Myra's coif. "If she had not been about her way. We need not such a snoop as she, around."

They all laugh at the tiny sprite, fearless for her small size. "It is plain that Myra is in very capable hands,' says Merlin from the future.

• • •

"Morgana can cause us much trouble," Merlin from the future is saying later that evening, with the six of them up in Merlin's rooms. His long robes drag the floor as he uneasily paces back and forth. "Can you," says Merlin from the future addressing his counterpart, "keep her mind on other tasks, while we attempt another solution?"

"Most certainly I can. According to you, it will be a few years before she devises the idea of conceiving a child with Arthur, which occurs after the adultery of Guinevere and Lancelot. This is also the same time she will imprison me. I will dispel any ideas she may have of your pending motherhood, and focus her thoughts on 'stealing' my power from me."

"Haghery, I wish you to eavesdrop on any conversation of young fertile maidens who may have an attractive eye for the King," says Merlin from the future.

"Yea Merlin, if there be a lass so inclined, influence her I will," boasts Haghery. "Never know what hits them, they won't."

• • •

A few days later, they assemble again, Merlin from the future asks, "Haghery, have you found any maidens who might captivate King Arthur."

"There aplenty of pretty lassies there, no doubt. Even a few who find Arthur tempting, but to go up against Guinevere, none there are. Too much in love with her is King Arthur, not a chance would they stand of enticing him into adultery," the little man pauses for a brief moment and begins again. "With Gawain I heard Morgana speaking, suspects Guinevere and Lancelot already she does, they having strong feeling for each other. Said she notice it on more than one occasion, the sly looks they give each other. She's suggested that he say something to Arthur about it. And he is, I think."

"Yes, that memory is still strong with me," Merlin from the future sighs. "She started the rumors of Guinevere's unfaithfulness to Arthur. And when Guinevere was formally accused, her honor needed defending. Here Lancelot received a mortal wound, and I intervened in order to save his life. Eventually this brought about the actual affair. Arthur found them together in the forest, asleep in each other's arms and in his rage plunged Excalibur into the ground between them. It so happened that Morgana and I were in my underground chambers, and as I was speaking a curse on Morgana to halt her evil plans, the sword cut into the spine of the dragon, affecting me. This caught me in a bind and Morgana seized the opportunity and reversed the curse onto myself. She then stole the spell for the Charm of Making, using it to imprison me. That very night she used it on Arthur, blinding him to her identity. He thought she was Guinevere and she conceived Mordred. From that, the kingdom went into decline. For decades, the land was devastated; Arthur's knights went in search of the Holy Grail. Perivale finally located it. Just when it appeared that the land and the King were restored, Mordred challenged Arthur for the throne. And you know the outcome. I witnessed it all from my prison. I tried to influence things from their dreams, but I failed. Arthur was killed, and died without an heir, for, before his death, he killed Mordred."

"From what I am hearing so far," says Merlin of the past, "there is no reason to change these events; doing so will alter history too radically. You should move forward into the future a few more years and try another strategy. I probably will not be here, if Morgana has her way." At this point Merlin of the past walks over to Myra, "My dear child, it is an honor to have met you. Please remember if you must make this sacrifice, it will be to save all humanity. A sorrow for you, I know. Should it become necessary, console yourself with the knowledge that this not only provides a future for your son, but also any other children you may have. Without this, none of us have hope."

"This plan, so far, is going nowhere fast," says Adrian despairingly. "It would seem the only choice Myra and I have is to give our unborn son to others to raise in this time frame. But we *are not* willing to do that. If our son is the only hope, and he must stay here in the past, then Myra and I will stay here also and raise him ourselves. Just how to introduce him as King Arthur's son is beyond my ability to see. I may be Arthur reincarnated, but I cannot pass as his twin. There is little resemblance and you will never convince anyone that I am a long lost brother or cousin. It will be a battle to try and seize the throne; one at a great cost of life, even if we found enough supporters. Not to mention the threat on his life if it is found out whom he is. Morgana already looms as a possible menace to his life even before he can be born."

Myra sits on the sofa with silent tears running down her face, "I cannot bear this agony, married barely a week and I learn of my pregnancy; that it is a boy, as well as a king and that I must give him up all in the very same week. No, I agree with Adrian, even if it means I will never return to the future nor see my parents again, we will stay here."

"Do not cry, Lady Myra," pleads Sleyvia, "Haghery and I will remain with you and see that you and your baby are well protected. He will have all the powers of his father as well as the wisdom of the ages. We can teach him all that he needs to know, and he will be the most loved King of all times." The little sprite flutters to Myra's shoulder, where she remains.

"I think that Merlin is right," says Merlin from the future. "I will summon the Keeper of Time tomorrow and we will discuss the best time frame to enter. If the two of you do remain at Camelot, maybe it will serve our purpose better to be further into the future than we are."

That night is a sleepless one for Myra and Adrian; she lies cradled in his protective embrace, feeling that he can protect her and their son from any and all dangers. When she does catch a nap or two, her dreams are of being bound in tight roots of surrounding trees, while a baby's plaintive cries are deafening, and she is unable to rescue him. She awakes with cries, and struggles to free herself, only to come to the realization that Adrian is holding her close.

"Myra, wake up, sweetheart," Adrian tries to soothe her and free her from the demons in her dreams.

Fully awake now, "Oh Adrian, it was a horrible dream." Myra relates the details of her nightmare through occasional sobs, as she tries to control her emotions.

"This is not good for you, you know."

"Yes, I do know. Adrian we must admit to ourselves the fact that, however incredible it may seem, it will take our son to save the Universe." Myra pauses for a minute. "We can and we will stay with him. There is no other choice."

"Yes, Myra. I already know that. Tomorrow we will ready ourselves to remain here in the past."

The next morning after a light breakfast, they once again call on Eydasi. They must let her know their decision to move forward.

Merlin from the future takes the staff and raises it over his head while standing at the window, "Eydasi!"

The air in the room begins to blow strongly, the hangings at the windows flap, but nothing else in the room is disturbed. The wind picks up in intensity until it forms a whirling purple vortex, which dies away, leaving in its place Eydasi. Her skin is a light sky blue, her hair is a dark thundercloud with lightning bolts shooting from it, and her garment is made of transparent silk, which ripples with the slightest breeze. Her eyes are glassy-like amethyst, and on her finger is the ring of the sun, around her waist is the belt of stars, and from her neck hangs the crescent moon.

"Merlin, you called," again the many voices coming from all directions.

By now, they have grown used to Eydasi's different guises, and wonder what she will be the next time they call her.

"Yes, I did," responds Merlin from the future.

"What have you decided?"

"It is necessary for us to move forward about five years."

"Why five years?"

"It is after my imprisonment, or at this time, my counterpart's imprisonment," he waves his hand in the direction of Merlin of the past, who bows to indicate his willingness to accept his lot.

"Also, it is the same time as Mordred's conception and I wish to be present to see how he matures. Myra and Adrian have definitely decided to stay here to raise their son. I agree with them. There is no one else whom I could trust with his upbringing. We know his life will be in danger, and he will need magical aid in his defense. I will also stay. I wish to regain my previous appearance, so that no one will recognize me, especially Morgana."

"So be it," exclaims Eydasi, as she extends her arms, and the room expands into the size of the mountain. Again, there appears the giant hourglass with the red Sands of Time flowing smoothly into the future. Eydasi claps her hands once and the sands increase in speed, while the walls reflect the future. It shows the wars with the Saxons and Arthur's many victories. It reveals the prosperity of the land; crops grow in abundance, there is very little sickness, only the very old die and above all peace flourishes. When they arrive at the Time of Guinevere's and Lancelot's betrayal, Time slows back to normal.

"It is time to transfer," commands Eydasi.

The five of them, Merlin from the future, Adrian, Myra, Haghery and Sleyvia move toward the ripples in the Time they will enter. Before they proceed through, Merlin of the past gives Myra a fatherly embrace and clasps

Adrian's hands, "Thank you dear children for the sacrifice you are about to make. And Merlin, I wish you well and may the blessing of the one God be with you."

"Thank you, my Counterpart; we will merge again in the future. You will be able to see everything that happens, as I did. Time will pass quite swiftly for you, so trouble not. Farewell, for now."

Merlin from the future turns to Eydasi, "We are ready."

As before, Merlin steps through the time frame, and when he does, he returns to his former appearance. He has entered this time frame, materializing in his own hideaway, deep in the forest. It is a simple two-roomed hut, made from the bark of trees with a roof of dry thatch. There is a small cot against the mud walls, a small fireplace, and a wooden table with one chair.

"Myra, Adrian come through," he calls.

Together they step through Time, and then Haghery and Sleyvia come through together.

"Wow! Merlin, what is this place?" questions Adrian.

"This is my sanctuary," replies Merlin. "It is here that I recuperate when I am exhausted from expending the power of the dragon. I know it is small, but I only sleep when I am here. It must blend with the surrounding forest to prevent anyone from becoming suspicious and scrutinizing further inside. I am very vulnerable when I am here; for my power is often drained and I sleep very deeply. There is nothing that could awake me, were someone to find me. We are over five miles deep inside the forest, and the building material used in constructing the hut, camouflages it almost totally. We should be very safe here."

Merlin opens the old plank wooden door and steps outside into the glen and the others accompany him. It is a glorious autumn morning, mid-November. It is chilly but not freezing, which is a delight, for it had been very frigid in the castle. So far, they have journeyed through Time in the same month as when they departed the 21st century. The trees are in their full autumn splendor; dark reds, bright yellows, vivid oranges are abound, and the wind tugs the leaves from their branches, tossing them unmercifully to the earth. There is the call of ravens as they soar swiftly through the forest heading for unknown destinations.

Myra pulls her cloak closer to ward off the slight chill. Adrian notices and pulls her close to his side. "Cold, darling?"

"Just a little."

"Inside we should return," says Haghery. "A fire we need."

"Indeed, my friend," agrees Merlin. "Sleyvia, work your magic!"

"Aye, aye, Sir," she answers and flies into the room. "Merlin, you and the others best wait out here. Wouldn't want you injured by flying debris," she giggles.

"Just the inside, Sleyvia, not the outside, and do not increase the dimensions of the hut," instructs Merlin.

"Understood Sir," she replies as she hovers near the ceiling. With a flash of her wand and a shower of fairy dust, the interior of the room melts, as a painting might run when doused with water. When everything is black, items grow up from the new floor, which is no longer dirt but soft carpets. Two good-sized beds replace the cot in the back room, along with a dresser and mirror. An oval table constructs itself in the middle of the front room with four chairs.

The fireplace grows until it takes up nearly one complete wall, having all the amenities a 'modern' fireplace of this Time period should have, and it now comes alive with a roaring fire. Against the other wall, is a huge cupboard containing all the dishes, cookware, glasses, and eating utensils that they will need. Another wall has a pantry filled with food stocks using 21st century canned goods; she also cheats a little when she adds an inside hand water pump, which should not be invented for many centuries yet. Each room has one window, from which Sleyvia hangs heavy drapes that help ward off the cold. She also adds a sofa in the front room and several armchairs in the backroom.

She flies over to the front door, "Your Lordship and companions, you may enter," she sweeps her arm in an open invitation.

"Lassies first," says Haghery.

As Myra steps toward the door, Adrian surprises her by sweeping her up into his arms, "Since this will most likely be our home for sometime now, I think we should initiate it properly by me carrying you over the threshold."

"Certainly, my Lord."

After they are inside, Adrian kisses her before letting her feet ease to the floor. Merlin and the wee folks follow them inside, then cheer, and clap at their open display of affection.

With Adrian's arms still holding her, Myra looks up at him, "This will be our home away from home. We must make the best of it. I can cook and clean, you can hunt, and in the summer, we can have a small garden. I know it will be a solitary existence, but we can manage, you'll see."

"As long as we are together, anything is possible," he glances toward Sleyvia, "especially with this little nymph with us. I don't think we need want for anything."

Myra lays her head against his chest, closing her eyes for a moment while she envisions what the future holds in store for them.

CHAPTER FOURTEEN

THE FIRST ATTACK

The months have been uneventful; autumn with all its beauty soon deteriorates, until the trees are naked and the snow deep. Myra begins to feel the symptoms of her early pregnancy, but with Haghery's knowledge of herbal remedies, she is relieved of the worst of it, and by her third month, it passes. They spend time playing games brought from the 21st century, courtesy of Sleyvia.

Soon Myra's pending motherhood becomes quite apparent as her abdomen swells with the growing child. Adrian keeps a watchful eye for any abnormalities that can crop up unexpectedly, silently swearing that should the lives of his wife and son be in the slightest danger, they would return to the 21st century for the proper medical attention, even if it meant they could not complete their mission.

• • •

Myra sits at the window in one of the straight-backed chairs, her arms resting on the windowsill. It is the middle of March, still the snow lies thick on the ground and more is falling. She has entered the fourth month of her pregnancy, and has felt the first flutter of life. At first she thinks she imagines it, but moments later she feels it again, and there is no mistaking it this time. Yes, her son is alive and making his presence known. She is home alone except for Sleyvia, who will never leave her. She stares out into the darkened forest, the leafless trees cradling snow on their boughs; will spring never come? Back home in North Carolina it never snows this late in the year, why even in April the dogwood blooms. Myra sighs for she longs to see her mother. She has a great need to tell her about the baby, but it seems that her parents will never know or see their grandchild. Why was this burden placed on her young shoulders? Adrian still plans on finding a maiden to bear Arthur a child and maybe luck will be with them. They can only pray.

As she stares out into the snowstorm, a movement catches her eye. At first, she is sure it is Merlin, Adrian and Haghery returning and she makes for the door. As she opens the door pulling it inward, a black shape comes hurling toward her; it is big, tall and furry, a bear! Myra screams as she attempts to slam the door shut, but the bear forces his weight against it, throwing her to the floor.

On hearing the commotion, Sleyvia soars into the front room and sees a huge black bear standing over eight feet tall and reared up on his hind legs, with front paws raised threateningly in the air, snapping his jaws, and snarling vociferously. Brandishing her wand, Sleyvia gives the bear a powerful jolt of electricity, sizzling his hide, but he does not back down. He makes straight for Myra, slashing out with his huge paws, as if it is only her that he sees. Myra manages to get to her feet, running to the back room seeking cover. The bear lumbers on all fours after her, again Sleyvia zaps him, and the stench of burning fur can be smelt, but it does not so much as slow his attack. He has Myra cornered on the bed; she pulls the covers up to her chin, as if they might give a measure of protection. When the bear lunges for her again, she let out a piercing scream that fills the cabin and travels out into the forest. Bravely, Sleyvia continues her assault with her wand, jolting the bear with a high voltage of electricity, which would kill any other wild beast, but only succeeds in slowing his attack. With each bombardment, he halts long enough to bat a huge claw at this flying menace, thus saving Myra from being mauled, at least for now.

• • •

Earlier that morning, even though there is still snow on the ground, Merlin needed to find out all he could about Morgana. They have assured Myra that all is well, they will be extra careful and with Sleyvia, she will be safe. They dress in peasants' clothing and with Haghery in tow, they conjure up a donkey and an old beaten down cart and take their leave.

They are now returning from Sir Hector's castle, where Merlin has learned a good deal more about Morgana. Hector did not recognize Merlin, and told him how the Sorcerer was missing, and, many thought, hiding somewhere waiting, for what, no one knew. He told them of Guinevere's banishment to the monastery after her adultery with Lancelot, and that Lancelot had fled the land. King Arthur was in declining health since learning of Morgana's trickery and her subsequent pregnancy. They had bidden their host farewell and headed back to the hut.

They are traveling by donkey and cart, keeping the illusion alive that they are just poor traveling minstrels, going from town to town seeking to entertain the masses, in exchange for food and lodging.

Merlin pulls the donkey cart to a stop, "Adrian, did you hear?"

"I did, it's Myra! She is under some sort of attack! Merlin can you hurry?"

"Heard it as well, I did," shouts Haghery.

Merlin jumps from the cart and take his staff, holding it above his head, "I call upon the Four Elements; take us to my dwelling deep inside this forest!"

The orb swells in size, and, as it becomes large enough, it surrounds the two men, rises immediately in the air over the tops of the trees, carrying them off, then settling them onto the snow covered earth at the door of the hut. It shrinks to its normal size and returns to the end of Merlin's staff.

Adrian is first to rush into the cabin; seeing the immediate danger and with no thought to his own safely, he flings his body onto the back of the enormous bear, wrapping both arms around its thick neck. This is how Merlin finds them when he enters. Once again, he holds the staff high, "I call on the Element of Fire, destroy this beast!" Adrian jumps away when he hears Merlin shout. A giant fireball leaps from the orb, and engulfs the bear completely, burning it to cinders in a matter of seconds, while not even scorching anything else.

Myra heaves exhausted sobs as Adrian takes her into his arms.

"Merlin, a bear, this time of the year? They hibernate 'til after the snows melts," says Adrian. "Sleyvia, tell us what happened."

"Your Lordship, this was no ordinary bear. It was bewitched. I zap him continuously, and the best I could do was to slow him up. I could have moved Myra, but switching tasks would have given him enough time to kill her. I intensified the volume of her screams, hoping you would hear, and make it back in time to help me save her."

"You were wise, Sleyvia," says Merlin. "Obviously this is Morgana's work. Somehow she has learned of this pregnancy and its significance. We arrived after Merlin's imprisonment. When she stole the Charm of Making from him, she may have read his mind. She knows! She is pregnant also, probably as advanced as Myra. It is a race to see which child is born first. The child that is first to be born, will be the heir. To us it matters not, for we know that Mordred will perish, but Morgana knows not all of this. We are no longer safe here without a barrier. I will erect one of invisibility. Of course, it will not prevent Morgana herself from entering, only any animal or man she may send forth. However, I believe she will not risk her unborn child to pursue us herself. That at present is to our advantage."

Myra has regained her composure, and she sits upright on the edge of the bed as she sips the hot cup of tea that Haghery has prepared for her. "I have never been as terrified as I was today. Not even when we fought the demon. This time I have an innocent life as well as my own to protect. I don't suppose there's anymore we can do that we aren't doing already."

"This is a world fraught with danger and with a sorceress hunting you, the danger increases dramatically," says Merlin. "Henceforth, either Adrian or I will remain with you."

"Don't forget me," cries Sleyvia.

"No, you are not forgotten, our little heroine," says Adrian, "If you had not been here, that bear would have killed Myra. No, no, definitely you are not forgotten!"

"Not forgotten Haghery," pipes in the leprechaun, "Be here also, I will."

"Certainly you will, Haghery," assures Merlin, "Were you able to return the donkey and cart here without problem?"

"Indeed I did, came after you as fast as the beast could pull, used a little magic to lighten his burden, and hurry him along, I did. Got here in time to hear you speak of Morgana. An invisibility barrier you say, laugh at it, Morgana will. Better than nothing, I suppose. Speak with the animals, I will. For to give warning should another beast come under a spell cast by Morgana."

"I shall call the fairies and elves also," injects Sleyvia, her dragonfly wings beating rapidly with anticipation. "They will be more than glad to help. You know they will do anything for you Merlin."

"Then the leprechauns, I'll call," says Haghery, not to be outdone once more by Sleyvia.

"I am certain all of your efforts will be of great assistance," laughs Merlin. "With so many protectors, we should be victorious in any battle with Morgana. I anticipate the birth of the child, Seth, to be about the 19th of August. I am hopeful we shall not be troubled by Morgana, until after the birth of both children."

"Merlin, what did you call the baby?" asks Myra.

"Seth will be his name."

"Where did you hear of this name?"

"During my captivity, this name was mentioned by the Druids' priest; it is the name of one of their monks who rescued many from starvation during the potato famine in Ireland, during the nineteenth century. Hearing this name brings thoughts of security to many in the British Isles. I think that it is fitting for this child, do you not?"

"We haven't talked much about a name," says Adrian, "with so much going on, but I do like the sound of it. It's one I've never heard before. I think I like it, how about you Myra?"

"A unique name for a unique child, yes I like it," Myra smiles up at her husband.

"Okay, Seth it is."

The next morning, Merlin does as he had promised. He steps out into the yard and the new fallen snow is well above his knees. At the edge of the forest, he holds his staff high, "I call upon the Element of Wind to issue forth, and surround this place with an invisible shield!"

The orb churns and from an unseen exit the Wind gusts forward, out into the world, unseen but felt, it creates a whirling vortex around the perimeter of the hut.

• • •

Spring finally arrives in the forest, the daffodils break the ground a little after the crocus and their bright yellow blossoms bring welcome color back to the landscape. The warming sun melts the winter snow, and small rivulets form, temporarily, to carry the once frozen water to the creeks and streams and finally the river. The first indications that winter has finally given up for this year, begin to appear. Brightly colored butterflies and industrious honeybees compete with each other for the sweetest nectar among the flamboyant wildflowers of the meadow. The nightingale has also returned, for his melancholy song permeates the night air.

"Adrian, do you hear that?" asks Myra. Myra and Adrian are sitting just outside the door on a wooden bench. "I've never before heard such a beautiful song from a bird."

"Yes, it is extraordinary, what kind of bird is this, Merlin?"

Merlin stands to the right of the door taking in the sweet night air, "Ah, my children, that is the song of the nightingale."

"Nightingale," whispers Myra in awe. "How lovely is its voice. I heard its song last night, and it did not cease singing 'til the dawn."

"Yes. There is a myth about the nightingale. It is said that it sings all night to keep itself awake."

"Why does it need to stay awake?" asks Myra, getting very interested in the story.

"At the very beginning of Time, the bird is alleged to have had only one eye, so it stole the legendary single eye of the glowworm. Since then the vengeful glowworm searches every night for the nightingale, to take back its eye. Thus the bird must stay awake, and in order to do so, it sings all night with its breast pressed against a thorn."

"Oh, how sad for the nightingale," sighs Myra. "I wish I could see one."

"It might be possible to arrange that," says Merlin. "When a nightingale senses danger, it cries out in a series of short chirps, repeatedly, warning the other forest inhabitants. It would be the best sentinel you could have."

"Get a nightingale for you, I could," volunteers Haghery. "Not too many can sneak up on a nightingale, its hushes its singing whenever someone comes near, but one of the wee folks could easily snare one."

"I can create for it a beautiful cage," says Sleyvia. "And arrange it so the nightingale would have its freedom but still stay close to you."

"That is settled then. Haghery tonight you and your clan shall capture for Myra a nightingale," Merlin bows his head towards the leprechaun as he speaks.

• • •

True to their word, Sleyvia and Haghery have summoned their kith and kin, and now the forest is full of fairies and leprechauns. They keep watch diligently for any out of place beast or being, and there have been a few that they deemed necessary to escort to the edge of the forest. The peasants whisper that the Black Forest is haunted, and the few that dare travel through it, make great haste to do so. None but the bravest dare venture far off of the beaten path, to do so bring unknown peril.

Haghery ventures out late that very night, and, using the cunning known to his species, he goes about unseen. The Black Forest earned its name, for it is so black at night that a walking stick is needed to help feel the way. The fairy folk are exempt from this inability to see at night, and Haghery makes good time as he hurries to the old hollow tree in the very center of the forest. As the little man walks, he hears the night crickets chirping at him to take his leave from their domain; ignoring them, he continues on his way. After a lengthy march, he arrives at the Old Hollow Tree. The tree is an ancient oak; it is nearly ten feet in diameter, and carved out of the bark is a small door. A greenish light filters out from around the door; there is a quaint little lantern hanging from the lowest limb, sending a welcoming glow for nighttime visitors. Haghery raises his fist and pounds on the door.

"Be you man or be you beast, if you mean us harm, we will grind your bones to make our feast," a strong warning comes from the other side.

"Haghery it be, open the door so me to see," Haghery answers in like fashion, not to do so would bring suspicion to the residents inside and they might take him for an enemy and rush out to do him bodily harm.

The wooden door springs open, and several leprechauns hurry out to greet him, "Haghery! Haghery! Haghery!" They are exuberant to see their king as they take his arms and usher him inside.

"Glad are we to see ye, what forth brings ye hear? Done we have as ye requested and kept the varmints and villains at bay."

Inside of the Old Hollow Tree are a mass of wee folks; fairies, leprechauns, and elves alike, all are assembled here. The walls of the interior of the tree divide into small cubicles, which is where each one of the wee folks lives. These brightly painted cubicles go all the way to the top of the tree and all the way to its roots, and each level has a half floor that goes the circumference of the tree. To reach these cubicles, if you can't fly, are various ladders of vines and roots. Sleyvia's parents are here and fly over to ask about their daughter. Haghery takes the time to tell them all that is going on with Adrian, Myra, and Merlin and especially the new babe due to be born very soon.

"And what bring you about here on this dark night, Haghery?" ask Sleyvia's father, King Quaff.

"A nightingale we be needing."

"A nightingale? Whatever for," asks the Queen,

"Lady Myra has heard its song and is struck with its beauty. Have one she must. Its song will sooth the babe in her womb and let My Lady sleep in peace."

"So, bewitched is she by the nightingale's hypnotizing song? That is the danger for most mortals, who hear the nightingale on its first night back in the land of Britain. A curse it can be, for often the wanting is better than the getting."

"Aye, know this well I do, but Merlin wants the nightingale for Myra's lookout. For a warning will the nightingale give should danger be near, and Sleyvia will be its trainer."

"Well then, since it's Merlin who wants the nightingale for Myra, then a nightingale Myra shall have," says the King. "I need elves and leprechauns to volunteer for an undertaking."

Leprechauns and elves hurry forward, "What might that undertaking be?" inquires a leprechaun.

"We need a nightingale," answers the King. "Since they have only arrived back in Britain last night, they probably have not paired up yet for breeding. A single male we need. Haghery, select three each of elves and leprechauns, with yourself, that will be seven. Seven as we all know is the number of completion. Since the beginning of Time it has always taken seven to locate and capture a nightingale."

Then going over to an old dilapidated trunk, the King opens it and retrieves a net of gold; he faces the group Haghery has selected, and hands the golden net to Haghery, "With this enchanted fishing net, you will capture the nightingale with no injuries to the bird or yourselves."

Haghery takes the golden net, and eyeing his brigade, orders, "Troops, march."

The wooden door swings open, and out into the night they go. After some distance from the Old Hollow Tree, they pause as Haghery get his bearings, "Listen we must for the bird's song."

As each member strains his ears, a melancholy tune wafts in on the wings of the night breezes; it is the nightingale. He is a great distance, for the tune is faint and broken.

"From the North it seems to be coming," says Hermes, the tallest of the leprechauns.

"North it is," says Haghery as he leads the way.

The melody is closer now, they are within sight of the nightingale but picking out its dark plumage is proving more difficult than expected.

"A light we need," says one of the elves.

"He, he, he," a wicked sounding laugh is coming from nowhere.

"Who be there?" calls Haghery.

The darkness moves, but still no shape.

"Answer, or be cut down."

"And who will be doing the cutting," a shrill voice demands. "It will not be the likes of you."

"Show thyself, thou specter of the night!"

THE CURSE

At that command, a figure appears from the thick underbrush; it is an old hag. She is stooped and very old, "Why do you wander about my garden in the wee hours of the morning? What are you trying to steal?"

"Steal, we do not. We but seek the nightingale whose song we heard," replies Haghery.

"There are no nightingales, say but the one in my garden, and he is mine. Away with you, for the other nightingales have not yet returned to Britain. Seek your bird elsewhere! Be gone, before I turn you into swine!"

Haghery is undecided, for if this is the only nightingale in Britain, then this is the one Myra heard, and this is the one Myra must have.

"Buy him from you, we will," says Haghery. "Name your price, for a leprechaun has much gold."

"You do not have enough gold to purchase this fine bird, for this is an enchanted nightingale. He was in my garden one night many years ago; he was devouring my silkworms. I cursed him, now his feathers are copper and silver. He can no longer fly. So in my garden he has no choice but to stay. He delights me with his song on the nights that it is hard for me to sleep, and I will never release him. So you best take your leave or you'll find yourselves rooting around in the mud!"

"Take our leave, we will," says Haghery. "Good morn to you dear lady," as he tips his cap and bows low. He and his band start off into the forest.

"Leaving are we really?" asks Ernie. "But it is daylight in but an hour, and no nightingale have we."

"Leaving? No, we are not," injects Haghery. "A magical bird this be, and have it we must. Buy it we can't, so steal it we will."

The seven little men surround the cottage and its garden. The nightingale continues its song, but they cannot see him. The old hag goes inside of her cottage; by now, they well know that she is a witch, known to the peasants as the Hag of the Black Forest. Many peasants seek her out for potions and spells; they bring her beast and fowl as payment.

Haghery advances into the garden; he leaves his men with simple instructions, come when he yells. The song continues and Haghery unerringly follows it to its source, an old bent cage made of twigs and rope, and inside is the most beautiful nightingale he has ever laid eyes on. The feathers that should be brown are a shimmering copper, and his breast is gleaming silver. The eyes are black as ebony and the beak and feet are gold. The sheer beauty of this magnificent bird is enough to make your heart race. Taking the golden net he carefully opens the cage door, the nightingale hops onto the edge of the opening, Haghery throws the netting over the bird that screams at this insult, which of course brings the old hag running from her cottage.

"Why do you scream?" she calls to the bird.

And surprising to all, the bird answers, "I am caught by a leprechaun and he is carrying me away!"

The old hag gives chase after Haghery and the others, and with her old pointed hands, throws imaginary fireballs at them, that materialize into the real thing and explode all around, digging up the earth and splattering them with dirt. All the while, the nightingale screams in the high-pitched chirps used to warn of danger. Haghery has him securely wrapped in the gold net, and turning to the others, he yells, "Haste must we make, boys. Head into the rising sun, for it will blind her." Although this is not the direction from which they came, it seems the only strategy that will work just now. The old hag hurls insults at them all and casts a curse that is intended to turn them into swine. Sadly, it is only the elf bringing up the rear that catches the curse; in full stride, he changes from running on two feet to running on all fours, and squealing his protest; but nevertheless he keeps up with the rest, even passing a few much to their shocked surprise.

The old hag gives up the chase, after all she is very old, and turns back to her cottage. Panting heavily, Haghery halts the troop, "We must now go south, if home we go."

He holds up the gold net to admire the nightingale, "A nightingale that speaks, I've never seen. Under a magical spell are you."

"I've never seen a leprechaun until this day, myself. Are you also under some magical spell? Why do you take me from the old woman?" the nightingale's voice is as musical as its song.

"A lovely young lassie that is great with child heard your song and wishes to see you. We did not know that the birds had not yet this spring returned to Britain, so we went in search of one, which led us to you. A prize you are, much more magnificent than any ordinary bird. You will do nicely to sooth the unborn child and allow the lady to sleep."

"Why were not my feelings considered in your quest? Maybe I liked it there with the old woman. She fed me and in winter took me into the cottage to stay warm."

"Occurred to me it did not, that you would not want to escape from your prison. Back to Merlin I could not go without that which I sought."

"Merlin, the Sorcerer?"

"The one and the same, the greatest wizard there is. It was he that bade me bring Myra a nightingale. Should I release you so you may return to the old hag?"

"No, I will go with you gladly, I wish to meet Merlin. But you can release me from the net, I will stay with you."

Haghery removes the net, and the nightingale hops upon his shoulder and starts singing. His metallic feathers gleam in the morning sun as back to the Old Hollow Tree they go, one nightingale, four leprechauns, two elves and one little piggy that said wee, wee, wee, all the way home.

• • •

When Haghery returns to the hut, he presents Myra with the enchanted nightingale, "This nightingale, My Lady, is charmed. Say 'hello' to your new mistress."

Much to Myra's delight, the nightingale speaks, "Glorious day to you Mistress."

"You can speak? Look everyone, a nightingale that talks as well as sings. Your voice is as musical as your song."

"You have a unique bird there, Myra," says Merlin. "How did it happen that you are spellbound?" he asks the nightingale.

The nightingale begins to sing, and it sings the story of his enchantment. When he has finished, Myra reaches out to him, for he is in a silver cage, and dutifully he hops upon her finger. "Oh you poor thing, as beautiful as you are, you have lost the ability to fly, and thus your freedom. I shall give you back your freedom, but I can do nothing about your flying."

"No, but I am able to do so," says Merlin. "I will return flight to you and you may keep your feathers of precious metals."

Merlin speaks the Charm of Making and the nightingale takes flight, around the perimeter of the forest he flies, and eventually back to Myra's shoulder. The nightingale is Myra's constant companion; his silver cage's door is always open, he may come and go as he pleases, but he likes to stay with Myra, singing to her and her unborn son. Myra's spirit is lifted whenever he sings for her, she does not worry so much about coming events and thus she enters the final stages of her pregnancy, her eight month.

CHAPTER FIFTEEN

THE DRAGON AND THE BIRTH

July as usual is hot; even in the forest the noonday sun bears downs on the inhabitants, draining them of their energy. The forest animals are more active now in the early morning than after the sun has set in the evening. The grasshoppers' unrelenting buzz steals the peace from the forest. Rolling thunderstorms come up and just as quickly roll by, leaving the hut degrees cooler and the air sweet smelling.

• • •

Barely a month to go until the birth and they have heard nothing from Morgana. Merlin is very suspicious. He does not think that Morgana will let the birth happen without one more attempt to eradicate the unborn child. Another afternoon summer storm brews in the distance; the lighting strikes before the thunderclaps can be heard. Myra is very heavy with the baby now and her movements are slow and deliberate. She stays outside behind the hut where Adrian has planted the garden. They have had plenty of fresh vegetables this summer; he also cultivated sunflowers and deep blood red roses. Honeysuckle grew wild around the back of the garden. She and Sleyvia as well as Nikkei, the nightingale spends the most part of their afternoons out here.

"Oh, My Lady," sighs Sleyvia, "It looks as if we are in for another storm."

"So it would seem," agrees Myra. "But I think it is some ways off, there is no need to go inside just now."

Nikkei perches high in an oak tree, singing his little heart out. A gust of air breaks through the wind barrier grabbing the little bird and throwing him toward the ground. The nightingale manages to take flight before it is too late, and as he swoops up, he screams the alarm that danger is close.

Adrian rushes around the cabin to see why the nightingale has sent out the alarm. He stops at Myra's side, "Darling, I don't see anything, but to be safe let's get you inside."

As Adrian assists Myra, a thunderous flapping sound comes above them. Looking up, they make out the shadow of an enormous hawk, many times the normal size. The little nightingale is very frightened; hawks are a number one killer of many small birds including nightingales. Bravely he stays near his mistress continuously sounding the alarm, but the hawk is after larger prey this day. He dives towards Myra with talons spread wide in the posture of attack. Sleyvia once again bring out her trusty wand and throws a lightning bolt toward the giant bird; when the bolt of lightning strikes its breast the bird splits in two.

"Well that was easy," says Sleyvia, but before she gets the words out of her mouth, the two halves grow into two complete hawks.

Adrian knows they are in real trouble, the wind barrier did not stop this bird of prey and now he is certain that it is bewitched. Staying in front of Myra, shielding her with his own body, Adrian has only his hands with which to defend Myra, but remembering his powers when in Hades, he thrusts them forward and sparks fly from his finger tips. Each bird in turn charges with its feet stretched out toward him; one of them scratches his cheek causing blood to run down the left side of his face. Merlin is gone to the Old Hollow Tree; and whoever this is seems to know that he is not at home.

"Myra do you think you can make it to the front of the hut? Sleyvia, go with her. I will draw their attention long enough for you to get inside."

"Adrian! No! You will be killed," Myra screams and hangs on to his left arm.

"Myra! Do as I say! GO inside!"

Reluctantly, Myra turns and heads for the front, Adrian runs out into the middle of the garden drawing the attention of one bird, but not the other. This bird never takes its eye off of Myra and plunges down toward her, whilst Adrian battles the first hawk with the sword that appears in his hand, this from Sleyvia. He slashes out and manages to slice off its claw, but another claw grows in its place; this is not working, any damage done to the conjured birds seems only to make them stronger. How can he alone, defend against two? He sees out of the corner of his eye that the other hawk is trying to get past little Sleyvia. She manages a shield of sorts between herself, Myra and the hawk. The fowl hovers in midair, which they normally can't do, and stabs at the shield. Sleyvia does not use a weapon against it, for it is obvious this is the wrong way to defeat this bird, all she can do is defend. Adrian fears the worst; he is unable to fight both birds at once. While one bird keeps him occupied the other goes after Myra.

Just before the second hawk can grab Myra, another, extremely large birdlike creature sails through the sky. It wingspan is forty feet; it has a reptilian body, lizard-like head, and claws with talons three feet long. Black smoke snorts from its nostrils and red flames from its mouth. A dragon! And guiding this enormous beast is Merlin himself.

The dragon bellows fire at the first hawk; its feathers go up in flames, and soon it is plunging to the earth where it crashes with a thud. Elves and leprechauns rush out from the forest and proceed to secure it with ropes.

The second hawk makes to escape by heading straight up into the atmosphere. Merlin leaps off the dragon, the dragon then sets off after the other hawk.

"Myra, Adrian, is everyone safe?" Merlin checks to assure himself that he is not too late, and that no one is seriously injured.

"Adrian is hurt," says Myra, as she holds a cloth to the wound on his face, "but I'm okay as far as I can tell. Was that a real fire-breathing dragon?"

"It was indeed," beams Merlin. "I was certain Morgana would not abandon her evil schemes and I also knew she would not make any attempt with both Adrian and me here. I waited for her to move and she fell into my trap. I did not know exactly what she would use, but I did suspect something that could get through the wind barrier. Something that could fly. I must admit she chose well, which means she is getting stronger."

As he speaks he looks up, "Observe! . . . The dragon!"

All heads gaze skyward; the dragon catches the second hawk in his claws and with his teeth tears the fowl into shreds, which he gobbles up before any can rejuvenate. In minutes, the dragon has devoured his feast. The mighty leviathan glides above the clouds, circling the clearing where the little hut stands.

"Evidently he was hungry," laughs Merlin. "That meal should last him awhile. Would you care to meet your champion?"

"Meet a dragon? Are you serious, Merlin?" asks Adrian.

"Indeed. I am aware that he wishes to meet Myra. He has observed her from a distance and knows our story, but I asked him to wait so that I could prepare you for his visit. He is now awaiting my call."

"Then by all means, call him down," urges Adrian.

Merlin looks up and calls loudly, "Manfred! . . . Manfred!"

"Manfred?" questions Adrian. "For a dragon?"

Merlin shrugs his shoulders, "He chose it himself. It did not seem sensible to oppose him; would you have done?"

"No, not I," says Adrian, as he puts up both hands palms first and steps backward.

Manfred, the dragon, on hearing his name begins spiraling down, until he glides to a landing as graceful as any swan. He folds his enormous wings as close to his body as possible and still they cover the entire garden. His body from nose to tail measures about twenty feet, with the serpentine tail another twelve, he has four legs jutting out from the side of his torso, much like a lizard's. His snout is long but blunt, with tiny web-like structures framing each nostril; the mouth is the most intimidating, with jagged black-blue teeth, a long forked tongue, eyes glowing phosphorus red, and blue-green scales covering his body.

He lowers his head in a bow and snorts billows of pale steam as he speaks, "My Lord and Lady, pleasured am I at our meeting."

Myra and Adrian are a little taken back, they do not know what to expect, but certainly not this formal pattern of speech.

Myra responds, "As are we, kind sir. We are most grateful for our rescue. You are our hero." Myra cautiously leans forward and kisses the dragon on the tip of his snout.

If it were possible, Manfred would blush to the tips of his wings, "Oh your Ladyship, it is I who is grateful to serve you."

"I thank you as well," says Adrian.

Manfred nods his head and his scales twinkle with specks of light and tinkle like wind chimes. His red eyes change color to a deep blue-green, as his aggressive nature becomes more passive.

"The Universe will forever be in your debt. None knows just yet of the impending doom, nor would they care, for it will not happen in their lifetimes, but it is quite possible to happen in mine, for, you see, dragons can be immortal."

"What kind of creature are you, for we always thought dragons to be myths?" asks Adrian.

"Dragons, like serpents, have a bad reputation, only because of the disobedience in the Garden of Eden. The serpent was cursed to crawl on its belly in the dust for eternity, while He gave the dragon immortality, so that He could guard against man's return to Eden after his banishment. We are creatures of shadows; no one is ever certain that we actually exist. Merlin discovered this at the beginning of Time and I for one have been ready to serve him ever since."

"Are you then the only one?"

"No, there are five hundred of us, but a few have gone the way of transgression, and lost their virtue. Those are the ones who give us our bad reputation."

"As bad as that is, still we are glad to meet you," says Myra.

"The babe, when is its birth?" inquires Manfred.

"We anticipate the delivery in thirty days time," Merlin answers.

"May I be here at the time?" Manfred asks.

"But of course, good friend, you are welcome any time," encourages Adrian.

"We must remain on guard against Morgana; twice she has tried to destroy Myra and the baby; with barely a month left, she will again make the attempt." Merlin emphasizes his words.

"I must take my leave now, but should I be needed I am but a call away," Manfred spreads his wings and with a mighty beat that sends the dust spinning, he lifts up into the sky, spiraling upward over the clouds until he is a mere speck, and then nothing.

● ● ●

July soon ends with no more encounters directly with Morgana, although the elves and fairies do continue patrolling the forest staying on the look out for strangers. They report regularly to the hut to calm any fears that Myra may have, for she now finds it hard to spend much time outside; she only does so when Manfred circles overhead giving her a sense of security. Sleyvia and Nikkei stay close by, but try not to intrude any more than needed on her privacy.

● ● ●

August, and it is only two weeks into this month and they are on the final countdown to little Seth's birthday. Morgana has not yet had her son and both women are due anytime.

On this day, 12th of August, Myra awakes with the knowledge that her son will be born in the next twenty-four hours. Although she feels contractions there is no pain; she understands this to be a gift from Merlin. She lies very still in bed next to Adrian, listening to his deep breathing, thinking she need not awake him just now. The sun is just breaking the eastern horizon, sending sunbeams out to awaken the sleeping Earth. On the other side of the barrier erected by Merlin to give them their privacy, she hears Merlin stir, and Myra thinks that, 'yes Merlin knows that it is today.'

She eases out of bed, sitting on the edge and placing her hand on her abdomen as another contraction comes, but still no pain. She smiles to herself, as she walks to the front room, and starts a fire in the fireplace to make breakfast. She knows magic could do this, but it is more fulfilling to do things for yourself. With her coffee in hand, she goes out the front door and sits on the bench to savor the sweetness of the morning. As she sits, small animals, rabbits, squirrels, weasels, and others begin filtering out from the edge of the forest, coming up into the yard and forming a semicircle about ten feet around her. Nikkei flies over to her shoulder and continues his sweet melody. Soon more birds fly into the surrounding trees, now deer poke their heads out from behind the foliage, and a tinkling sound draws her attention from above, it is Manfred circling overhead. Now fairies and elves are suddenly flying around, and leprechauns slip through the barricade and come close.

Myra laughs as she looks at all of her forest friends, "I guess all of you know what the day is, correct?"

"Correct," the fairies, elves and leprechauns, say together.

"With all of you here I should be well protected but you may have a long wait, you know."

"Yes, we know," they all reply.

• • •

The day passes fairly slowly for those waiting outside, but babies have a way of entering this world in their own selected time; nothing can be done to hasten Mother Nature, so patience is the best attribute. Myra remains very comfortable during all stages of her labor, and now as the sun wanes, the final stage that urges the birth begins. Myra feels the pressure and the need to push.

"Adrian, I think Seth is ready to make his début," Myra informs her husband, so he can be in position to receive the infant. They are in the back bedroom where Myra has retired only a half hour before, for she is thinking the time is very near and it seems she is correct.

"Hold tight, honey."

All but Sleyvia leave the room; Adrian has Myra turn transverse on the bed, "Pull up your knees, and when you feel the next contraction push with it." Adrian gives her instructions.

The next painless contraction begins growing in intensity; Myra grabs each knee and raises her body to a semi sitting position and pushes. She feels the head start to crown.

"That's good Myra, relax and take a deep breath, wait for the next contraction to push," Adrian peers up over the sheet that covers the lower half of Myra's body to see how she is faring. Her color is good and there is no sign of distress.

Sleyvia stays at Myra's head also whispering encouragement with each contraction. "You are doing great Myra; you will soon have your son in your arms."

The next contraction comes almost immediately and Myra once again works with it, the head delivers.

"Relax, darling, and take another deep breath," says Adrian, as he suctions out the mucus from the infant's nose and mouth.

"You're doing great, sweetheart, one more contraction and our son will be born."

Myra feels the next contraction and the infant delivers quickly.

"Great, Myra!"

Adrian lays the infant face down on his hand as he strokes his back to further drain mucus from his lungs. As he does, little Seth takes his first breath and cries, Adrian then lays him on his mother's abdomen while he cuts the umbilical cord.

Out in the yard, shouts and cheers arise from the throng when the birth cries come through to them.

Myra raises her head and coos to her baby as his father cuts the cord that binds mother and child. Little Seth looks up at his mother with his violet colored eyes, then ceases his cries and blinks.

"He knows you Myra," says Adrian. He then bundles Seth into a towel and with great care, proceeds to cleanse the birth fluid from his face and body, while the babe gazes into his father's face.

"Myra, you are not going to believe this, but he has your white hair. I thought the trait was only passed down through the females," Adrian hands the child to Myra as he speaks.

THE CURSE

"No, that can't be," exclaims Myra, examining her son while the delivery bed is cleaned and tidied by Sleyvia. Adrian completes the postnatal chores, and helps Myra to a more comfortable position in her bed.

"Well, unless I am color blind, his hair is white; we can't be sure of his eyes for a few more months, but right now they are violet," reiterates Adrian.

"Adrian, what can this mean?" Myra asks with great concern.

"It means your son is destined for greatness," this from Merlin as he enters, knowing the child is born. "We all heard his birth cries and there was rejoicing at the sound.

"Little Seth is not only Arthur's heir but mine also. Did you forget my mother had a sister from whom Myra descends?"

"You had this plan in mind way back, before the time you aided in the deliverance of Mariah and the Lost Souls, didn't you, Merlin?" asks Adrian.

"Yes, when the demon dared to once more interfere in my family, I knew I must act. You know the rest of the story. The curse lifted with Seth's birth and he inherits the trait even though he is male.

"We must allow the multitude who waits outside to see Seth, and if you will permit me, I will proudly present him to them." Merlin looks to each parent and they both nod their consent.

Gently the greatest Sorcerer of all Time takes the babe in his arms; the child is naked, having only a blanket. Merlin stares at this tiny being, and remembers when he first held Arthur. This time, however, he will not have to take the child from his mother, due to the decision and sacrifice his parents have made to stay and raise him.

He steps out to the front and cheers rises up from the gathering, "May I introduce Master Seth Ertian Grey, the next King of Britain!"

Merlin holds the naked babe up over his head, turning from one side to the other, so all may have a glimpse and the ovation continues. Then suddenly all is silent as red and pink rose petals fall slowly to the earth, and the strong scent of roses permeates the air. The roses gather together and form a human figure.

"Eydasi?" questions Merlin, for he had not called her.

"Yes, Merlin. It is I," she answers with the sound of many voices coming from all directions at once. She wears a garment of red rose petals, her flesh is the palest of pink, her coif is green rose leaves and her eyes are aquamarine, around her waist is the belt of stars, on her finger is the ring of the sun and hanging from her neck is the crescent moon.

"I have come to christen the child and to validate his claim to the throne."

Adrian from the doorway speaks, "I thought we were to be given the chance to find another heir to the throne."

"There will never be another; your son has more than the required blood line, he also has the power. He is our next King." With that statement, she draws the babe to her, where he floats in mid air. The child does not cry, and his eyes have the look of understanding and of wisdom.

"In the name of the most High, and His only begotten Son, I validate this child as the next King of Britain, Prince Seth Ertian Grey!" She then showers him with a spray of rose oil, returns him to Merlin, and he in turn hands him to his father.

"Should any harm befall this child the consequences will be astronomical to those who seek to destroy him."

Eydasi then collapses into a pile of rose petal that the East wind picks up and carries away. Adrian carries the baby back inside to Myra, he places him in her arms and sits down on the bed, "Myra, Eydasi has just validated Seth as the next king. There is no possibility of another child being born to Arthur."

A tear forms and runs down her cheek, "I already know," is all she says. She pulls the baby close to her breast and he begins suckling. Sleyvia and Nikkei return to comfort the new mother, and the nightingale sings her his sweetest song as the night falls.

CHAPTER SIXTEEN

THE OTHER BIRTH

Morgana stands at the castle window, she is far into her pregnancy, the sun hangs just above the western horizon and she feels the pangs of labor beginning. She pulls the rope that calls the servants, and a maidservant approaches her and curtsies, "You call my lady?"

"Yes, send for the midwife, I am ready to give birth to my son."

"Yes, my lady."

Morgana fumes, for the white-haired wench had her son just moments ago; he is the elder and is the true heir to Arthur. She is vague on how this came about; Merlin is still in his crystal cage, she checked on him not two days ago, so how is this couple receiving so much magical aid. She understood a little from when her mind mingled with Merlin's, at the time she stole the Charm of Making. She still cannot deduce how the maiden came to be pregnant by Arthur, but with what she had seen, the truth of it she cannot deny. She failed in several attempts to murder both mother and the unborn child. She needs to do the task herself, but she did not want to jeopardize her own pregnancy, so she held back. Her spies kept her informed, and they did quite well, but only an hour ago a vision came to her of the birth of this child.

She let Arthur know of the other maiden, and argued viciously with him, but he denied ever having had an affair with anyone but her, and he did not even remember the night of incest with Morgana.

• • •

This night passes into the early morning hours of Friday, the 13th of August and her labor pains are getting more unbearable. When neither potion nor spell eases her agony, she orders all from her bedchamber, screaming she will have her baby alone. A few hours later as the sun peeps over the eastern horizon, Morgana, alone, reaches between her thighs and pulls her son from her womb. He is born exactly twelve hours after his half brother.

His birth cries carry all through the castle and throughout the countryside. "I'll call him Mordred."

• • •

Deep inside the Black Forest, Merlin looks out toward the rising sun and knows of the unholy birth. "Mordred has been born," he whispers to himself.

He enters back into the still sleeping hut and checks on baby Seth, the babe sleeps in his mother's protective embrace, with Adrian sleeping by her side. Adrian awakes and sees Merlin, he also whispers, "Mordred is born." It was a statement not a question.

"Yes."

• • •

Morgana recovers fairly quickly from the birth and engages a wet nurse for Mordred; she does not wish to be tied down with the chores of motherhood. She does not love Mordred with the love of a mother, no, he is only a step to get what she thinks is rightfully hers, the crown and all that it entails.

Two mothers, two sons, but each with a different approach to rearing children. One mother gives her all and the other mother only takes.

• • •

A month after the births, Morgana cannot rest, for it eats at her that her son is born second and thus not entitled to the throne. She goes to her brother Arthur. Arthur is not well. When Morgana is announced, he receives her in his own room, rather than the throne room.

"Morgana, what do you want with me now?" The King reclines on a lounger and his voice is very weak. His hair is untidy and his beard is in need of a trim.

"I have come to let you know our son is born," Morgana's red hair is pulled back into a high ponytail on the top of her head, she wears a rich burgundy robe over her gown, September has arrived with a bit of a chill.

"Yes, so I was informed," sighs Arthur.

"Well, since you have not been to see the boy, I've brought him here. I think he looks a great deal like me."

Morgana claps her hands three times rapidly and the wet-nurse carries in the baby. Morgana take him from the nurse and walks over to Arthur to show him.

"Here take your son. I have named him Mordred. See how good it feels to hold your own flesh and blood. You are not only his father but his uncle as well. Can you not see he is more entitled to the throne than the other wench that you coupled with? Her son is born also, twelve hours before mine, or did you know of his birth also?"

Arthur looks down at Mordred, and no bond forms between father and son. The child is handsome enough; he has his mother's light green eyes, but the child's hair is a pale blond, and he can see no resemblance to himself. Feeling the coldness of his father's embrace, Mordred abruptly cries and Arthur hands him back to Morgana, who in turn hands him to the nurse. "Take Mordred out," she orders.

"I want you to announce at the next gathering of the round table that Mordred is your legitimate heir, and do it before that tramp can lay claim to the throne for her bastard son," Morgana threatens.

"I have told you more than a few times, I know of no other maid or another son. And furthermore, I will not pronounce Mordred as heir. Begone with you and your son."

"Arthur, I strongly warn you, either recognize Mordred as your heir or you will live to regret it."

"I regret it already, the child is unholy. His conception was in error as was his birth. Now take yourself and your devil child from Camelot and do not set foot near me again!"

Morgana's face turns as red as her hair, but she says not another word, for the guards rush in at the raised voices coming from the King's personal chambers. She turns quickly on her heels, her skirts flaring, whilst giving Arthur a contemptuous glare.

"Escort my dear sister and her child to the gate, and she is not to return to Camelot, or anyone from her household."

• • •

November settles in with the first frost of the year, the autumn colors are at their most vivid and only gladness prevails at the little hut. Many visitors came to pay homage to the new little prince. Even the Old Hag of the Black Forest begs to come visiting, and Merlin grants permission, [after she has removed the curse from the elf that she turned into a pig.] They now discover her good nature. She takes an oath never to reveal the location of the hut. She visits often, and offers Myra advice on caring for an infant and even help with the household chores.

The first day of November is the first wedding anniversary of Adrian and Myra, it is a quiet celebration and everyone sees just how happy the young couple is and just how much they love each other. There is never an angry word spoken between them; not that they don't disagree at times; they just seem to know it is not necessary to disrespect each other to get across a point. Baby Seth, by the time he is two months old, is growing plump on his mother's milk and the good care he receives from all. His Great Uncle Merlin takes the greatest delight in watching his young nephew grow into such a happy and healthy baby. Merlin had no actual involvement in Arthur's rearing; in fact, he did not see him after his birth until his sixteenth birthday, at which time Arthur became King.

A routine develops and life is good, there have been no assaults and they almost forget the menace that surrounds them. This has Merlin more than concerned, for he knows Arthur has banished Morgana and Mordred from Camelot. This cannot leave Morgana in the best of moods; she plans an attack but just bides her time until an opportunity presents itself.

• • •

Morgana paces the floor of her bedchamber, Mordred fusses and the nurse cannot hush him, forcing Morgana to play mother. As she bounces him on her shoulder whilst pacing, she fumes inwardly and speaks aloud, "I will not wait much longer to allow that child to live!"

She looks to the nurse who sits quietly to one side. "Well, what do you think I should do? Wait and let my brother declare him King? No, I think not. I shall take care of the matter myself. If you want things done, you need not expect others to do them for you." Morgana looks toward the nurse waiting for her to agree with her. "Well?"

The nursemaid looks at Morgana when she realizes that Morgana is waiting for her to answer, "Yes, my lady," she stammers. "You are indeed right."

"Yes, and I have a plan. They will not expect me to appear myself, and that will be their undoing. I shall visit Merlin in the caverns and use his spells to work out a scheme. I am not sure just what I will do, but it will be spectacular."

• • •

Early the next morning before daylight, Morgana leaves her castle on horseback, riding out alone; she rides until she arrives at the base of a mountain. Dismounting quickly she leads her horse into an almost invisible opening in the mountain's side. She then, alone, descends steps leading down deep inside of the cavern, which is lit by phosphorus illumination. There are stalagmites rising from the floor of the cave and stalactites dropping from the ceiling, the walls reflect the rituals of everyday life going on in the world. There is every conceivable color of the light spectrum, and in the center of it all is a large solid crystal block and encased inside of the wedge is Merlin. He looks frozen; only his eyes prove that he lives. He watches Morgana as she enters the cavern and every move she makes as she circles around him.

"Well Merlin, I do not know what sort of tricks you are up to. Are you powerful enough still to influence the lives of others? I know who this maiden is now. She is the one that visited you once about five years ago. I thought then that she was gestating, but it was certainly not with this child. How did she become pregnant by Arthur? Did you trick her as you tricked my mother? When you helped Uther to seduce her, so that she begat Arthur? Have you done it again, old man? This time it will not work. My son, Mordred will become King. I will destroy this imposter myself if I must. I would rather die than this child be heir to the throne."

"Morgana!"

"Merlin? Are you able to speak from there? I see not your lips move. What is it that you want, you old fool?"

"This child is of Arthur's blood. This child is of my blood. This child will do what Arthur is unable to do. Mordred will never become King. Seth will take the throne in eighteen years time."

"Ahhhhhh!" Morgana screams in a fit, she rushes at the crystal case and beats it with her fists. "You fool, who do you think you are toying with? I have the control here, not you! Never you again! You will never leave this place until one comes who is pure of heart and innocent of the ways of the world, ignorant of carnal sin, willing to sacrifice all to save you."—Thus, Morgana had cursed Merlin, a curse that had lasted for fifteen hundred years.

Furious, Morgana recites the Charm of Making. As she speaks, a mist rises up enveloping her in a white fog, electric sparks fly from this cloud, then suddenly it is sucked away, leaving in its place an identical image of Myra.

"Well, what do you think Merlin?" it is still Morgana's voice. "Do you not like me as a blond? I think I shall enjoy myself in a guise such as this. That husband of hers will never know what has happened. I will just walk in, pick up the child, and walk out. They will think I am his mother. They will not know until the mother returns and asks for her baby. Then it will be too late. I will kill him as soon as I am out of the forest. The forest is too infested with fairies and elves for me to attempt such a thing while still within its confines."

Merlin blinks, but nothing more comes from him.

"You can do nothing, you old fool. This time *I will win.*"

With a rustle of her skirts and her head held high, she quickly leaves the cavern. Merlin hears the hoof beats of her horse, signifying that she is gone. Concentrating with all the power he can muster, Merlin seals the entrance to the cave. No one, including Morgana will ever be able to open it again, not until the breaking of the curse that Morgana placed on him and, unknowing to her, his descendants.

• • •

It is a cold day in late November, the skies are gray, and there is the smell of snow in the air. Inside the hut, a cozy fire blazes away in the fireplace, coffee perks hanging from the hook that attaches to the grate. Myra checks on Seth who is three months old now. He is contently just gazing around his little world. Haghery has made him a mobile out of the little carvings that were gifts from the different leprechauns, and Adrian has attached it to his cradle. There are butterflies, birds, hearts, a cat, a dog, a bunny and other animals spinning slowly to the delight of the baby.

"Hi there my little man, how is Mommy's baby boy?" when his mother speaks, Seth grins and kick his feet and waves small fists in the air. He loves the sound of his mother's voice and at times, she is the only one who is able to quiet him when he cries.

Seeing that he is fine, Myra speaks to Adrian, "I am going to the garden to get some dried rosemary, watch Seth for a bit."

"Would you rather I get the herb for you," Adrian offers.

"No, I need a change of scenery and a little exercise. It seems good that it is just you and I for a change. I won't be too long, too cold to stay outside."

Myra goes out and Adrian leans back in the armchair with the book he is reading. After a bit he starts feeling drowsy, and lays his head back against the headrest. Soon he sleeps.

The front door silently swings open and Myra comes back inside. She sees Adrian sleeping and smiles to herself. She walks quietly over to the baby's cradle; he too has dozed off. Very gently, she picks up the sleeping infant and heads for the front door with him. She turns once more and looks at Adrian, he stirs and Myra holds up her hand as if to stop him from waking, his head flops back down on the headrest. Myra smiles, and leaves, softly shutting the door after her.

She heads off across the yard at a fast walk, but she doesn't quite make it, the real Myra rounds the corner of the hut just in time to see a rendition of herself with Seth in her arms crossing the front yard.

"Hey! Stop!" she yells, dropping the herbs.

The imposter turns and looks at her and then runs for the trees. Myra runs after her. "Stop, you cannot get away. HELP!" Myra screams with all of her strength. "HELP! . . . HELP!" she screams again.

She is still running after the kidnapper, and gradually, is catching up; the imposter does not want to stop to battle with her; this will take too much time, time she does not have. Seth has started crying and the sound breaks Myra's heart. The imposter turns and faces Myra, it is Morgana, and she taunts Myra by holding Seth up by just one of his legs. She has no compassion for the child and would just as soon kill him now in front of his mother, but that luxury is not hers just yet. The baby screams and Morgana laughs.

"Oh please Morgana, do not harm my baby. You can have the throne. We never did want it. Lay my son down and you can leave the forest safely. No one will follow you. We will return to our homeland and that will be the end of it. You will win. PLEASE!"

"No, that will only happen after I destroy this child. The throne will never be mine until he is dead!" With that, she speaks the Charm of Making, the ground breaks open as the roots of trees grow longer and as quick as a thought, they entwine themselves around Myra, holding her fast. Seth's cries continue as Morgana heads out of the forest with him. Myra sobs and screams as she realizes her worst nightmare has come true.

• • •

It seems like hours before Adrian comes to her rescue, as he unties her she tells him what has happened. "Adrian, we will never see Seth again. Morgana is determined to kill him. I don't know why she didn't do it here in front of me. I know she wanted too, but something held her back."

"What held her back was the forest and what inhabits it. She somehow drugged me either with a drug or with a spell. I thought she was you coming in, but I was asleep and was dreaming or so I thought. I only came out of it when your screams woke me, I knew then it was not a dream."

"She won't harm Seth as long as she is inside of the forest, to do so will only endanger her own life and Mordred's. Already there are many searching for her; Merlin is riding on Manfred. They are circling the forest, no she won't get far." Adrian doesn't sound as sure as he would like.

• • •

Morgana holds the baby close not caring that he screams with the tightness of her grip. She has left her mount at the edge of the forest; there she plans to kill the baby. She will not take him any further than she has to, for she does not care to be holding him now.

Out from every corner there is movement, leprechauns have spotted her and sound the alarm. "She is here! At the southern end of the forest. Hurry! Hurry! Before she makes it to the outside."

All the while, they run at her heels, hitting her legs with sticks and throwing stones. Morgana stops, kicks back, then dangles Seth by his leg again, "Move back! Or I'll drop him into the briars!"

Knowing she will do it, the leprechauns back away, and stop their assault, but continue to follow her. Morgana hastens her pace, she can see the clearing now; if she can reach it, her powers will once again be strong, she will murder the child and be on her way before they can do anything about it.

At the last tree before the end, she pulls from her cloak a dagger, and places it at the crying child's throat, just as she steps free of the Black Forest.

She pulls the knife across the infant's throat and throws him to the ground; she runs for her horse and mounts, but the animal rears up and throws her from the saddle. She lands hard, and makes to get up again, and then she sees what spooked her horse. A ferocious dragon is breathing down on her. Its eyes are glowing red and hot flame blasts from his mouth.

"Not yet, Manfred," the voice is familiar. A tall man wearing a purple cloak sits between the shoulders of the ancient beast. He has long white hair and beard. He holds in his right hand a staff with a large orb at the tip. Inside the orb churns a milky looking liquid, "We do not want to end her existence yet. Greetings Morgana."

Morgana whirls around when she recognizes who it is, "Merlin! How can it be you? I saw you but this morning sealed in your crystalline case."

"Yes, so I am still," Merlin smiles at her, toying with her mind. Now was his time for vengeance.

"And why do you look older?" she asks, as if she does not believe.

"I look quite well to be fifteen hundred years old, do you not think?"

"No matter, you are too late. The child is dead. My son, Mordred will now be King. Not even you can bring back the dead."

"What child is dead? I see no child."

Morgana turns to look where she tossed the baby's body. There was a corpse there but it was not a child.

"I regret Morgana, but I see only a pig."

"A pig? I had a child in my arms. A real live child. That is not a pig. You are only trying to trick me. I have killed the challenger to the throne. Mordred will be King!"

"I tell you he will not. Seth will be crowned in eighteen years."

Her plans thwarted once more, Morgana seizes her hair with both hands, pulling it out by the roots, and then falls to her knees screaming. Manfred sends a hot flame toward her, burning the clothing from her back and her hair from her head; her face and hands are severely blistered. She cries out in agony, and then naked and scorched, she mounts her horse, and rides on toward her castle.

"Why did you not let me burn her to cinders, Merlin," asks Manfred.

"What she has now is worse than death. Her beauty is gone. She will have to use much magical energy to restore herself. Besides, she has Mordred to rear. Come old friend; we must return Seth to his parents, and apologize for using him as bait for Morgana."

Merlin climbs onto the shoulders of Manfred; the beast beats his wings and in one stride is in the air.

"Tell me Merlin, just how you knew Morgana would try this," asks Manfred as he soars through the darkening sky.

"A little bird told me, so to speak," replies Merlin loudly over the roar of the rushing air. "My counterpart, Merlin, trapped in the mountain sent a message to the birds in the area and they carried the message to Nikkei, you remember, the nightingale. Of course, the nightingale told me first. Merlin, my counterpart still is not strong enough to focus far from his prison, but one day he will be."

"What did you do then?" Manfred asks.

"During the night, I changed baby Seth for a pig, which the Old Hag of the Black Forest then placed under a curse, as in reverse. She is adept at those you know. I left the pig in Seth's cradle, and the baby with the Old Hag. Sleyvia and Haghery are with her also. I could not tell Myra and Adrian, for fear they would be unable to pretend well enough to deceive Morgana. Understandably, they will be very upset with me, and, as they say fifteen hundred years from now, I will probably be in the doghouse for a while," Merlin laughs and Manfred with him, as they approach the Old Hag's cottage. After retrieving the baby, Manfred carries them all, Haghery and Sleyvia as well, back to the little hut hidden deep in the forest.

• • •

Adrian and Myra had learned what had happened at the edge of the forest from the nightingale, so their grief was short-lived but at the moment they could not be consoled for it was very real to them both, at the time. They hear the unmistakable sound of Manfred and they rush outside and watch the great dragon slide gracefully to the patch of ground in front of the hut's door. Not waiting for Merlin to dismount, Myra and Adrian quickly take the baby from his arms and as all three cry, they re-enter the cottage.

Inside is a joyful reunion between parents and child. Manfred pokes his head inside long enough to wish them all well and for Myra and Adrian to thank him properly, Myra with a kiss on his nose. Nikkei, the nightingale sings baby Seth a lullaby, confident in the knowledge that had it not been for himself and his feathered friends, the other Merlin could not have gotten out the warning and things might have ended quite differently.

Later in the evening, Merlin tells them the truth of what had happened. They are not too hard on him, for their son is back, safe and sound in his mother's arms, and Myra tells him of her dream so many years ago, that had come true this very day.

• • •

Morgana arrives at her castle in a very sad state; she calls for assistance from the guards. They rush to her side and seeing her condition, take her from the back of her horse, while shielding her from view, and carry her inside to her bedchamber. The maidservants hurry to tend their mistress's wounds. She is totally bald, her flesh scorched, and she is in a great deal of pain.

"Look at me!" she cries.

"Oh no, my lady. You do not wish us to see just yet. Give yourself some time to heal," they argue with her, for they know her wrath and do not wish to be on the receiving end of it.

"I said, look at me!" she orders again.

This time they obey, looking at her pitiful state, but then immediately leave the room.

Morgana does not hesitate to scrutinize her condition. She stares at herself, then, as the realization of just how bad her physical state is sinks into her irrational mind, she lets out a shattering scream that resonates through the halls and to the outside, so that the birds on the rooftop take flight.

CHAPTER SEVENTEEN

THE GARDEN PARTY

Seth is a very delightful baby, with purplish-blue eyes and cottony hair; he is a reflection of his father but with Myra's unique coloration. He shows extraordinary intelligence for an infant, and his motor skills are extremely advanced. He is sitting on his own at four months and walking by the time he is eight months. He didn't bother to crawl, "The floor must be too hard for him," laughs Myra. He undoubtedly comprehends when they speak to him, and responds with recognizable words. Myra potty trains him effortlessly at fourteen months. Haghery displays for him beautiful colored rainbows, and he recognizes all the colors at just eighteen months. His communication skills far exceed the typical child. When he is two, Merlin takes it upon himself to begin schooling him in language and mathematics.

For his second birthday, Myra has a gathering of pixies, elves, fairies and leprechauns, as well as many small creatures of the forest, and of course, Manfred the Dragon makes his appearance. The Old Hag of the Black Forest volunteers to bake his birthday cake, which makes Sleyvia jealous. Myra soothes her hurt feelings by suggesting she do the magical decorations.

• • •

They have the celebration in the rear of the cottage where the garden is located. Sleyvia, flying high over the grounds, starts with an enchantment:

"Floras and fauna hear my voice,
"Speech and movement you have your choice.

"One day only is granted to thee,
"Enjoyment for our guest is a gift from me!"

With a swish of her wand, starbursts spew in every direction, and whenever a spark settles on a flora, it instantly show signs of vivacity, with small faces situated in the center of the blossom and its foliage in motion.

When the embers alight upon the small animals, they receive the endowment of human speech, although Nikkei, the nightingale, already has this ability, and he now sings in his human voice with the same mesmerizing effect as before. Many feathered friends gather in the tops of trees and cheerfully chirp with the music. The small forest animals chatter away with each other, while butterflies, dragonflies, ladybugs, fat green beetles and honeybees, hum tunes and buzz around the blossoms.

"Music we need on this day,
"Pipe, flute and viola play,
"The sweetest music you'll ever hear."
"To fill every heart with gleeful cheer!"

Sleyvia waves her wand; this time fairy dust swirls in a mist and as the mist disperses, a musical instrument appears and directly starts performing.

When Sleyvia completes her decorating, Haghery steps forward, "Right it be, lads, our gifts we now present."

The leprechauns begin popping in one at a time, and as they do, each sets his bag of gold coins down and around the perimeter of the garden. The canvas bags begin untying the cord holding them closed. And as each opens, magnificent rainbows swell up and over each one, forming colorful arches. Soon lucent rainbows envelop the garden, while golden stars emerge and glitter in the middle of the afternoon.

The Old Hag of the Black Forest ambles her way slowly to the backyard; although the August day is rather warm, the old woman has a white knitted shawl about her thin shoulders. Beside her, four elves, one of which is the one that she had changed into a pig, carry a huge two-tier birthday cake. The cake has white icing with purple trimmings; atop of the cake are two rather large birthday candles, and positioned between them is a toy dragon that very much resembles Manfred. This toy moves and flaps its wings and blows small flames from its mouth, just like the real thing. Flowers that decorate the sides are talking and looking about, although they are made of frosting.

Manfred, the dragon, is spotted circling overhead; he looks for a place to touch down without upsetting everything. Haghery signals to him and he lands on one side of the hut. Soon fairies, pixies and elves, make themselves comfortable on his back, for they love Manfred. He is a very good friend and protector to the little people, and they always love to gather around him. He lies on his stomach with front legs folded up beneath him. Every once in a while he asks a fairy or elf to scratch him behind his ear, or on his back spines, or even his tail tip, and moans with delight as his requests are carried out.

It is a glorious summer afternoon, this 12th of August, and Seth will be two at 5:45 in the evening. Since the disfigurement of Morgana, they have heard nothing from her in these two years. Everyone has been on guard for any retaliation but so far, there has been none.

• • •

Myra, along with Adrian, who carries Seth, appears around the back corner of the hut, and when they come into view, "Happy Birthday Seth," rings out. The child's bright eyes light up with merriment when he sees the décor; the shimmering rainbows, twinkling stars, lively flowers, and even the trees have happy faces on their trunks. Adrian puts his son on the ground where he starts to skip about. He crouches down by his side, "Hey Seth, what do you make of all of this for your second birthday?"

"Father, I like it. Can I play?" the toddler's little face glows as he inspects the garden.

"Sure son, you go ahead. Uncle Merlin is on his way, and said for no one to eat the cake before he gets here."

"Great, Uncle Merlin!"

The Old Hag of the Black Forest calls to him, "Do you have a birthday hug for your old Granny?"

Seth runs over to her and climbs onto her lap; he wraps his small arms about her neck as she gives him a little squeeze and kisses him on his fat baby cheeks.

"Granny made your favorite cake for your birthday, and I have a very special gift for you later." The hag's voice cracks with age, no one knows how old she is and she won't tell.

"Oh lovely, Granny, I can't wait."

"Now Seth," says Myra, "Manfred is on the other side of the hut and he wants you to go see him. He's too big to come over here."

"Okay, Mother."

He hops down from Granny's lap, and with two leprechauns who are just about Seth's height accompanying him, for Seth is never alone, they hasten to where the gentle giant awaits.

"Manfred," shouts the toddler.

"Seth," responds Manfred. "Come climb up onto my back, and we will talk."

With the aid of four leprechauns who perform acrobats by climbing on top of each other's shoulders, they form a ladder, which Seth climbs until he is safely settled on the dragon's long neck.

"How are you doing Seth?" asks Manfred.

"Oh I am so happy today, Manfred. "How are you?"

"Well I can't complain too much, my bursitis is acting up a little. I must be showing my age, I am five hundred next year you know. The Hag gave me a potion for it and I am feeling somewhat better now. I have a special gift for you, but you must have permission from your folks before I can give it to you, okay?"

"Okay!"

Sometime later Merlin arrives at the Garden Party, and Seth rushes into his arms when he sees him, Merlin scoops him up, "Happy Birthday Seth. You are two years old today, how does it feel?"

"I don't know, Uncle Merlin. Am I supposed to feel another way?"

"Well, do you not feel older?"

"Uncle Merlin, I just turned two. You can't feel 'older' at two!" says Seth with a matter of fact tone; the child's response brings rounds of laughter.

"Very well said, my child," laughs Merlin. "Uncle Merlin needs to give you a birthday gift, but I have naught for you. For a boy who has most of what he desires, I have decided instead to give you a wish, but it must be a sensible one. Do you understand?"

Seth nods, "I understand, Uncle Merlin."

Merlin sets the toddler on his feet, preparing to produce some magic, "Well Seth, what will it be? A pony perhaps? No? A kite? A merry-go-round? Name it, and it shall be yours."

Myra embraces Seth, "Do you want Mother to help you choose something Seth?"

"No Mother, I know that I have the best there is. I can wish for nothing more. The only other thing I wish to have will not require magic."

The three adults look at each other, amazed at the wisdom the toddler always demonstrates. "Well then, Seth, what have you in mind?" Merlin asks.

"I was just speaking with Manfred and I would love to have a piggy back ride, high over the clouds," Seth waves his arm over his head indicating where he would like to go.

Myra gasps, "Oh no, Seth that is much too dangerous! Don't you have another wish that would keep you on the ground?"

"I understand your feelings Mother, but I will be very safe if Uncle Merlin will ride with me," he turns his pleading violet eyes towards his Great Uncle Merlin.

Merlin looks at both parents, knowing this is a hard decision for them to make, "He is right, of course. With Manfred and myself, there will be no danger. But it is too late to ride now, as darkness is falling. We shall fly tomorrow morning if everyone agrees."

Adrian looks at the others and says, "Hadn't we best ask Manfred? He may not want to do this."

"Not to worry Father, it was his idea," explains Seth.

"We should have realized that," laughs Merlin. "Well I am sure we are all ready for the birthday feast. Let it begin!"

After the feast, they gather around the huge birthday cake, the Hag snaps her fingers and the dragon on top of the cake spits a small flame to light each candle. The party guests sing the 'Happy Birthday Song', although not written for centuries yet. Seth kneels on the chair at the table, in order to be tall enough to reach his cake.

"Alright Seth, close your eyes, make a wish, then blow out the candles in one breath or your wish will not come true," instructs his mother.

The toddler closes his eyes, makes his wish and then blows as hard as he can, out go the flames and everybody cheers. Merlin hands him a knife, "Seth, you must cut the cake and grant me the first piece."

Seth uses both small hands to hold onto the handle of the knife, then carefully lines it up and cuts into the big white cake, carving out a wedge then placing it on his uncle's plate. Seth then yawns and Myra sees her young son is getting sleepy. The sun set a few hours ago, and it is nearing his usual bedtime, "Seth, would you like me to finish up for you?"

"Yes Mother," Seth replies.

Myra cuts Seth his slice of cake and hands it to him. When he puts the first piece into his mouth and closes it to chew, suddenly he is not there!

"Seth!" they cry.

"Yes, what is it?" then he is back and has spit out a small stone into his hand. "Look what I found in my piece of cake."

He holds out for everyone to see, a bean sized turquoise smooth stone.

"Hag, is this what I presume it to be?" asks Merlin.

The old woman laughs and says, "What do you think it is, Merlin?"

"Is it the Stone of Invisibility?"

"Yes, yes," chuckles the Old Hag. "I wanted to give Seth a gift that he does not have, or possibly will ever receive. It is a smooth river stone that saw its creation deep in the bowels of the Earth. It is billions of years old, and there are only a few dozen of them. They are very hard to find. This one I 'borrowed' from a giant, I just forgot to give it back. But not to worry, he is long dead and needs it no longer."

"How interesting," says Merlin. "By what name was this giant known and was he distinguished by having one eye in the center of his head?"

"That's a Cyclops, isn't it?" asks Adrian.

"Yes," answers Merlin, "And the owner of the stone may be dead, but I believe he has two brothers, who may want the stone should they learn of its whereabouts. Is this not so, Hag?"

"Yes, yes, yes," she answers, "But the stone is rightfully mine and I have the right to give it to anyone I want. I wish to give it to Seth to provide protection from Morgana. We all know she has not finished with the boy."

She speaks, before anyone realizes what she is saying and has time to stop her. Before anyone else speaks, Seth looks at his uncle, "Who is Morgana, Uncle Merlin?"

"She is of no importance," he replies.

"That's okay, Uncle Merlin if you don't wish to tell me. There must be a good reason."

• • •

The next morning, Myra has problems with Seth; he is so excited about his 'piggy back ride' on Manfred that he doesn't want to eat or take his bath, but getting dressed is the one thing he does agree to.

"Now Seth, if you don't eat breakfast you will not be able to go with Uncle Merlin and Manfred, do you understand me?" says Myra in a stern voice.

"Yes Mother, I'll try," the toddler replies. "When are they going to get here?"

Adrian enters the front room, "Well son, are you ready for your first flight?"

"He's more than ready," laughs Myra. "I can hardly get him dressed, he wriggles like a worm. I don't know if Uncle Merlin will be able to handle him, he is so excited."

"Oh, they'll do just fine," assures Adrian. "Merlin is going to keep the flight short, and just give him a bird's eye view, or in this case a dragon's eye view of the forest and Camelot. Seth wants to see the castle, isn't that right, son?"

Seth's mouth is so full he just nods and continues eating as fast as Myra will let him. A flapping sound outside alerts them that Manfred has just touched down in the front clearing of the hut. After a moment the hut's door swings open and Merlin looks inside to say, "Are we ready Seth?"

"Oh he's more than ready," laughs Adrian as he carries his son outside. Myra follows with Seth's jacket.

"Here you may need this, I know it is August but when the wind blows you may get cool," she pulls the linen coat over his head, for it was more like a poncho. She kisses her son's warm cheek, "Merlin I know I don't need to tell you to please be very careful, and don't be gone more than an hour."

"Mother, you worry too much about me, I am always safe when I'm with Uncle Merlin, and Manfred can whip anything if he wants to."

"I know, Seth. Have fun!"

"Don't worry Myra, I will protect him, never fear, Manfred is here!" says the dragon as Merlin mounts his broad back, quickly climbing into the saddle and then taking hold of the reins they've fashioned for Manfred. Adrian then hands Seth up to him. Merlin places the child in front of him, and when satisfied that he is secured, gives Manfred the signal. The big dragon then spreads his huge leather-like wings and, with a mighty thrust, he rises into the air.

From the vantage point on the back of the dragon, Seth sees the little hut growing smaller, his parents too, as they wave at him, then they are so small he no longer can see them. He feels Manfred's strong muscles as he beats his massive wings that are keeping them aloft, as they sail across the countryside.

"How do you feel, Seth?" asks Merlin.

The wind rushes past Seth's ears, but he does catch what Merlin asks, "I am doing very well, Uncle Merlin."

Merlin has one arm wrapped around the child, while guiding Manfred with the other. The tops of the trees in the forest look like small bushes, while the land has a patchwork pattern, some blocks being clay colored, while others are green and brown.

"Is everybody comfortable back there," calls Manfred.

"Most comfortable" calls back Merlin. "Are you feeling tired?"

"Who me? No, I could glide up here all day, just catch a good updraft and let the wind do the work."

They aren't as high as the clouds, but there are hawks gliding around up here searching for their next meal. Below is a long and winding dirt path, and horse carts can be seen traveling on them. Further down the path is a castle, a huge structure straight ahead.

"Uncle Merlin, is that Camelot?"

"It is indeed, let us glide in for a closer look. We must keep silent so that no-one may see us. Manfred, take us down a little lower."

The dragon spirals down closer to the castle; the moat, the drawbridge and the courtyard that the castle walls surround can be seen. There are about six mounted knights moving about, as if making ready to go out on a crusade. As it would happen, one knight looks up, for a shadow has passed overhead, drawing his attention. He nudges the others and soon Manfred with his passengers are the center of attention. The knights see that the dragon carries people and motion for them to land.

"They are signaling us to land," says Manfred, "Shall I fly up and away from them?"

"They have already seen us, and if we leave they will think they are under attack. Let us land, and await events."

Merlin waves to the knights and motion that they are landing. They fall back forming a circle and then more people come out looking skyward. Merlin suspects that the knights will take them into custody once they are on the ground, but he is not too concerned, as he knows he can escape if need be. He has more power now than most people suspect, but he does not often reveal his magical abilities, wishing them to remain secret.

Manfred starts the spiral downward and since the courtyard is fairly large, he has no trouble settling gently to the ground. Merlin turns in the saddle and eases down to the ground, holding onto Seth the whole time. A senior sentinel approaches, "Just who might you be, and what is your reason for circling the palace on this beast. Why do you have this child with you?"

Seth until now has been quiet following his uncle's orders, but now pipes up with, "This is my Uncle Merlin and my name is Seth Grey."

A vociferous whisper runs rampant through the crowd, for they have heard the name 'Merlin' but nobody has seen him in almost three years.

"Did this child call you 'Merlin'? Merlin the Sorcerer? And what else? Yes, Uncle Merlin, that's what he said." The guard comes closer to take another look; Seth suddenly wraps both small arms tightly around Merlin's neck.

"Uncle Merlin, I'm scared. Can we get back on Manfred and go home now? I want to see Mother and Father. And I'm getting hungry."

"You need not be frightened Seth. This is a knight; you may greet him.

"Merlin, it IS you!" exclaims the knight. "Why are your hair and your beard so white and long? Where have you been these three years? Do you not know just how ill the King is?—Ha! And leave it to Merlin to tame a dragon!" (At this remark, Manfred snorts steam but holds his tongue; he knows it is disaster if he speaks.) "Most folks are scared of them you know, for much of their lands are burned due to dragons' attacks."

"Yes, it is I. I will answer your questions in due time. This is my great nephew, my mother's sister's daughter's son. He is two. But first, I must meet with Arthur; I was not aware that he was so sick."

"Everybody stand back, make way, come with me Merlin," instructs the guard as he leads the way into the castle. "Arthur is in his chambers; give me a few minutes to send word you are here." The guard summons a page, and gives the boy the message to take to the King. The lad hurries away.

Ten minutes later the page return, "His Majesty wishes you to come to his rooms," he then hurries away to return to his chores.

Leading the way, the guard guides them towards the stairs that they climb up to the third floor and Arthur's rooms. Seth, like the typical two-year-old, chatters nonstop about all that he is seeing. At one point, the guard stops and looks at Seth and then at Merlin, "Did you say he's only two?"

"Yes," replies Seth before Merlin can answer, "I was two yesterday."

"Yesterday," repeats the guard, "He talks better than most adults I know."

"Yes, he is highly intelligent," replies Merlin.

They have arrived at Arthur's chambers, "Wait, and permit me to announce you." He enters the room and after a short time, returns, "You may enter now."

"I'm afraid, Uncle Merlin," Seth buries his small face in Merlin's shoulder.

Merlin pulls him back so he can look into his violet eyes, "You need not fear Arthur; he is a very gentle person. He will not harm you. You do want to meet the King, do you not Seth?"

"Yes."

"Very well, then," Merlin puts the small boy on his feet, "Now you walk ahead of me and bow to the King. You understand?"

"Yes sir, Uncle Merlin."

The guard opens the door; the small boy squares his shoulders, throws back his head and walks determinedly into the darkened room. Merlin follows and after a second they see the king on his couch; Seth walks up to him, bows low, then speaks, "Good morning, Your Majesty."

Arthur sits upright as he sees this child, this little boy, which speaks with the diction of a scholar. "Who are you, boy? Come closer so I may get a better look at you."

"I am Seth, sire," he replies, "Seth Grey. Adrian and Myra Grey are my parents. We live with Uncle Merlin at his hut in the Black Forest."

"Uncle Merlin, did you say?"

"Yes sir."

"Where is Merlin?"

"Arthur, I am here also."

Arthur turns his attention on Merlin, "You do not look like Merlin, but you sound like him. You and the boy come closer, into the light. Move those tapestries," he instructs the page.

Daylight floods the room as the page pulls open the heavy draperies.

"That is better. Merlin, why do you have white hair and beard, and so has this child white hair. Come here, son, and sit by me."

Seth looks to Merlin, "It is well, Seth, be seated by the King."

"Okay Uncle Merlin," he walks to Arthur, the King looks closely at him and then holds out his arms, and Seth walks into them. Arthur picks him up.

"How old are you Seth?"

"I am two years old yesterday, Your Majesty."

"Yes, you cannot be much older than that, how is it you speak so well?"

"I am very smart; I have a very high IQ."

"IQ? In heaven's name what is an IQ?"

"Well, Your Majesty . . ." Seth starts to explain.

"Never mind, I do not need to know," says Arthur. "So you are two years old?"

"Yes sir."

"That makes you the same age as Morgana's son, Mordred. I wonder," says Arthur as he strokes his chin. "Merlin?"

"Yes, Arthur."

"At the time these boys were born, Morgana tells me of another maiden who was with child, which was supposedly fathered by myself. Now tell me truthfully; is this the boy?"

"Yes, Arthur, he is your son, but not in the usual fashion," replies Merlin.

"I dare say not in the usual fashion, for unless I was bewitched, I remember no such encounter with any maid other than Morgana. Her son is mine. To that, I do affirm, though I would rather not. So, please explain this. And how is it he is your, how did the guard say, great nephew?"

"I cannot tell you how he is related to you in a way you would understand or even believe, but he does have your blood flowing through his veins, to this I swear. He is my great nephew by my mother's sister Eileen; you were never acquainted with her and she is now dead. It is her granddaughter who is Seth's mother. His white hair comes from her. Mine, on the other hand comes from age."

"So he is your distant cousin really and not your nephew. Well that explains your relationship, but not mine."

"As I said, I cannot explain it; you must trust me in this matter."

"So it would seem, but you are not old enough to have white hair, and where have you been for these three years?"

"I have been guarding Seth's parents, and eventually him, from Morgana. We keep well hidden, it is necessary or Seth would . . . well the worst." Merlin stops in time for Seth is there and has an enquiring mind.

"Yes," agrees Arthur, "knowing my dear sister. We have not heard very much from her since I banished her and her kin from Camelot forever. But with the betrayal of Guinevere and Lancelot, things have steadily been in decline. My health is failing, the land is desolate, and famine and disease covers my entire Kingdom. Lancelot deserted me, Guinevere is at the monastery and I have lost Excalibur. Then when I needed you the most, you were nowhere to be found. It was rumored Morgana had done away with you and stolen your powers. However, it seems there was no truth to those rumors."

"Some truth," answers Merlin. "It has taken a long time, but I have recovered."

"Yes, and glad we are that you are back, old friend," says Arthur as he slaps Merlin on his back. "I have sent my knights on crusade, to seek that which I have lost. We have no answers. Will you help me, my old friend, to regain my kingdom and my glory?"

"At this time, Arthur, I am unable to help. You must realize yourself what it is you have lost, and only you can regain it. My power is weak. It is the time of men, not of magic and sorcery. I must return to my sanctuary and complete one final mission in my life. However, Seth and I will visit you again, if you wish it."

"Yes, I would like that very much. When you are ready, the guard will escort you out. I grow tired and need to rest." Arthur motions for the page to draw the drapes and he lies back on his couch.

Merlin picks up Seth, who has been very quiet during the conversation between Arthur and Merlin. The child has learned a great deal from listening to the adults talk and he knows that things are not as they should be.

"I think we must journey home, my son, before your parents start to worry."

"Yes, I think so too, Uncle Merlin."

• • •

Back in the courtyard, Manfred still waits, while a crowd mingles around him. They touch him and talk about him, but they do not know that this dragon knows what they are saying.

"Are you prepared to leave now, Manfred?"

The dragon stands from a crouching position and winks at Seth as he nods his massive head. The two climb aboard with help from the guard, and with a mighty beat of his wings, Manfred sends dust swirling as he lifts into the air. Soon they wing out of sight and back towards the Black Forest.

• • •

During their flight back home, another palace come into view, "Uncle Merlin, whose castle is that?"

Merlin knows exactly to whom it belongs, but does not want Seth to know. However, curiosity overcomes caution for Merlin, as he wants to see what is happening with Morgana. "That is merely a neighbor of King Arthur's; we will fly over if you wish, to observe."

The mighty dragon circles high overhead, and Merlin increases his vision and hearing so he tunes in to the happenings at Morgana's castle. There is a beautiful redheaded woman walking about holding onto the hand of a small boy of about two; it is Morgana with Mordred. 'So, she has used the Charm to restore her beauty,' thinks Merlin. 'It must take all she can muster to retain this illusion.'

Mordred is having a tantrum, and Morgana shakes him to try and stop this behavior, but it is not working, so she turns the child over to the nursemaid and goes back inside.

"There is little to see there, Seth."

"Why is the little boy crying Uncle Merlin?"

"He must wish for something which his mother will not grant to him, Seth."

"Oh," says Seth.

"Let us return to the hut, Manfred," orders Merlin.

• • •

After they are back at the hut, "No, we really weren't worried," Myra is saying, we just had the feeling that everything was fine, but you were gone most of the day, instead of the hour. I was just concerned that Seth would get hungry and overtired; he still is pretty much a baby you know. We kind of forget that about him." Myra has Seth on her lap as he drifts off to sleep for his overdue afternoon nap.

CHAPTER EIGHTEEN

TRAINING FOR KNIGHTHOOD

Seth's education continues; he spends two or three hours each morning in some type of scholastic activity. Merlin tutors him in mathematics and language arts, but Seth's favorite lessons are conducted outside with the Hag, where he learns the ways of the natural world; the healing as well as the destructive properties of plants. Sleyvia and Haghery teach him to use his magical abilities and his father shows him how to use his psychic powers. Myra is content just to read him his nursery rhymes, but more likely than not he reads to her. He receives his spiritual instruction from everyone; he studies the Bible daily and learns the greater purpose that God has for man. They do not tell him of his part in saving the Universe; he is much too young to handle the enormity of that knowledge.

He grows straight and tall and especially handsome, his ashen hair curls, unlike his mother's, and he has the deepest violet colored eyes, with a few freckles running across his nose. Merlin has taken him back several more time to visit the King, and Arthur grows much attached to him. At the age of seven, Arthur requests that he begin training for the knighthood; this stage of his training will lasts for seven years, until he is fourteen. He is assigned as page to Sir Sagremor, one of the few knights that has not gone out on crusade, but who stays behind to guard Camelot. Myra's heart feels ripped from her chest when she contemplates her son not being under her constant attention. She knows the palace is not the best place for him as far as his safety is concerned, for it is the last place Morgana wants him. Over the last few years, she has continued her attempts at destroying the boy, but he is just too well protected. Morgana, herself, has never tried to harm him again, but she still casts spells over creatures of the air, field and forest to try to get her wicked work done for her. Every time she uses the Charm of Making, she exposes her disfigurement, for she is not strong enough to maintain her beauty and control the spells she casts.

Nevertheless, Myra relents and approves of Seth's training, but insists that Merlin stay with him while he is at Camelot. Myra and Adrian knows that Adrian cannot go to Camelot, for any contact between him and Arthur would be disastrous, and Myra doesn't want to be separated from him. Merlin agrees to stay at the castle three weeks out of four, and return to the hut for one week, with Seth. This is not the usual arrangement made for pages, they normally only see their parents twice a year after training starts, but Arthur concedes and gives special consent for the monthly visits.

• • •

Now after eleven years of training, Seth will be eighteen this August; he is in his fourth year of being a squire. It is the month of May and he and Merlin make their monthly visit to see his parents back at the hut. As always it is like having a family reunion, all the forest inhabitants, the leprechauns, elves, fairies, Manfred, the Hag and Merlin, gather together for a grand feast.

• • •

Myra, now in her mid thirties is still a very beautiful woman, not showing any sign of ageing. She wears her hair very long; it now reaches her knees, not having had it cut since they came here. Adrian in his mid forties has a touch of grey at his temples, but still retains the lithe frame of a much younger man. The eighteen years of living here in the middle ages has done them no harm; Myra has learned the ancient ways of homemaking and Adrian has all the skills of a hunter and farmer, as well as carpentry. He has added to the hut another two rooms and a corral out back, for their three horses. There seems always plenty to do, and for the most part magical help is no longer sought, it is much more fulfilling to do things for themselves. Merlin, on the other hand has not changed at all in these years; he is still advisor to the King and many seek his advice on various things, from romance, to the ravages of the land.

∙ ∙ ∙

On his third day back home while finishing up their morning coffee, Seth speaks to his parents and Merlin. Seth has things on his mind and so, "Mother, after I help you out in the garden this morning, I think I will take a long ride through the forest."

"Are we boring you, Seth?" Myra asks with a gleam in her eye. "I know we can't offer the same entertainments as Camelot, you must be feeling restless."

"What's this about feeling restless?" questions Adrian as he comes in from the back room.

Merlin leans back in his chair; he knows what is on Seth's mind but decides not to interfere with what Seth wishes to do.

"Seth wants to go riding this afternoon, after his chores are done," Myra informs him.

"Well, that will be fine; I'll get my horse and ride with you."

"If you don't mind, Father, I wish to be alone for awhile. I want to think over the King's offer of allowing me to omit my last year as Squire to Sir Sagremor, and be knighted on my eighteenth birthday. That way I would skip three more years of training, and I am not sure if I am ready for it."

"What brought this on?"

"I'm not really sure, but rumors are that Morgana and her son are plotting an attack on the peasants of the kingdom, to capture some of Camelot's lands and add them to her own, so as to build up her armies. He will need faithful and trained knights. He seems to think that I am as ready as I will ever be. But I am not so sure."

"Merlin, did you know of this?" asks Adrian.

"Yes, Arthur discussed it with me; my advice was that I believe Seth could handle knighthood now. So prior to leaning, he put the proposal before Seth, in order that he could consider it whilst at home this week."

"Oh Adrian, isn't he far too young for this," asks Myra. "I thought knighthood started when they reached the age of twenty one. He is still a squire now; he has had no training for battle, has he?" Myra looks anxiously at her husband.

"Yes Mother, I have had more than the other squires, and I often wondered why. I understand now."

"Okay son, if you feel you need the time alone, I will respect your wishes. Just promise your Mother and I, that you will not leave the confines of the forest, for inside you have a measure of protection, outside you do not."

"I promise, Father."

• • •

Sleyvia, forever with Myra, even when Myra is not aware that she is near, hears this conversation, and makes an unscheduled visit to The Old Hollow Tree. She has a quick meeting with her parents, the King and Queen, and explains what she needs for that afternoon. Her father orders one third of the elves and fairies to follow Seth through the forest to see to his welfare, without Seth's knowledge, and report back to the King should there be any trouble. If it becomes necessary, they will intervene on Seth's behalf, should anything threaten him.

• • •

They have lunch out back of the hut, the weather is warmer after the long winter, and everyone is anticipating the summer months. Their discussion centers on Seth's training and how well he is doing. He far exceeds what is required for a squire; he already shows the physique of a young man. He is the height of his father, with developing masculine muscles. His horsemanship is superior to all the other squires and in the use of weapons, he is the best swordsman. The squires carry no sword, only a small dagger on their belt, and are well versed in its use.

"Lunch was delicious Mother, I will take my leave of you now, and I will return before dark." Seth leans over and gives his mother a kiss on her brow.

"Father, is there anything you need from me before I leave?"

Adrian stands, and looks fondly at his son, pride swells up in his heart, the pride of a parent, the pride of a man and the pride of a human. "No Seth, not at this time. You go and enjoy your afternoon, get rid of some pent up energy. I know when I was your age, it seemed I could go on forever, and never get tired. Your training has been hard I know, go, relax and have fun. But, be very cautious and return by dark."

"I will Father, Mother," and he strides over to his chestnut, mounting the horse with ease. He reins the horse around, looks at his parents, gives a salute and spurs the horse away.

• • •

He enters the tall trees not following any path and urges his horse into an easy gait. The sweet smell of late spring greets his nostrils; his horse's hooves are cushioned by the thick carpet of pine straw, and directly over his head, small birds dart about, winging from tree to tree, their chirping resounding through the dark forest. Also, unseen and not sensed by Seth, the elves and fairies glide from plant to tree, to keep up with him.

Seth breathes deeply, relishing his newfound freedom; no one to give him orders, no one to watch his every move lest he should come to harm. No, for the first time in his young life, Seth feels like a man, a man with a great future. He will be one of the greatest knights there ever was. He will seek what King Arthur has lost; none of the knights from the round table has found the secret and many have lost their lives in the attempt. Yet, they continue with the quest, and King Arthur lingers somewhere between vigor and frailty. He cannot die, yet he does not live, and the land outside of The Black Forest grows more desolate; the people are hungry, they can barely gather enough to keep body and soul together. Death and disease are constant companions; many peasants work too hard, and die too young. They are unable to force the land to produce, to recover, to reinvigorate, no, there is no joy and only death brings solace.

• • •

Seth slows his steed down to a steady walk; for a moment, he has lost his bearings, for he does not recognize this section of the forest. He and Merlin, riding on the back of Manfred, have investigated all sectors of the woodland, and this one is strange to him. It is still daylight, and he trusts his own sense of direction to guide him home, so he does not worry about the strangeness of his surroundings. He presses on.

There is a noise not too far distant, the clink of metal, the rustle of leaves, the pounding of horse's hooves; he decides to investigate. This brings him to the edge of the forest, a large clearing, a flattened meadow where two knights on horseback are engaged in jousting practice. They wear complete suits of armor; one is clearly an instructor, for he is giving advice to the other on errors made.

Seth watches for a brief time, secluded by the trees. One knight wears golden armor, with a helmet shaped in the form of a human face and head. He carries a shield with an unrecognizable crest; his horse is a golden palomino, there is a sword hanging from his waist and he balances a lance on his right arm. He rides to one end of the field.

The other knight wears black armor, his helmet is shaped like the face of a hawk, his shield's crest is a hawk, he also has a sword hanging from his belt, and carries a lance; he rides a black stallion and he goes to the other side of the field.

There is a long improvised fence made of rope running about two hundred and fifty feet, dividing the meadow, and each knight positions himself on the opposite side of this barrier. For the first time, Seth notices that there is a squire with the knights, and he is standing on a large rock just between the two knights but spaced away from the battle field; he holds a red scarf, he signals that he is about to drop the flag, he does. The knights spring into motion, spurring their mounts into a full gallop. With lances lowered and aimed at their opponent, they dash unwaveringly towards each other. Seth sees the ends of the lances are blunt, proving this is only a practice match. They close in on each other, and, as they meet close to the middle of the barrier, the black knight's lance strikes the shield of the other, unseating him and flinging him to the ground, where he lands hard on his back.

The black knight reins his stallion around and returns to where his opponent has fallen; at his approach the fallen knight stands up, and both remove their helmets. The black knight is an older man with black hair, beard, streaked with grey, the other is a young lad, about the age of Seth, and he has long reddish blond hair. Another young man trains for the knighthood, but Seth is not familiar with him.

• • •

"You are improving, Mordred," the older man is saying, "but you hold your shield too high. Had I chosen I could have gored you full in the belly. Next time lower your shield and keep your lance more to the front. You leave yourself exposed. Now mount your horse and let's try again."

"I don't see how it was you unseated me again. I had my weapon as you directed, but still I was defeated."

"At the beginning of the run you did, but you did not maintain your posture to the end. You cannot let down your guard. You must hold your position for the entire joust, not just at the beginning."

"All of this is a waste of time," says Mordred. "I've have trained for over a year now, I think I am ready to take on Arthur."

"Your Mother will have the final decision on that," replies the Black Knight.

Seth, on hearing this, decides to leave, but his efforts at turning his horse cause the steed to neigh in protest; this draws the attention of the Black Knight. The knight halts the match; he reins his stallion to a stop, while holding up his lance vertically. Mordred stops his charge and faces the direction the sound comes from.

"What is it, Sir Garther?"

"Someone is hidden in the thicket," he replies. "You there!" he shouts towards the thick groves of trees, "Show yourself!"

Seth hesitates briefly, but, thinking it is best to reveal his presence, he spurs his horse out into the open meadow. His chestnut trots across the field, and Seth guides him towards the two knights. They wear full armor, while Seth is wearing a dark maroon tunic and blackish blue leggings with ankle high black suede boots. As the knights await his arrival onto the field, they remove their helmets placing them beneath their arms.

Seth speaks first, "Greetings gentlemen, I regret disturbing you."

The Black Knight rides his mount up to him and asks, "And who might you be, lad?"

"I am Seth," is the short reply.

"Whence forth do you hail?"

"I live at the castle, Camelot."

"At Camelot, eh?" he murmurs. "Are you training for the knighthood?"

"Yes," he answers.

"Why are you riding here in the Black Forest?" the Black Knight asks. "You do know it is haunted, do you not?"

"Well no, I did not, I have never seen anything that might indicate such."

"The peasants will not travel through the forest unescorted. But why are you here, so far from Camelot?"

"I am visiting my parents who live on the other side of the forest," says Seth, not revealing the exact location of the hut.

"It would seem you are a far way from home. I am Sir Garther of Linse," he says with a bow of his head, "and this lad is Mordred, Son of Morgana and King Arthur."

"Yes," speaks up Mordred, "if you live at Camelot, no doubt you have heard of my Mother, have you not?"

"Yes, I have heard her name spoken," Seth answers, keeping a wary eye on Mordred, as Mordred guides his palomino to circle Seth.

"In what matter have you heard of my mother?" he asks with a smirk on his handsome face. "What do they say about her? You know she and I have been banished from the castle?"

"Yes, I did know," Seth sees no point in not answering his questions, for it has been nearly eighteen years, and it is now old news.

"I have heard of you, too," sneers Mordred. "You would not have guessed that, would you?"

Seth shakes his head, and turns in his saddle to keep his eyes on Mordred, for he continues to circle Seth.

"How is it that you are the King's son?"

This question stuns Seth; he cannot comprehend why Mordred asks such. "I do not know the meaning of your question, Sir."

"I am King Arthur's son," replies Mordred. "I was born on the morning of August the thirteenth, but your birth preceded mine by twelve hours making you the legitimate heir to the throne. I, by rights, should be the heir; after all, my Mother is also King Arthur's half sister."

"My father is not the King," states Seth emphatically, "as I say, I am visiting my parents this week, and I do not know how you came by such false information; but swear to you, I do, that I am not King Arthur's son."

"Well I know different," disputes Mordred. "My Mother told me all about it, that you are a bastard, and not fit to rule."

"I do not wish to 'rule', and a bastard I am not," says Seth through clenched teeth. "'Tis you who are the bastard, your mother laid with her own brother, like a bitch in heat to begat a king! She is trying to steal the throne from her brother, using you as her weapon, so that she can rule Camelot herself. You would be merely a puppet. You? King? It will never happen!"

Mordred's face turns more red than his hair, "How dare you, you son of a harlot! I shall have your head for that remark," he clumsily draws his sword and takes a swing at Seth.

Seth reacts quickly enough to avoid a slice at his throat, but takes a searing slash to his left forearm. He grabs his arm, and blood starts oozing from between his fingers. The black knight knows this argument has gone too far, and hastily steps in; he seizes the hilt of Mordred's sword wrestling it from his grip.

"Enough, Mordred!" he shouts at him, as he shoves Mordred's horse backward with his own. He then turns to Seth, but he is taken aback by the sight before him.

Seth is surrounded by elves and fairies as they wrap the wound with large leaves and they then form an elfin shield in front of Seth, so that he is surrounded by their imparting energies.

"What manner of boy are you?" he asks in bewilderment, "You have the protection of the mystical ones. How is that?"

"That I am unable to answer," Seth's voice is steady and calm; he has no more pain, anger is swelling up inside, and his heart pounds with his fury, but he hides it well. "I will not allow this attack to go unchallenged. We will meet again, Mordred, you and I, and you will regret this day!"

"No, no, there is no need for that," the Black Knight attempts to sooth raw nerves. "Mordred was impulsive, and reacted without thinking to your insult of his mother. You boys are far too young for combat, the King would not allow it, you would need stand-ins; you are healed, so no harm's done. You go back to your home and we will do the same. I will see to it that you never meet again."

The whole time the black knight is speaking, Mordred is straining to get around him and back at Seth, but the knight keeps him under control by holding onto the reins of his mount.

"Take your leave now," he orders, "and do not come back to this meadow again."

"This time you have the upper hand, Mordred, but come another time I will take from you the most precious thing you own."

"And what would that be, squire?" sneers Mordred.

"Your life!" he replies with the coldness of steel, and the look of promise in his eyes. He reins his horse in the direction of the black forest, as Mordred shouts insults at his back all the while, with a hint of fear in his voice. Seth does not look back but continues on towards home.

• • •

Seth arrives back at the hut just as the sun turns the skies pink and gold; he dismounts from his horse and leads him to the small corral out back, he gets feed and water and begins to brush the animal's red coat when Adrian enters.

"Seth!"

"Here Father!"

"Son, how is your arm?"

Seth shakes his head and laughs, "I see the wee folk have arrived here before me. It is well, they took immediate care of me, and surprised me for I had no idea they were about."

"Well that is good to hear, here let me see, for your Mother's sake."

The wound was completely healed, but the tunic was cut, and caked with blood at the site of the attack.

"Well, we'll get you all cleaned up, when you get inside."

"Father, I have questions," Seth begins.

"Yes, son, I know, we will talk once we go inside."

• • •

Myra is nervously pacing the floor and Merlin sits at the table drinking a goblet of ale when Seth and Adrian walk through the front door. Myra hurries to Seth's side, "Seth, you should never have left the forest; you cannot be protected beyond its boundaries as you can within. You know we told you, why didn't you listen?"

"I know, Mother," answers Seth a little exasperated, "you warned me when I was younger about not leaving the forest, but the reason you gave then was meant for a child. I am no longer a child, and I need to know the truth. I am afraid I have learned more today, about who I am, or might be, than in my entire life. How am I supposed to be Arthur's son? Mordred himself declared me to be. I know you two are my true parents, this you could not have hidden from me, but the two of you are concealing something, and I need its revelation now."

At this precise moment, a florescent green light filters in through the hut's small windows, traveling down across the floor and along the walls and the ceiling. This eerie glow merges in the center of the room and swirls clockwise until a feminine figure forms, it is Eydasi, the Keeper of Time. She wears a shimmering floor length robe of green grass, its hood completely covering her face, her skin is sky blue, and her eyes are flashing emeralds, she has the belt of twinkling stars circling her waist, the radiant sun glows blindingly from the ring on her finger, the silver crescent moon hangs from a necklace of pale moon stones.

"Eydasi!" Merlin, Adrian and Myra speak at once.

Seth wears a look of total shock, and stammers, "What manner of being is this?"

"I am Eydasi, the Keeper of Time," she speaks with many voices coming from all directions at once. "I have come to reveal our next King, and his role in saving the Universe."

"No!" screams Myra. "It is not the time."

"Of what does she speak?" asks Seth. "I demand to know!"

Myra rushes to Seth's side and throws her arms around his shoulders, "No, Eydasi, he is still a boy, he needs more time."

Adrian walks over to his son and wife, "Myra, darling, come sit by me, he needs to know now."

Eydasi focus her glowing green eyes on Seth, "Seth Ertian Grey, you are the next King of Britain; you are the son of King Arthur. You are the only and last hope of the Universe."

For a long moment, Seth does not answer, and all in the hut is silent. He walks up to the Keeper of Time, and reaches a hand out to touch her, "You may not lay hands on me, to do so would destroy you!"

Seth withdraws his hands and cups them in front of him, he waits a moment then asks, "I need answers, Lady. How can I be the son of King Arthur?"

"Your father is King Arthur. King Arthur reincarnated."

"I still do not understand."

"I will explain all. Be silent and listen closely, what I am about to say will be unbelievable, but I will show you proof."

Seth looks at both parents and then Merlin, who says, "Be seated Seth, and listen to what this seraph has to say."

"In the distant future," Eydasi continues, "a false heir sits on the throne of England. King Arthur dies without a successor. After Arthur and Mordred's death, there is no King for two hundred and fifty years. The land divides and warlords rule individual territories. This is known as the 'Dark Ages.' And very little can be found in the history books of this time frame. The Quest for the lost Grail, when successful, restores prosperity to the land for a short period of time, but then it once again deteriorates.

"The land dies and its people; the promise given by Abraham cannot be fulfilled. After centuries of constant clashes among themselves, they realize a common enemy, the Saxons, and unite, choosing a King from among themselves. So for thirteen hundreds years the crown has passed down a fraudulent, non-pure blood line. The Throne of England is the Throne of David. When the ten tribes of Israel were lost to history, the tribe of Ephraim settled in the British Isles, this is the throne Christ will occupy when he returns to the Earth.

"But an impostor sits on the throne and defiles the crown and bloodline; Christ cannot return until this is righted. The heavenly host has waited patiently for this to happen; it has not. So unless it is corrected the Universe will begin collapsing back in on itself, back to the beginning of Time. Yahweh would have to begin again, which would take billions of eons. Yahweh does not want to see failure in his creation, so we have one more chance to right the wrong.

"He appointed me, Eydasi, the Time Keeper, the final task of restoring Time to its original position, or it is over; the Universe as we know it, will be lost. I have been given more than my usual powers to regress Time itself, as far back as is needed. Merlin gained the position of Prophet and Magician by defeating the demon Thanatos, thus releasing many held in his power for centuries; Arthur was granted rebirth by Yahweh, his spirit reincarnated in your father Adrian, thus you are King Arthur's legitimate son and heir to the throne.

"I brought your parents, with Merlin, back to the time frame in which time went astray, which was twenty years bypassed, in order to restore Time to its true state. They are on the final episode of that mission. They have sacrificed all to remain here in the past to raise you themselves. They could have returned to their own Time and left you here to be raised by others, but chose not to do so. They, with Merlin and the mystical ones have protected you from many dangers, and enemies, Morgana the prime one. But she never understood that there was no possibility of Mordred becoming King. His conception was defiled by incest and prompted by Thanatos, against the wishes of Yahweh.

"Guinevere's adultery with Lancelot further doomed the kingdom and brought disgrace to the throne. Arthur should have executed both of them for treason; his refusal to do so was the further downfall of Camelot, and it came under a curse from which it was never released, not even in modern times.

"The only way to right this wrong, was to travel back in time and give Arthur an heir. It could not be done by the Arthur of old, so this way was found. We had a virgin, who helped in the liberation of spirits trapped by Thanatos, and with their release came the opportunity to save the Universe. This virgin, in marrying Arthur, brought back the glory and respect to the crown, the throne, and the kingdom.

"With their union, the Universe once again has hope. Merlin survived being trapped in the caverns by Morgana for fifteen hundred years. It was through the use of his mind that he became immortal and very powerful; without Merlin this day may never have come about. Arthur will recognize you as heir and you will rule."

Merlin stands, "Thank you, Eydasi. That was a long tale and difficult to relate." He turns and looks at his companions of nearly twenty years; Adrian has his arm around Myra's shoulder as tears run down her face, and Seth sits with a dumbfounded look on his young face.

"We have further challenges to face; there is a reason Arthur has chosen to knight Seth now, even though he himself does not fully realize its implication. Morgana and Mordred plan to attack the castle in early autumn; this will be the beginning of the end for Camelot, unless an heir is declared before then. Seth, return to Camelot at the end of this week; your training for battle will intensify, you will not return home to the Black Forest until the battle is won."

Seth now also stands, and, gazing on the faces of the ones he loves most, speaks, "Somehow all of this seems very real and quite true, as well as believable. I do understand it, and I accept my responsibility. I knew I owed Mordred a debt, I just did not realise how huge it was."

Seth walks over to his mother, "Please Mother, do not cry, it will all be as our God has planned. You and father will have many grandchildren. I will aspire to be the greatest King possible. I was raised for it, and I will accomplish it."

He looks at Eydasi, "Thank you, Eydasi, the Keeper of time."

"I am honored to disclose to you your destiny, King Seth. Rule long and well." With that, Eydasi spreads herself out on the spring breeze and disappears.

CHAPTER NINETEEN

SIR SETH

August is upon them before they realize it; Seth returns to Camelot and gives King Arthur his decision to forgo any more service as squire, and accept his knighthood now. His training is long and arduous; at night, he is so tired that often he falls into bed whilst still clothed. Merlin now trains Seth himself, for battle as well as survival techniques. He learns more of chivalry, and hones his psychic abilities. He has dreams that tell him he will be the one who kills Mordred, instead of Arthur, as history has recorded it.

• • •

His birthday is tomorrow and he has the day off from training, for he will be knighted along with squires three years older than he. The ceremony will be held at one in the afternoon; afterwards, the new knights will participate in a jousting contest. Their opponents will be drawn by lots and no one knows whom he will come up against until the final few moments.

• • •

Adrian and Myra arrive at Camelot late in the afternoon prior to the day of the ceremony. Adrian is secretly escorted up to Merlin's rooms so as not to risk direct contact with King Arthur. Merlin and Seth await them in the reception hall.

"Mother! Father!" Seth greets the both of them and hugs them. "It has been a very long time since you have been to Camelot, has it not?"

"Not since your conception," says Merlin. "They had to leave because of Arthur's possible contact with your father. I doubt seriously if Arthur will remember your mother or father, for he has not seen them in twenty-three of his years, but still we must not take any chances."

"Well, this place has not changed much over the years," observes Adrian.

"Some things never change," answers Merlin, "and then some things always do."

"Adrian, you and Myra take my sleeping chambers tonight and I will stay in Seth's rooms with him. I will have dinner sent up for the two of you if you would prefer not risk facing Arthur. But you make the decision. I think it will be possible to keep you separated if you wish to join the guests. Arthur has planned pleasant entertainment after the dinner tonight."

"I think we would like to come down," answers Adrian. "It has been a long time since Myra and I have been away from the hut. I think we would both enjoy a change of scenery, yes, thank you."

"Good, I should wish to introduce you as Seth's parents; that would make me very proud, and I am certain Seth would feel similarly."

"Most certainly I would, Mother, Father. I have much to be proud of," he replies and looks thoughtfully at his parents.

• • •

Later in the evening, Adrian and Myra make their way down to the very large dining hall. Myra wears an off the shoulder deep purple velvet gown, with only a sparkling tiara holding her smooth ashen locks in place. Her eyes appear even more violet with the enhancement coming from the gown. She wears no other jewels, save for her wedding rings. The gown is a figure flattering a-line form, with a short train at the back hem of the garment. Adrian is clad in mushroom colored leggings and a crimson velvet tunic with black suede knee-high boots and an umber beret. These styles have never been seen in this century, but Sleyvia conjured them, saying that none would wonder and that Myra would be setting a fashion trend. Seth is clothed completely in hunter green from head to toe, and Merlin wears a robe of inky blue trimmed in silver braid. As always, he carries his staff, with the orb churning on its tip. There is a silver headband, encrusted with rubies, placed over his waist length white hair; his very long white beard lies straight and smooth down the front of his robe.

Just before they are seated, Merlin introduces them to Arthur, "Sire, you may not remember but these are Seth's parents, Adrian and Myra. They were first introduced to you some twenty years ago."

Arthur looks up from his sitting position; his face has aged, he looks frail and tired, and his dark hair is streaked with grey. "Ah yes, I think I may remember the two of you. Who could forget such a flaxen-haired beauty? Your son, madam looks a great deal like you."

Then looking at Adrian he smiles weakly, "You, sir, are the one with the shocking touch."

Adrian laughs and replies, "I am afraid you are right. It may be better not to shake hands then, don't you think."

"My thought precisely, please be seated. I wish to say what a fine son you have. He has been like a son to me in many, many ways, a complete pleasure to have at Camelot."

"Thank you, sire."

The seating arrangement are much as they were those many years ago, with Seth given a place of honor to Arthur's left and Myra and Adrian next to him. With every one now seated, the first of a four course modest meal is served, along with ale, for the grape harvest had been non-existent and thus no wine for the cellars of Britain. Conversation is light, but there are many empty seats at the round table, with the absence of the knights out on crusade, or who have been killed whilst searching for the Holy Grail.

As the meal is finished and the dishes cleared, King Arthur rises from his seat, and taps lightly on the table with his knife, "May I have everyone's attention for a moment, please." All heads turned in his direction expecting the announcement of the evening's entertainment but instead, "I want to introduce to you a very fine young man. Seth of the Black Forest. Seth, would you please stand."

Seth rises from his seat, somewhat confused as to what is coming next.

"I suspect many of you are already acquainted with this young Squire; he has been in the service of Sir Sagremor for many years now. Seth will be forgoing his last three years of service and I will knight him tomorrow during the annual ceremony. I think many of you are aware of this and may not be surprised, but I also want to announce that I am naming Seth Grey of the Black Forest, as heir to the throne after my death. He will be your next king and not Mordred!"

Cheers and shouts of approval ascend from the crowd in the dining hall.

"Mordred," continues Arthur, "will bring only disgrace to Camelot and ultimately its destruction. Although Seth is not my son by birth, he does have a blood link to me, although a weak one. He is also the third cousin to Merlin, thus his qualification to rule the kingdom is strong. I will make it official tomorrow at the celebrations. So now, bring on the minstrels and dancers for your entertainment. However, you must excuse me, I am feeling tired, and must bid you goodnight." With that statement, Arthur retires.

• • •

On the following day, the ceremony is being conducted in an outside arena that has seating stands on either side of the gaming area. The King has a booth, which is closed in on three sides with a blue and yellow striped fabric roof; inside there are two thrones with two seats on either side of each throne, then three more rows behind them. Two armored and armed knights stand at attention at the back corners of the podium.

Shortly before noon, the arena begins filling up, the King and his entourage arrive just minutes before events get underway. The throne next to Arthur is noticeably empty; Merlin is on his right, Adrian and Myra to his far left. Sir Hector, Sir Kay, Sir Sagremor and their ladies fill the remaining seats.

Two horsemen dressed in dark green leggings and yellow tunics and carrying long thin brass trumpets, ride out into the center of the arena; they turn and face the King, and play a short burst of notes. This introduces a third horseman, who rides out with a scroll placed under his arm; he stops in front of the first two. The horses wear blue and yellow caparisons that almost cover their hooves. The trumpeters again raise their instruments and play another fanfare, at which the announcer unrolls the scroll and begins the ritual.

The announcement is concerning the squires who will be knighted; in no particular order, their names are called. They ride out and stop their horses in front of the King, he stands and taps each shoulder and pronounces them Sir. Four are called before Seth, then his name rings out across the countryside.

"Seth Grey, of the Black Forest!"

Suited for the first time publicly, in armor, he rides out his chestnut before the crowd; his horse wears a shorter caparison of white trimmed in red, his armor is silver, his bronze shield bears the crest of the White Dragon, Arthur's crest. He guides his steed close to the King, removes his helmet and lowers his head. King Arthur draws his sword and taps him first on the left shoulder and then the right, "In the name of God, Saint Michael and Saint George, I give you the right to bear arms and the power to meet justice as a Noble Knight of the Round Table. Rise Sir Seth!"

Applause and cheers ring out from the audience.

Seth raises his head and looks at the King, and replies, "A duty I do solemnly swear to keep as a Knight of the Round Table."

Sir Seth then kisses the tip of Arthur's sword, and before he can leave to take his place beside of the others, the presenter speaks again.

"May I have your continuing attention please? For those who were not present at the feast last evening, the King has important information for you." There was a long and very pregnant pause, as all eyes focus on Arthur.

He remains standing, "I am proud to decree Sir Seth Grey of the Black Forest to be my one and only true heir. He will rule in my stead should I become injured or in the event of my death! Mordred, son of Morgana will not receive my blessing as heir! Nor any of the wealth of Camelot." Arthur then sits as the crowd goes mad with happiness at this news, for none wants to be ruled by the tyrant Mordred is proving to be.

Seven more are knighted, and they all line up facing the King. The trumpeters again play a fanfare. The announcer, certain he has silence and the attention of his audience proceeds, "Lots will now be drawn to see which knights will face each other in the coming joust."

A squire holds a large clay bowl; the knights file by in single order to withdraw a name; of the twelve, only one receives his own name and needs to draw again. Seth has drawn the name of Sir Collins and they are fifth of the six contests. The joust is underway and all are in high spirits at their first competition; the lances are not blunted so there is a very real possibility of injury, but battle to the death is forbidden and mercy always granted.

Sir Seth and Sir Collin are facing each other at each end of the arena; the flag is dropped, each prepare to charge, then unexpectedly from out of nowhere another horseman penetrates the field opposite Sir Seth. Coming up behind Sir Collins, he violently shoves him from his horse and takes his place on the field of combat. He rides a golden palomino; his armor is gold, and his helmet in the shape of a human head. Immediately Seth recognizes Mordred. "What is this rogue up to?" wonders Seth aloud.

Mordred pauses briefly, as he holds his lance vertically, signaling he is ready for battle. Seth is uncertain the match will be allowed; he searches for the King's approval and gets it. Seth holds his lance vertically towards Arthur, signaling that he will accept the challenge. Both knights look to the flagman, he drops the red flag and the joust is underway.

Seth lowers his lance and deliberately plunges into the charge with the intention of meeting this challenge with all his strength and knowledge. Urging his chestnut into a full gallop, he narrows his range of vision to include only one object, Mordred.

Mordred reacts likewise; their horses' hooves kick up billows of dust as they charge violently forward. Like demons straight out of hell, the two furiously begin their assault towards each other. At the precise moment of contact, their lances converge, and then splinter as they bypass each other, but neither is unseated. They go to their respective ends of the field and each receives a new lance. Merlin has hurried over to Seth's station when he sees Mordred enter the competition. He now speaks to Seth.

"You are aware that this is Mordred?" he asks.

"Yes," is all he answers.

"Arthur wants to know if you wish the competition discontinued."

"No."

"You understand, Mordred will not hold himself bound by the rules of competition, he will try to injure or even kill you. Do you understand what this means?"

Seth raises the faceplate of his helmet, looks at Merlin and nods.

"You are prepared for any trickery from him?"

Again, Seth nods.

"Go then, God be with you."

After receiving a new lance and a damp cloth to wipe the dust from his eye, Seth turns and stares down the field towards Mordred. He holds his lance vertically to indicate he is ready for the next round; Mordred returns the gesture. Shields up, lances lowered, they wait for the drop of the flag, then rush forward again, concentrating only on each other, on their anger and the need to settle scores. Dust clouds swirl from the horses' hooves almost obscuring them as each steadily makes his advancement towards the other. Mordred focuses his lance just below Seth's shield, trying to gouge him in his right side. At the moment of impact, Seth's horse rears up and climbs into the sky over the head of Mordred, who stares in confusion at the other rider sailing over him. Even Seth is taken by surprise at the ability of his horse. The beast touches back down to earth and Seth regains control of the reins.

Up in the King's tent, Adrian realizes immediately that this chestnut is the very horse he rode into battle with Cromwell, it is Tranquill the stallion. Secretly Haghery had brought the stallion here, given him to Seth without anyone being in the least suspicious, and this makes Adrian feel much easier about this battle with Mordred.

"Myra," Adrian nudges his wife, "do you know what horse this is that Seth is riding? It is Tranquill, the very horse I rode into battle with Cromwell. The one at your parents' home."

"Yes, it is. How did Seth get him?"

"There is only one leprechaun."

"Haghery!" she exclaims.

"The one and only, not said a word to a soul about it."

"Bless that sweet little dear," she says with tears gathering in her eyes. "I must give him a well deserved kiss when I see him again. Somehow he knew that Tranquill's talents would be needed."

Arthur gets their attention, "What manner of horse is this? From where did he come?" He asks, and then answers his own question, "Merlin? Am I right?"

"That's a very good guess, sire" Adrian replies.

• • •

Mordred takes the stance again and raises his lance, vertically signaling he is ready, Seth responds in like fashion, they lower their faceplates and their lances and raise their shields. The red flag drops; they charge, and the gallop seems to go on without end. Seth feels the strong beating of his own heart, his lungs filling with oxygen, and his blood rushing through his veins; his whole body gearing up for the challenge. His anger and need for revenge grows like a beast inside of his chest; the need to destroy, totally, this foul excuse for a human, takes complete control of his rational mind, and only Mordred's death can ease the pain. They are within a few feet of each other now, so close, they can see each other's eyes through the slits, their breathing is as rapid as the horses' hooves, their lances at the ready. Mordred's lance hits hard on Seth's shield creating a dent, but while Mordred's aim is off, Seth's is on the mark. He aims lower, holding firmly onto the shaft of the lance, steadying it, he feels the give of flesh as it spears Mordred's right thigh, then with the lance jerking loose from Seth's grip, it lodges in the wound.

Mordred screams but is not unseated; he grabs the lance and pulls it from his leg, black-red blood gushes from the gaping hole in his thigh. As he jams his hand over the wound to quell the gushing blood, Seth draws his sword and dismounts with intentions of continuing the fight on the ground. The administrator rides up to the combatants, "The bout is ended. Tend to this man's wound."

Mordred is led off of the field by his squire. Seth mounts and rides in the other direction, up to Arthur's tent, "Sire," he bows his head.

"Yes, Sir Seth?"

"Why was the match stopped? I could have killed him," he spat between clenched teeth.

"We could not have allowed that here, not today. Your chance will come. Go and rid yourself of your armor and join us for the remainder of the games."

"Yes, Sire" he nods his head and turns his horse around, but before he can leave, a carriage is racing across the area to where they are, the driver pulls on the reins and halts in front of Arthur. The door busts opens with a terrible force and Morgana angrily exits the carriage. She faces Arthur with extreme rage, "So . . . you named that bastard your heir, after all. I warned you Arthur, there would be repercussions for this action. I was very serious. You ignored my warning. Mordred will take Camelot by force. I will see this impostor slaughtered, as he should have been years ago. Mordred will rule, and you will live to see the new kingdom, then you will die!"

"Your threats mean nothing, Morgana. I told you once not to tread upon Camelot soil and I now order your removal. Take Mordred with you. He has been wounded; you are fortunate he was not killed, and, except for the rules of chivalry, he would have been!"

"Who dared!" she screams.

"Seth Grey, my son and the next King of Britain," this from Myra, who still remembers the night Morgana tried to kill Seth when he was but an infant. "The one you tried so many times to murder." She is standing, and her anger reflects in her stance and in the stormy fire of her violet eyes. Adrian stands close behind her holding her by the shoulders. He will not interfere whilst Myra vents years of pent up rage, but he will see to it she comes to no harm.

"Yes, I remember you," says Morgana. "So you are the bastard's mother. You left your husband's bed to sleep with my brother. Tell me, how did you manage to get away with it? The penalty for treason is death, which should have befallen Guinevere. But my brother is weak when it concerns his women."

Adrian pulls a reluctant Myra back toward the rear of the booth, fearing Morgana might use some form of the black arts against her. Seth draws Morgana's attention saying, "Mordred lives for now, but his days are numbered, as are yours. I will eradicate him; I swear this on the cross of Christ!"

Morgana turns towards Seth and snarls, "Well, we will see who lives or dies! Camelot will be mine and Mordred will be King. And you . . . , you will be no more than the dirt on his shoes." With a toss of her head and a swish of her skirts, she climbs back into the carriage, leaving the arena without Mordred.

• • •

Myra and Adrian stay on at the castle at Arthur's insistence, "You will be better protected behind the castle walls should Mordred decide to attack."

"We will stay for a short while," says Adrian. "But the hut has its own defenses, and we have come to call it home."

• • •

Myra and Adrian decide to stay at Camelot longer than planned. Merlin has told them their presence will help Seth and they will have more knowledge, living at the castle, about any further actions of Morgana and Mordred. For, with the decree that Seth will be Arthur's only true heir, the danger to Seth increases ten-fold. During their extensive stay, it is obvious that the King is in poor health for he stays in his rooms most days, only coming down for formal dinners.

Merlin and Seth are together constantly, improving Seth's skill with a sword and with his fighting hand-to-hand combat, in full armor. Everyone at the palace knows that war with Morgana and Mordred is imminent, and when Morgana has healed Mordred's wound, an attack could be likely at any time.

Arthur sends out the order for all knights on crusade to return to the palace in preparation for war. A few knights at a time filter in and immediately begin training for combat; none has so far found the secret of the Holy Grail, and Arthur still languishes from day to day.

Late one evening the castle guards excitedly ask for an audience with the King. They are granted permission to enter the King's private chambers and the two guards escort Sir Percival into the room. Percival is still dusty from his journey, not having taken the time to bathe before seeing the King. He holds in his hand a golden chalice.

"Sir Percival," Arthur rises slightly from a reclining position, "what have you that is so important?"

"I have found the Grail and learned its secret," he approaches the King.

Arthur looks up at Percival, "I am wasted away. I cannot die, yet I cannot live."

"You and the land are one, drink from the cup of Christ," Percival holds the cup up to Arthur's lips, "and be reborn and the land with you."

Arthur drinks from the chalice, and his eyes open wide as he looks around his chambers, "Percival, I did not know how empty was my soul, until it was filled."

Arthur stands with new vigor, "Ready my knights, together we will ride again. Mordred and Morgana will find us a relentless foe. I am a true King once more!"

CHAPTER TWENTY

ARTHUR BATTLES MORDRED

It is early autumn, and the harvests of the summer's crops are unexpectedly abundant; King Arthur has revived and the land with him. Once more, the inhabitants of this land find prosperity and joy; the twenty-year nightmare ends, but a new one looms.

The next few weeks are used to prepare for invasion by Mordred, as a call issues forth for all peasants to come to the castle for sanctuary behind its walls. All the quest knights filter in as they learn of the King's orders; many young men volunteer to be squires or soldiers, as needed. In due course, everything is made ready, if it is possible to be totally prepared for war.

One frost-covered morning, with just a few of his knights around him, including Seth, Arthur sets out for the abbey where Guinevere took refuge so many years ago. Ordering his knights to wait outside he enters alone; minutes later, he exits, but he is not alone, a nun all in white is with him. He has his arm around her shoulder and a sword in his right hand, Excalibur!

"My Knights, I have good news. Guinevere will return to Camelot as my Queen," he announces. He holds the sword of power high and exclaims, "Excalibur is returned to us, Guinevere kept it safe these many years. Might, as well as right, is on our side. We ride against Mordred on the morrow!"

The Knights of the Round Table all draw the swords from their sides and hold them aloft in tribute to Guinevere and the return of Excalibur. Their shouts of anticipation echo through the hills.

• • •

The call to arms resounds through the palace, three hours until dawn, and preparation for combat nears its completion. The knights are to assemble in the main courtyard; a small garrison will remain to guard Camelot.

• • •

"Seth, promise me you will take no unnecessary chances during this battle," Myra, Adrian and Merlin are seeing Seth off.

"I promise you Mother, but I will do what I need to do to defeat Morgana and Mordred."

"Seth will have more than the usual protection, his shield is blessed and his own mystical abilities have increased to the point where I was fifteen hundred years ago," says Merlin. "He has trained hard; he is strong in both mind and body. He will do well."

Adrian is also suited up in armor, but he will stay at the palace as part of the defending force, as will Merlin. Surprisingly Myra is very calm as she sees her only son and husband head for war.

There is a tap on the door of Merlin's rooms; Merlin steps to open it, there stands Guinevere, "May I come in?" she asks.

"Yes, please enter," Merlin steps aside allowing her entrance.

"Merlin, it is a pleasure to see you again, I do not believe I would have recognized you with the hair and the beard. We all heard that Morgana had imprisoned you; it appears that was not true. I was so misguided those many years ago, and I am not sure why Arthur should still love me, but I am very grateful for his forgiveness. But that is not why I am here, I wish to meet the young man who will next rule Camelot."

Seth steps forward and bows, "Ma'am."

Guinevere takes a long and studying appraisal of this tall and charismatic young man. "I am not aware of all the reasons for Arthur naming you as his heir, but the ones I do know are very compelling, as far as I am concerned. I know I do not deserve the right to voice my opinion, but I am so grateful that he has discovered a young man such as you. He says you have been coming to the castle since you were two. So young! He tells how Merlin, riding on the back of a dragon first brought you to Camelot. It would seem Arthur looks on you as a son; the son I should have given him, and not his sister. He is very proud of you, you know."

"I am honored to hear that," Seth replies.

"He says that there is a weak bloodline between you two, but he is not sure just how that comes about. Also, that you are third cousin to Merlin, so you must seem like a son to him also."

"A very true statement," says Merlin, placing a hand on Seth's left shoulder.

"Well, enough, I came to see if Myra would remain with me whilst the two of you are gone. I do not wish to be alone and I rather think that neither will she."

"I think that would be splendid," injects Adrian, who had been secretly worried about leaving Myra on her own.

"Yes, I would love the company and the chance to get to know you better," says Myra.

"Very good, I shall go for now; desire a page to escort you to my rooms. We can breakfast there if you wish." Guinevere turns and exits.

After she has gone, Myra turns to Adrian, "Oh, Adrian, it is so sad. We would not be in the predicament we are, had it not been for the affair between Lancelot and Guinevere."

"You forget Myra, Guinevere is barren, there never would have been any children from her," says Merlin.

"You're right, I did forget. But still theirs is a very sad story. Well never mind, there are greater things to deal with on this day," Myra heaves a sigh.

• • •

Ah hour later, all the warriors of Camelot await their King; he soon emerges with Merlin at his side. Arthur gazes on the faces of his most loyal subjects, "Knights, men, I will not make a long and flowery speech. We go into battle against a foe with unscrupulous morals, one who will use the devil himself to gain the Kingdom of Camelot. We must not be blinded by the promises they make. Direct your minds to the main objective, to destroy Morgana and Mordred's claim to the throne and to the land. The land is renewed, I am reborn, Guinevere is once again Queen, and the future of Camelot, of your lives and the lives of your children depends entirely on the outcome of this conflict. With the blessing of God, we charge into battle! Merlin, do you have any words for these brave knights?"

Merlin steps forward, holding his staff at arm's length. The four elements are now visible to all who gaze upon it; they churn, slowly changing the color of the orb to red for fire, to blue for water, to white for wind and to green for earth. All who behold this mystical sphere, marvel at its soothing effect on their inner minds.

"I have here the elements of the Universe, earth, wind, fire and water. These will aid us in our struggle with Morgana and Mordred. Do not be deceived. Morgana delves into the Black Arts; a demon is her accomplice. She has become very powerful and evil. She will not cease until she has attained her goal, or until her death." Holding the staff higher, Merlin commands, "I call upon the Element of Water. Spawn for us a fog, a thick penetrating fog, to shield our advance on Mordred's camp."

The orb swells, becoming watery blue, as a dark violet mist condenses through the sides of the globe, growing in intensity, becoming murky as it rapidly spreads throughout the countryside. Soon enclosing them is a dark mist, but somehow they are not dampened by its heaviness.

"I called upon the Element of Fire," shouts Merlin.

The orb turns fiery red, as flame leaps through the sides of the crystal, forming a ball.

"The Element of Fire will be your guide to the campfires of Mordred. Without it you will become confused and lose your way. The mist will hide your advance, and the flame will keep your path true."

Arthur looks at the new miracles conjured by Merlin, and for the first time, feels he has a real chance of defeating Morgana and Mordred.

"Ready my Knights?" he asks.

"To battle!" they respond.

Arthur takes the head, then a squire follows, carrying a red pennant bearing Arthur's crest, the white dragon, which flaps in the breeze created by their forward movement. Turning in the direction of the drawbridge, "We ride!" is the command. With the fiery sphere leading, they spur their steeds into the fog-shrouded countryside. Only by the light given by the ball of flame do they see where they are headed, for the mist is so thick, it is suffocatingly heavy, and they can only make out the man ahead of them.

• • •

In Mordred's camp, anticipation for battle is jubilant. Morgana has placed spells on the shields and swords, giving the men a feeling of invincibility. She has added greed to their thoughts, for she has promised land, great wealth and power, to her generals should they defeat Arthur. Mordred heads for his mother's tent, "A mist is rising, Mother. I thought there would be no fog, it will go against us in battle."

Morgana looks on her son with pride. Once a very beautiful woman, she now expends much magical energy to conceal the scars inflicted on her by the dragon and Merlin. She holds a deep grudge against him and her need for revenge outweighs her rational thinking.

"It cannot be, I conjured a spell for a clear day," she hurries outside of her tent. "This is Merlin's doing. You prepare the men immediately, for a fog like this might hide an army, and they may be upon us even as we speak. Go! Hurry! I will deal with this fog. It *will* lift."

"Captain!" calls Mordred, "Prepare the men for combat. Arthur may be in our midst!"

Suddenly the mist clears, and Mordred's camp is surrounded by Arthur's men, with drawn swords and raised shields. Morgana has eradicated the fog, but too late. The battle is on. The fight is fierce and bloody on both sides. Morgana, seeing that the battle is going against her, decides to use the Charm of Making. As she recites the incantation, griffins, hawks with the hindquarters of a lion, swoop down from out of nowhere and savagely attack Arthur's men. Using their forelegs, they grab the men by the shoulders lifting them off their horses, carrying them high while using their hooked beaks to rip off arms and legs, lay open chests to reveal still beating hearts, and plucking eyes from their sockets.

Seth and Arthur remain close to each other, guarding each other's backs, fighting courageously. Arthur wielding Excalibur, manages to ward off the griffins' onslaught; Seth, for the first time, calls upon his inner abilities and surrounds himself with a force field, where the slashes of swords bounce off but he is able to inflict damage on the enemy. So far, they have managed to stay on horseback, with Tranquill soaring into the sky after the griffins. Seth takes them on in the air and many are sent back to the hell they came from. Even with the blessing placed on the swords and shields of Arthur's men, Morgana counteracts the spell with one of her own. She hangs back from the main battlefield to see better where the conflict is failing and where to send reinforcements, in the guise of unholy allies.

Mordred also stays away from the main battlefield, proving him the coward Seth suspects that he is; but no matter, this will save Mordred for him and him alone. The battle rages for hours with none getting the upper hand.

"Mother," shouts Mordred, "Can you not do more? We are not gaining ground, my men are being slaughtered; use the Charm."

"Very well, there is one but it will drain all of my reserves," she answers.

"Do it! Or all will be lost!"

Morgana guides her horse further away so that she is totally alone; closing her eyes, as she faces the earth, she begins chanting. As the Charm takes effect, Morgana's appearance of beauty and youth begins fading. Her beautiful long red hair grays, and falls out, her flawless complexion shrivels and darkens, horrible scars draw the skin on the right side of her face, where she had caught the full force of the dragon's breath. Her lithe and curvy figure emaciates and twists into that of a living skeleton.

Mordred goes in search of his mother, but finds an old crone instead. "What have you done with my mother?" he screams at the woman.

"Mordred, my dear boy. My lovely son. It is I, Morgana, your Mother," her voice cracks and her gait is unsteady as she approaches Mordred with outstretched hands, her sight now almost gone.

"You lie! What have you done to my mother, old woman?"

"Mordred!" she begins.

"No!" he shouts as he grabs the ghoulish woman by the throat and squeezes the breath from her weakened body. Morgana wheezes and splutters, trying to ward off his assault. Her final thoughts are that she is dying at the hand of her own son, she will not get revenge on Merlin and Camelot is lost to her. Then blackness as death claims her evil life.

As the old woman goes limp in his grasp, Mordred throws the lifeless body to the ground, turns and heads for the battlefield.

But the Charm works, for the dead rise up from where they have fallen, whole bodies, bodies without arms, without legs, no heads, bodies that had been disemboweled, once again take up the sword and do battle. As each one is again cut down it gets back on to its feet, if it has feet. Those that don't, pull their mangled bodies across the ground in an effort to fight. It is a horrific scene, but Arthur's men are tiring; there is no rest from the charge of the zombies, slowly they are beginning to succumb to the unholy combatants.

There is a great shadow passing overhead; it is immense, Merlin riding Manfred, soars onto the vast mêlée. Circling the battlefield, he sees the fight starting to go badly for Arthur. The first fight centuries ago, he was not there to intervene, but this time things will be different.

Holding high his staff, he pronounces; "I call upon the Element of Earth. Construct a dust storm and bury the living dead!"

The orb glows green, then brown, as dirt filters through the crystal, forming a haze of dust, which engulfs all of the enemy who had died and risen, and the dirt settles on their mutilated bodies, burying them instantly.

Taking advantage of the hazy environment, Mordred, now finding his courage, urges his horse out onto the field. He has seen Arthur and creeps up on him unawares, catching him unprepared.

Half of Arthur's army is still holding its ground, not falling, not surrendering. Arthur and Seth are engaged in combat with the rest of

Mordred's men. As the dirt settles, Mordred, in his golden armor but without helmet, appears out of the murkiness, "Father!"

Arthur recognizes Mordred's voice and turns in his direction, but before he can react, "Come Father, let us embrace!"

Mordred, now on foot, has a lance leveled at Arthur, charges at him and spears him through the gut. With a groan, Arthur collapses onto his knees, grabbing the lance with his left hand, while reaching for Excalibur with the other as though preparing to counteract Mordred's vicious attack. But suddenly Mordred is challenged from behind . . . Seth!

"Face me, you coward. I do not have my back turned."

Mordred releases his hold on the lance, allowing Arthur to fall on his side still grasping the lance that protrudes through his belly. Mordred pulls his sword from its sheath and spins around to face Seth.

"Seth!" calls Arthur faintly. "Catch this," and he throws Excalibur to him.

The sword of power spins two times in the air before Seth catches it by the hilt, and twists swiftly around to face Mordred.

"So, you wish to stop me, you son of a harlot," sneers Mordred. "Our *Father* is dying and shortly you will join him in his grave."

"Boast while you still can, Mordred. But believe you this; my face will be the last you will ever see. A promise I make, a promise I keep!"

Seth crouches low as though making a small target; Mordred foolishly rushes head long with his sword leveled, just as he thinks he has made contact, Seth disappears. Mordred stumbles, as he touches nothing but air, "Where are you? Coward, face me!"

"I am right here," says Seth.

Mordred turns in the direction of his voice but sees nothing at first, then, suddenly Seth is standing just to his right. Realizing that Seth has the upper hand, Mordred growls like an animal, and slashes his weapon through Seth's side. Again, he vanishes, and Mordred's sword cuts air. Feeling this threat greater than any he has ever faced before, Mordred runs from the battle. The battlefield is still foggy and he does not see clearly; out of the mist, he runs right into a solid mass, Seth.

"Oh, are you leaving? But we have only just begun," taunts Seth, as he wields Excalibur across Mordred's left cheek, drawing blood for the first time in their third meeting. Mordred howls and grabs his face; it is only a flesh wound, a promise of what is to come.

Madly, Mordred begins swinging his sword without any idea where he is attacking. "Mother, where are you? I need your magic. MOTHER!" he screams and it resounds through the countryside, echoing again and again. "MOTHER!" again no response. "Mother, I am in trouble, help me! Please help me. The Charm of Making, use it. Hide me!"

"It is no use, Mordred. You have killed her. She is dead, and by your own hand."

"I have not killed my own mother, she is here and she will help me defeat you," he hisses as he plunges toward Seth, with his sword at a downward angle.

Nothing is there; again, Seth has vanished. "Over here." He becomes visible to Mordred's right once more. Another foolish charge, this time Seth meets Mordred's sword with Excalibur, using an excellent defensive move, he deflects the sword, and it recoils.

By now, Merlin has landed and rushes to Arthur's side and begins rendering aid to his fallen King; he only hopes he is not too late to save Arthur's life. Kneeling beside him, he helps him to a slight recline and cradles his head so he might see the clash between his two sons. Merlin has used the Charm of Making to slow the flow of blood from Arthur's deadly wound. The lance has carved a hole in Arthur's abdomen the size of a fist; he is not sure he can save him.

"How does Seth disappear like that, is this a trick of yours?" his voice is strained and low.

"Not I, but the Hag of the Black Forest; she gave him a river stone which when held in the mouth gives invisibility.

"Try to be silent, Arthur, I have summoned help. We will try to get you to Camelot, where I can better tend your wounds."

• • •

Back at Camelot, Manfred slides down to the center courtyard. Haghery rushes up to him, for none at the castle know that Manfred can speak. Seeing the leprechaun coming, Manfred lowers his massive head toward him, "Arthur is down, Merlin said to bring the doctor."

"Adrian? Help he cannot be. The two of them contact must not make," argues the leprechaun.

"Merlin has sent for me?" asks Adrian having walked up and hearing the conversation.

Manfred responds, "Yes, Arthur is gravely wounded, he needs you as a doctor."

"Haghery, get my medical bag, then tell Myra where I have gone, but wait until I have left, she will try to stop me." Adrian climbs onto the back of the dragon; Haghery has returned with his bag, it is four o'clock in the afternoon.

With a mighty beat of his leathery wings, Manfred is airborne and soaring toward the battlefield.

• • •

The fight between Seth and Mordred continues; Mordred has become very frustrated, as Seth continues to toy with him, "Why can you not fight me like a man, you bastard, and stay where I can cut you to ribbons?"

"I might consider it, if there were a man to fight; I see only scum!" Seth sneers at him, but all the same, Seth is also tired of this cat and mouse game and decides to end it. He knows Arthur is fatally wounded and he wants him to see Mordred die.

Suddenly Seth's stance changes and he swiftly closes in on Mordred as their swords meet and clang with each thrust. Seth gives no quarter as he relentlessly wields Excalibur with the ferocity of a man driven by vengeance. Mordred stumbles backwards, trying to evade Excalibur's sharp edge; Seth presses on, and finally Mordred falls, Seth falls on him, and sits astride him.

Fear is plain on Mordred's face, he manages to get one arm free and slash out at Seth; Seth feels the impact of the blow but it only serves to anger him further, as it knocks him momentarily to one side. Thinking himself loose, Mordred twists and attempts to pull away, but Seth recovers and regains his control. Seth holds him tightly with his knees as Mordred manages once again, out of desperation, to free his sword and just as he thrusts upward toward Seth's chest, Seth defends with Excalibur and stabs down and slices into Mordred jugular vein, delivering the deathblow. Mordred's eyes grow large and blood spurts from his gasping mouth, while his lifeblood flows freely out onto the torn and ragged earth.

Seth removes himself from the bleeding and dying Mordred. Mordred's eyes are open and stares at his killer, he jerks and convulses, fighting to stay alive, as his life-force slowly drains away, congealing on the ground. Seth watches as Mordred dies, with a certain satisfaction. Now he is still, respiration stops, eyes glazed and unseeing, dark thickening blood oozes from the cut in his throat, his head rolls to one side, body and limbs go limp.

Seth searches the battlefield. The men have ceased fighting and stood watching the fight between Seth and Mordred. They know that with Mordred's demise there is no need to pursue any further conflict. Seth speaks, "Do any of you wish to take up Mordred's sword?"

One man steps forward, "There is no need for more blood letting, we honor Arthur as King. Long live the King."

"Long live the King," echo the others, as they raise their swords in salute.

Seth holds Excalibur high, "Long live King Arthur!"

• • •

Whilst the salutation for Arthur is happening, a shape grows larger over the western horizon, just below the setting sun. Seth recognizes Manfred, and that he has a passenger, Adrian, Seth's father. Manfred glides to a graceful landing and Adrian quickly dismounts. Seth greets his father, "Hurry, you may be able to save Arthur!"

Together they rush towards Merlin and the fallen King. Merlin and Arthur are encased in a soft green vapor; Merlin holds the dying King's head on his lap.

"Stop Seth, Adrian" orders Merlin as he sees them approaching. "We are suspended in time, Arthur will die. I cannot save him. With all my powers gained over the centuries, I do not have the power over death. This event in history cannot be changed. Arthur must die and Seth will be King. Arthur wishes to speak to both of you. When I remove this veil, he will have only minutes, so listen carefully."

Holding high his staff, Merlin chants a few word of the Charm and the mist dissipates, leaving their vision clear. Both Seth and Adrian approach the King, "My King, what are your wishes?" asks Seth.

Arthur looks quickly at both men then turns his gaze on Seth. He labors to breathe and fresh blood once again flows from his wound. "Seth, you are now King." Seth nods with tears swelling up in his eyes. "I wish for Guinevere to continue to live at Camelot,—promise me," Arthur coughs and Merlin helps him to a straighter sitting position. Again Seth nods, too disturbed to speak.

"I know the kingdom is now in good and capable hands; with both Mordred and Morgana gone, there will be no challenge for the kingdom."

Arthur focuses his attention on Adrian, "Will you move into the palace and give guidance to Seth?"

Adrian looks at Merlin, who nods, "We will stay with him as long as is needed. Do not speak any more. I must see if I can stop this bleeding," this is the medical doctor coming out in Adrian, wanting to do something, but knowing he cannot.

Merlin mouths the word; 'No.' Adrian understands that it is still dangerous for he and Arthur to make contact.

Arthur waves his hand in the negative, "It is no use. The hole is too big, you will not be able to fill it," Arthur's attempt at humor fails as his hands drops back to his chest and his eyes lock in a vacant stare, his final breath escapes and he goes flaccid. Merlin eases him back down to the ground. It is finished.

Adrian, acting quickly now as a doctor, reaches his hand out to check Arthur's wrist for a pulse. It should be safe enough, with Arthur's spirit departed. He holds the limp arm up, fingers placed on the wrist; he looks at Merlin and Seth and shakes his head. This mighty man, a man of legend and myth is gone, they have not been able to change history after all but at least there will be a true heir on the throne of England.

Curious about the injury, wanting to know for himself if Arthur could have been saved, had he, Adrian, been able to administer medical aid in time, he pulls away the clothing at the site of the entry wound. He probes the gash with experienced fingers, feeling inside the dead King's abdomen, when suddenly, he experiences the same electrical charge he once had years ago, when he had touched Arthur at their first meeting. This time, though, he is not thrown backward away from Arthur, but instead feels a surge of energy flow from his body into Arthur's, and he cannot withdraw his hand from the corpse. A translucent blue human shape forms, a being that leaves Adrian's body and traverses the narrow space between the two men. Adrian is frozen, unable to free himself, and uncertain as to what is happening. This occurs so swiftly, that no one has time to react. The spirit, through the wound, enters Arthur. The blood halts its flow and surges back into Arthur's body, even the blood on the ground return to its host. The wound closes up, until there is no indication of it; Adrian is released at last and falls backwards, but appears uninjured.

Arthur's color returns to his waxen complexion; his eyelids flutter, his eyes open, he gasps a lungful of air. He is alive!

Arthur struggles to a sitting position, and, as he does his knights cheer and gather closer to him. Adrian takes another look at the wound; it has healed, Arthur's garments are torn but there is not even a drop of blood anywhere on them.

"Sire, this is amazing; what do you feel?" asks Adrian, as he takes Arthur by the shoulders to help him to sit up. There is no reaction to the contact between the two.

"I feel . . . splendid," replies Arthur as he touches his chest with both palms. "I last remember telling you not to concern yourself with me, then next . . . I am pulled away . . . out of myself. There was . . . this strange brightness . . . then an image of myself . . . it was rushing towards me . . . we collide. And . . . then I am back here with all of you. What has transpired? I was prepared for death. I think I did die."

"As yet, we cannot answer your questions, Arthur," replies Merlin staring hard at the King. "I will endeavor to ascertain how this miraculous phenomenon occurred."

Standing and moving away from the crowd, Merlin holds high his staff and in a booming voice calls, "Eydasi, I beseech you, appear before us!"

As soon as he speaks, the darkening sky grows even darker; the clouds swell and begin churning, a roar like a mighty wind erupts. Soon a purple funnel drops from the heavens and touches down on the earth, creating huge billows of dust and debris. The tornado dances toward the army of men, and then disappears leaving in its wake a misty figure. Slowly the mist clears revealing a feminine figure. Her garments are white, reflecting silver. Her skin is iridescent. Her hair is silvery, long and flowing in the unfelt wind. Her eyes are flashing sapphires, around her waist is a belt of shimmering stars, on her right hand is a ring of the blazing sun, at her throat is the silver crescent moon hanging from a rope of pale moonstones.

When she speaks, it is like scores of voices coming from many directions at once, echoing through the countryside.

"Are you ready to correct Time, Merlin?" she asks, ignoring the army beginning to surround her.

"Is this possible now? Is our task complete?" he responds looking up at her, for she is suspended in time and space.

"Arthur's soul has returned to him. Adrian is no longer the reincarnation of Arthur."

Adrian slowly approaches this magnificent angel, "Eydasi, then who am I now, if not Arthur?"

"You now have your own soul and personality. Your soul was stored in your sub-conscious until Arthur and his spirit could reunite. As you know, it could not happen as long as Arthur was living. His body had to be emptied of its spirit before he could accept it back again. In this Time, he dies; his spirit leaves him. When Merlin called it from limbo to be born again in the body of another, it was Arthur's spirit, with all that that specifies. Only in this way could Adrian have fathered a child in Arthur's bloodline. Now all is right with the Universe." Eydasi spreads wide her arms and announces "Let this Time now be recorded in history. The former passes away. History has changed!" The Earth moves and lightning flashes, while a lilac glow surrounds everyone and everything on Earth, as these changes are initiated.

Eydasi turns her attention to Adrian, "You and your wife, as well as Merlin will now be returned to your own Time."

"But we wish to stay here with Seth. He is our son. We will not leave him," argues Adrian.

"He is no longer of your blood, you are not his father. Arthur is. You are out of position with your Time; you must return. Neither you nor your wife will have a memory of this. You will return to the day before you left, back to the age you were. Only Merlin will be aware of what has taken place. There is now a different heir on the throne of England. I will tell you that it is a woman. Queen Elizabeth the Second now sits on the throne, the rightful monarch."

I think I must remain here also. Arthur and Seth still need guidance," says Merlin. He had missed terribly his old friend, and was now to leave his nephew, whom he felt to be a son.

"There cannot be two of you here in this time," replies Eydasi.

"Yes, I understand. It is regrettable my counterpart will not be released for another fifteen hundred years," says Merlin, with sadness in his voice.

"Ah, but you are mistaken, my counterpart from the future."

A voice booms from just over the ridge and as all eyes turn that way, Merlin of the Past is walking out of the mist, looking as he had when first imprisoned.

Without being asked, Eydasi explains, "This is another time line, a time line in which Merlin is not imprisoned in the crystal. All events have changed. This Merlin will remain with Arthur and Seth. You, Merlin from the future, must return with Adrian and Myra."

"Must we leave just now?" asks Adrian. "My wife is not here."

"Yes, you must return now, Myra will be with you at the same location. There is no need for farewells for you will not remember."

She raises her arms and as she vanishes, so do Adrian and Merlin. Back at the palace, Myra disappears from amongst the group of women, including Guinevere, with whom she is waiting for news of the battle.

224

EPILOGUE

"HELLO! Is anyone here?" a familiar male voice calls.
"It is us," another familiar, more feminine, one.
"Adrian! Myra!" Haghery and Sleyvia shout together.
"Oh children, please enter." Merlin offers a warm welcome.
Two very bright lights come bobbing up the cave corridor as their unexpected guests make their way toward the small group, carrying battery-powered lanterns. "We came to see you now," Myra was speaking as they came within view. "I couldn't wait until the holidays."

• • •

Merlin looks closely at his guests. They look just the same as they did nineteen years ago. Merlin knows that they have only just arrived from living in the medieval age for almost twenty years. Myra and Adrian are unaware of this fact and chatter happily with the two fairies.
"You two have a secret," states Merlin, "and I think I know what it is. Do you wish to verify my suspicions?"
"Okay, I will," grins Adrian. "Myra has agreed to marry me. And we are going to do it this weekend. Her parents will drive up tomorrow and we wondered if we can spend the night here with you?"

• • •

Merlin knows they will not have the fairy wedding they had the first time; this one will be more conventional. They will start their lives together, not with Adrian as the reincarnation of Arthur, but with Adrian as himself. Gone also are the memories of such. Adrian cannot remember that Merlin had told him that he was King Arthur; he only remembers the final battle with the demon Thanatos and no more. He is Dr. Adrian Grey, and no-one else.

• • •

Eydasi, satisfied with the outcome and certain she has altered the memories of those involved, smiles and goes to make a full report to Yahweh.

The End